Henrietta Alten West

I
HAVE
A
Photograph

HENRIETTA ALTEN WEST

This book is a work of fiction. Many of the names, places, characters, and incidents are products of the author's imagination or are used fictitiously. Any resemblance to actual events or locales or person living or dead is entirely coincidental. This book may not be reproduced in any form without express written permission.

Copyright © 2019 Henrietta Alten West

Paperback ISBN: 9781628062359
Hardback ISBN: 9781628062366

Library of Congress Control Number 2019910283

Cover design by Jaime L. Coston
Photography by Andrea Lõpez Burns
Interior design and layout by Jamie Tipton, Open Heart Designs

*This book is dedicated to the boys of Camp Shoemaker
and those of us who love them.*

CONTENTS

Cast of Characters, VII

Preface, IX

Prologue, XI

Chapter 1, 1

Chapter 2, 5

Chapter 3, 11

Chapter 4, 17

Chapter 5, 21

Chapter 6, 27

Chapter 7, 32

Chapter 8, 42

Chapter 9, 47

Chapter 10, 53

Chapter 11, 59

Chapter 12, 66

Chapter 13, 71

Chapter 14, 76

Chapter 15, 82

Chapter 16, 89

Chapter 17, 93

Chapter 18, 98

Chapter 19, 107

Chapter 20, 115

Chapter 21, 120

Chapter 22, 127

Chapter 23, 133

Chapter 24, 141

Chapter 25, 149

Chapter 26, 159

Chapter 27, 161

Chapter 28, 174

Chapter 29, 180

Chapter 30, 186

Chapter 31, 195

Chapter 32, 202

Chapter 33, 211

Chapter 34, 218

Chapter 35, 226

Chapter 36, 233

Chapter 37, 241

Chapter 38, 250

Epilogue, 259

When Did I Grow Old?, 262

Acknowledgments, 265

CAST OF CHARACTERS

Elizabeth and Richard Carpenter
Elizabeth and Richard live in a small town on the Eastern Shore of Maryland. Richard is a retired pathologist who did some work for the Philadelphia Medical Examiner's Office many years ago. Elizabeth is a former college professor and CIA analyst.

Isabelle and Matthew Ritter
Isabelle and Matthew live in Palm Springs, California. Matthew is a retired urologist, an avid quail hunter, and a movie buff. Isabelle has retired from her career as a clinical psychologist and now owns a popular high-end interior furnishings store and design business.

Sidney and Cameron Richardson
Sidney and Cameron have several homes and their own private plane. Cameron is a former IBM wunderkind who went out on his own to start several globally-known computer companies. Sidney is a retired profiling consultant who owned an innovative, successful, and fast-growing home organization business before she married Cameron.

Olivia and J.D. Steele
Olivia and J.D. live in Saint Louis. J.D. is a lawyer who gave up his job as a prosecuting attorney to found his own extremely profitable trucking company. He is a logistics expert. Olivia is a former homecoming queen, a brilliant woman who worked as a mathematician and cypher specialist for the NSA.

Gretchen and Bailey MacDermott
Gretchen and Bailey live in Dallas, Texas. Bailey is a former IBM salesman, oil company executive, and Department of Defense intelligence agent. He currently is making another fortune selling commercial real estate. Gretchen works in the corporate world as the head of an HR department. Because she is so competent at everything she does, she actually runs the company she works for.

Tyler Merriman and Lilleth DuBois
Tyler and Lilleth live in southern Colorado. Everyone suspects that Tyler flew the SR-71 Blackbird for the U.S. Air Force during his younger years. After he retired from the military, he made millions in commercial real estate. He flew his own plane around the country. Lilleth is a psychologist who works on a reservation counseling Native Americans. She is a superb athlete and a beautiful younger woman.

Theodore Sullivan
"Teddy" lives in Charleston, South Carolina. He is an architect and city planner and spends his time giving professional advice to cities and countries around the globe. He ostensibly travels to consult about historic renovations and architectural design, but some of his closest friends suspect he also does some kind of mysterious undercover work as he travels the world.

Darryl Harcomb and Elena Petrovich
Darryl and Elena live in a university town in the northern Middle West. Darryl is an academic historian who fell in love with his student, Elena Petrovich. Elena is living a lie. Some believe she is a former KGB sleeper agent who came to the U.S. to spy. She supposedly gave it all up when she fell in love with her college professor and decided to get her PhD. But can she ever really leave her past behind?

Conrad Watson
Watson is not really a doctor, but he plays one on TV. He's a lawyer who achieved instant fame when he joined the cast of the hit television series, *How To Live Forever*. He flies his own plane and plays the guitar.

Preface

Some of the most poignant musical lyrics, for me, have always been the lines at the end of the Simon and Garfunkle song "Old Friends/Bookends Theme." The music and words resonate with people of all ages. When I first heard this song as a young person, my heart was touched. Many years later, when I hear it as an old person, I am moved to tears. This book is written about old friends. The mystery centers around photographs and memories from the past.

Prologue

They came of age in the 1950s and 1960s. It had taken some of them more time than others to become adults, but all were product and progeny of that long-ago, traditional world. This year they were commemorating an important milestone. They had all lived long enough to see themselves and their best friends from childhood make it three-quarters of the way through their hoped-for one-hundred-year life spans. They were alive to celebrate their seventy-fifth birthdays. It was certainly a cause for excessive revelry, in case any of them were still up to engaging in excessive revelry.

The group of friends had been enjoying their long reunion weekends, with their current wives and girlfriends, every September for the past nine years. They got together to talk about old times and the times of their lives, to laugh together and drink some wine, to remember things, and to hope for things to come. They gathered to give thanks that they had lived so long and been successful. They had, at last, found happiness in love and even in marriage. It was a fun group. They'd held their reunion in New Orleans; Santa Fe; Depoe Bay, Oregon; Asheville, North Carolina; Bethany Beach, Delaware; Cabo San Lucas, Mexico; Phoenix; Little Rock; and the Big Cedar Resort in Missouri. This year they were meeting in Bar Harbor, Maine.

The main criteria for the gathering had become that they all wanted to stay together in the same hotel or inn or bed and breakfast, and the reunion always had to be held in a location that offered wonderful food. The coast of Maine certainly would be able to rise to that challenge. It would be lobster this and lobster that and lobster, lobster all the time. There was even a lobster omelet that one could enjoy for breakfast. It was made with bacon and freshly grated Parmigiano-Reggiano, and it was everyone's new favorite menu item that September.

Chapter 1

THEY HAD MET SUCH A LONG TIME AGO, WHEN THEY were very young. It seemed as if they'd always known each other, and they really could not remember a time when they hadn't been friends, when they hadn't been a group. Most buddies who remain close into adulthood have gone to school together. Groups who still get together for reunions when they are in their 60s and 70s, usually have attended the same high school or college or belonged to the same fraternity.

Perhaps the meeting place that had serendipitously brought these little boys together set them apart in a unique way. When they were eight years old, they'd met at church camp. They'd all been born in 1943, so they were all assigned to Cabin #1. Camp Shoemaker was an overnight camp run by the Episcopal Church. There was a boys' camp, and, at a sufficiently safe and respectable distance away, there was a girls' camp. Camp Shoemaker was not a fancy camp, but it provided all the fun activities kids could want. There was a big lake for swimming and boating and fishing. There were woods and fields and hills and secret places and wide open spaces to play baseball and volleyball and capture the flag. Located in the Ozark Mountains, Camp Shoemaker drew kids from all over the central part of the country.

In the late 19th century a wealthy parishioner had donated a thousand acres of real estate to her church diocese, and Camp Shoemaker had grown out of this generous gift. At first there had been just a few cabins, and most of the kids who spent two-week sessions there were from the local Episcopal churches. Camp Shoemaker thrived and grew. Its reputation as a place to spend a great summer began to draw interest from all over the state and eventually from throughout the region. Camper demand increased, and more cabins were built. By 1951, it was still a camp with a religious base, but there were Methodists, Baptists, Catholics, and a few Jewish kids who wanted to join the fun at Camp Shoemaker. There was a waiting list to get in, and campers came from far and wide. You could stay for a month, and then you could stay for two months. Scholarships were offered to those whose parents couldn't afford to pay.

The boys in Cabin #1 were from different states and different backgrounds. But they immediately bonded and became a force to be reckoned with. Their slogan was "We're #1!" Although they were, that first year, the youngest kids in camp, because of their camaraderie and their joie de vivre, they were noticed. They were one. They took the athletic prizes and the prizes in the scavenger hunts. There was never any question that they would return the next year. It had been too wonderful. It had to be repeated, summer after summer. Of course, the next year, because they were a year older, they were no longer in Cabin #1. They were in Cabin #3. But they let everyone know: "We're still #1!"

The years passed. One of the boys had scarlet fever and couldn't attend camp that year. Barring illness and tragedy, if they possibly could return to Camp Shoemaker for the summer, they did. They became teenagers. They became junior counselors, and then they became counselors. They stayed close. They remained a group. A few attended the same colleges. They were best men and ushers in each other's weddings. But as time passed and as too often happens with the friendships of youth, they grew apart as their priorities shifted. Wives and children, careers and chasing success, and all the other things that the years demand of one's time and energy, took over and dominated their lives. The boys grew into men with adult responsibilities, and they lost touch. Individuals stayed connected and communicated with each other, but the group as a whole experienced the diaspora of life's events.

A man walked on the moon. Woodstock happened. The broken came home from Vietnam. Miniskirts came and went and came and went again. Leisure suits were briefly in the stores. Babies were born. Grandparents and parents died. Shoulder pads for women became a fashion trend. Hair was lost. Weight was gained. Gym memberships and personal trainers were in demand. HIV/AIDS decimated. College tuitions for the next generation were paid. Shoulder pads for women as a fashion trend passed thankfully into oblivion. There were divorces. There were second and third marriages. September 11, 2001 became the day of infamy. Politics divided. Cell phones proliferated. The world sometimes seemed a place war babies no longer recognized.

In the year when they were all turning sixty-five, Matthew Ritter was thinking about retirement. As he looked back on his journey and remembered old times and old friends, he decided he wanted to get his group from Camp Shoemaker together again. He planned a weekend in Palm Springs and invited them all to come. He arranged for a great room rate at a beautiful resort near his home, and he made reservations at his favorite restaurants. Dale Chihuly's magnificent glass sculptures were on exhibit in a nearby public garden.

The reunion weekend was a huge success. Everyone who attended had a terriffic time; they had to do it again. And so they did. Every year from then on, they gathered for a wonderful long weekend of fun, eating, and being together. The wives and girlfriends, who had been dragged into the reunion from hither and yon, got along famously and formed their own bond. Everyone looked forward to the yearly reunion. It was a trip down memory lane, and it became a chance to spend time with people they'd loved when they were young, people they realized they still loved now that they were old. It was an extraordinary occasion by any definition.

The variety of places they'd chosen for their reunions all offered exceptional food and interesting things to do. The places they met were important. But, they had discovered over the years, the most important thing about the reunions was to spend time together. They wanted to remember old times, but they also wanted to share pictures of grandchildren, talk about the successes and failures of their lives, enjoy the cuisine and the wine of the area they were visiting, and laugh a lot. It was a gift of later life that none of them had been expecting. It was a gift of life that every one of them was delighted to have. It was a gift that anyone would envy. They were lucky. They were "Still #1!"

Chapter 2

WHAT COULD BE MORE BEAUTIFUL THAN Bar Harbor in September? It's an impossibly difficult place to get to, especially if you are coming from a small town or from any place west of the Mississippi River. You have to fly into Portland or Bangor or Boston or someplace else and drive to Bar Harbor, unless you have a private plane. The town is idyllic. At least it was before Carnival Cruises and others began to put it on their itineraries. This group of tourists, the ones who were celebrating their seventy-fifth birthdays, hoped that all the other groups of tourists would come and go before they arrived. They wanted the place to themselves. What they really wanted was the Bar Harbor of 1961, or maybe even the Bar Harbor of 1928. They were going to get the Bar Harbor of 2018.

The weather on the Maine coast could be cold and rainy in September. There might be a hurricane, or worse, a Northeastern storm. But this year, fate smiled, and every day of the long weekend was predicted to be sunny or, at worst, partly cloudy. Miraculously, it was not supposed to rain a drop. That didn't necessarily mean it wouldn't rain, but at least the forecast, however faulty it might eventually turn out to be, started out as a good one.

One of the members of the group had just had a hip replacement. He'd been doing physical therapy and hoped to be able to participate fully in the agenda. One of the wives was disabled. She used a cane all the time and had to have a wheelchair for museums. Some of the guys wanted to pretend they were still in their thirties. They spoke longingly of mountain hikes and mountain bikes in the Acadia National Park. One of them sent a video to the others in the group, ahead of their long weekend, of himself paragliding, just to reassure himself and the others that he still "had it." Not everybody knew exactly what paragliding was, but everybody in the group knew, after viewing the video, that one of their own could still do it.

The Camp Shoemaker alums took turns organizing the weekend from year to year. Matthew Ritter, who was organizing this year's trip to Maine, had never actually vacationed in Maine. He'd grown up in Tennessee and now lived in Palm Springs. He'd been to Maine once, many years earlier, to hunt for ruffed grouse and some other exotic birds. His memories of Maine were dim, and he'd never actually organized an event like this before. His wife had always done it for him, but this time, she'd told him, she was busy. He was going to have to do it himself. He solved his problem by hiring a concierge named Vanna. Who knew there even was such a person outside of a hotel? Didn't this person used to be called a travel agent? Ritter sang her praises to his friends and told them Vanna knew all about Bar Harbor and all about Maine. He repeatedly assured the others that she was more than earning her fees.

Elizabeth Carpenter began to suspect something was off when Vanna scheduled dinner at a Cuban restaurant on the group's last night together. A Cuban restaurant in Maine? Most people go to the Pine Tree State to eat whole lobsters, steamed clams, and lobster rolls. Elizabeth loved stopping at a roadside shack to buy a lobster roll for lunch. She loved going to the lobster pounds, which are fiercely proud of their lack of conventional ambiance, to select her own crustacean from a tank of lazy fellows.

Eating a lobster is not an elegant endeavor, even for the most proficient of lobster eaters. The lobster pound not only recognizes but embraces this. There is no standing on ceremony there, no attempt to be anything other than what it is, fighting to get the darn thing open and then indulging in the sweet meat. One's chin must drip with butter, of course, another inelegant but essential factor when visiting Maine. The Cuban place was supposed to be the latest "in" place and "fabulous" ... but really? Elizabeth kept telling herself that the group might be "lobstered out." Cuban food might be a nice break from the steady diet of shellfish.

Matthew's research led him to the Inastou Lodge, a hostelry and resort built more than a hundred years ago. He was reassured by a widely-traveled friend that the Inastou was first rate and well worth the considerable nightly room rate they charged. The inn was indeed historic and quaint and had magnificent views. It was located near the entrance to the Acadia National Park, convenient for all of the rigorous athletic activities that were planned by some in the group. One had to drive to the town of Bar Harbor, but for the seventy-five-year-old jocks, convenience to outdoor sports took precedence over proximity to shopping.

The Inastou was indeed old-school and charming, and the view was as advertised. But there were problems. The rooms were small, and the bathrooms were tiny, some equipped with sinks and other plumbing fixtures that were even more antiquated than any member of the reunion group. The furnishings in the rooms were dated, and most of the window frames rattled with the wind. One member of the group, who was not able to get a good night's sleep because of the noisy windows, stuffed magazines and newspapers, and even dirty clothes, into the gaps around the windows to keep the wind at bay.

Elizabeth Carpenter was handicapped and required a walk-in shower. She and her husband Richard had to stay across the street, in an entirely separate building, an old and somewhat rundown annex called Blueberry House. The Inastou did not have any handicap accessible rooms in its main lodge. Staying at Blueberry House was isolating and inconvenient for the Carpenters, but it was their only option.

But it wasn't all about the accommodations. It was about being together and enjoying each other's company. There were fun activities and wonderful restaurant meals planned. It was going to be another special reunion weekend. No matter what, this group of friends always managed to have a great time.

Their first night together, they met on the back porch of the Inastou Lodge for cocktails. The sun was just fading below the horizon into dusk. They were all together again. They had the long weekend in front of them. What could be better? The group had lots of catching up to do; much had happened since they'd last been together. White wine was popular, but Captain Morgan on the rocks was also frequently requested.

Sidney and Cameron had just been to Panama for expensive and, they claimed, effective "Fountain of Youth" treatments. They were convinced that the stem-cell injections had made them feel younger in many ways, including allowing Cameron to run farther and faster than he had in twenty years. He was convinced that the stem cells had caused his hair to change from white back to dark brown. He demonstrated that the treatments were enhancing his balance, and he wanted to share his experience with the others in the group. The others were skeptical. The two doctors in the group were particularly skeptical.

Matthew Ritter was a movie buff, and since he'd retired, he had watched hundreds, if not thousands, of Hollywood's finest. He had compiled countless lists of the movies he'd seen, dividing them into numerous categories. He handed out these lists to everyone, every year, and usually showed a movie montage he'd created. His audiences loved his movie montages. This year, he was frustrated because the Inastou Lodge was not able to provide him with a "smart TV" so he could show his montage. The technology required was not sophisticated. How could the Inastou not have at least one smart TV available? Who wanted dumb TVs anyway?

Gretchen and Bailey announced that their second grandchild, a girl, had been born that morning, two weeks early. They were beyond being excited and proudly passed around their cell phones to show everyone photographs of their beautiful offspring. Tyler introduced his friend Lilleth to most of the people in the group for the first time. She was beautiful and enchanting. Everyone immediately loved her, and all were thrilled to welcome her to the reunion. Olivia and J.D. had a large extended family with children, stepchildren, adopted children, inlaws, outlaws, and all manner of assorted grandchildren. It was always fun to catch up with what was going on in their complicated and energetic clan.

Richard and Elizabeth Carpenter were both writing books. Elizabeth had just published a second youth book written for her twelve-year-old grandson, and she had sent a copy to each couple in the group. Only one person had read it, but he was enthusiastically telling the others how much he had enjoyed it.

Everyone had something to talk about. Those who needed hearing aids put them in, and everyone listened as they caught up on the lives of the others. It wasn't always happy news. One member of the group had died two years previously, and everyone wanted to know how his widow was doing. She had adopted a second dog from the animal shelter, and she seemed to be doing as well as could be expected. She had been invited to continue to attend the reunions, but so far, she'd not had the heart to do it. Maybe next year?

Darryl and Elena always arrived late and left early. They were still working and couldn't spend much time away from the university. Darryl was old enough to retire, if he'd wanted to, but married to a much younger woman, he chose to stay in the academic fray. He tried to look and act younger than he really was, sporting trendy clothes and a trendy haircut. He was always on his iPad, no matter what was going on. He ate with his iPad and everyone was sure he slept with it, too, maybe more nights than he slept with Elena. Darryl and Elena were not there for the welcome cocktail party. Most of the time they didn't show up for the reunion at all. Apparently, they were so important, they couldn't take time off.

The group's first meal together was at the Inastou's dining room, and it did not disappoint. The famous warm popovers were the stars of the show. Some couldn't wait to dive into lobster world, and the bright red crustaceans arrived at the table, complete with bibs, claw crackers, and servings of melted butter.

The coast of Maine had been an excellent choice. Good weather was still predicted. Plans were finalized for the big biking event in the Acadia National Park the next morning. Originally eight people had signed on for the ride, but the numbers had dwindled to four. Gretchen announced that she intended to sleep late. Bailey and Richard were meeting for breakfast. Isabelle and Olivia planned to drive to Bar Harbor to do some shopping. The evening was a promising start to the reunion.

Chapter 3

THE FIRST SIGN OF TROUBLE ARRIVED IN THE FORM of a bike accident. All the bikes were rented, and there had been much discussion as the participants selected exactly the right bikes for themselves and for this particular itinerary. Lilleth Dubois, who was considerably younger than most of the others in the group, was the only female who opted for the bike ride. She loved to bike, and Tyler was proud that she was fit enough and had the stamina to keep up with the rest of the bikers who were all men, albeit older men. Tyler was beginning to feel his age, and Lilleth's participation gave him the mental push he needed to make the demanding half-day bike ride through the Acadia National Park.

Tyler had the de rigueur biking shorts and shirt, and of course everyone had to wear a helmet. Lilleth also had the right spandex biking clothes that looked wonderful on her slim and shapely younger body. J.D. and Matthew wore their khaki summer shorts. After making sure each one in the biking quartet had the perfect bike, they set off on their outing. They were just a quarter of the way through the ride when Tyler's bike's brakes failed. The bikers were sharing the road with the September traffic that was driving through the national park, and they were on a long downhill run.

Tyler's bike was almost brand new, and he was stunned when he realized he couldn't slow his bike. The downhill slope and the inevitable pull of gravity got the better of the situation before he could pull over to the side of the road. He was now stuck on a jet-propelled two wheeler, as it raced down the incline, out of control. Then, Tyler realized he could not operate the steering on the bike. His top-of-the line bike had suffered two critical and catastrophic failures. He couldn't stop, and he couldn't steer. Tyler was in trouble.

A sports car, moving way too fast on the narrow road, came around a corner, and Tyler tried to get out of the way. But of course he couldn't. The sports car nicked the back wheel of his bike and sent Tyler and the bike off the road and over the side of Cadillac Mountain. Tyler flew into the air and landed hard in the pine scrub. He rolled and rolled, down, down, down the cliff until his rapid head-over-heels fall was finally stopped by a large boulder. His bike, which had flown out from under him when he went off the road, continued its long, downward tumble into Borden Pond, the beautiful lake at the bottom of the mountain. Tyler lay still, unable to move. At first he was conscious and in pain. He could not understand what had happened. He always checked his equipment carefully, even compulsively, whether it was for skiing or kayaking or biking, and he had never had an accident in his more than seventy years of riding bicycles. He knew Lilleth and his friends would come to help him, and he allowed himself to drift into unconsciousness.

Only Matthew Ritter, who was bringing up the rear of the foursome had seen Tyler go off the side of the mountain. The other two bikers had been in front of Tyler and hadn't seen the accident. Matthew was a physician, and he immediately pulled off the road, disembarked, and called 911 on his cell phone. Mobile phone service was spotty in this remote part of Maine. In the early days, when cell phones were not as common, poor service was frequently the norm, but everyone with a phone was now spoiled, as cellular service became dependable and nearly ubiquitous. Here, in a national park on Mount Desert Island, however, service came and went at will.

Matthew had seen Tyler fly off his bike and roll down the cliff. He knew Tyler was hurt; he just didn't know how badly. Matthew spoke with the 911 operator, but he wasn't exactly sure where he was or where to tell her to send the EMTs. Then he called Lilleth, but she didn't answer. He sent her a text message. Then he called J.D. who answered his phone. Matthew told him what had happened and where he thought he was. J.D. was able to catch up with Lilleth who was in the lead and tell her there had been an accident. They turned their bikes around and raced back to where they hoped to find Matthew and Tyler. J.D. the logistician, always aware of where he was, knew the best way to tell the 911 operator how to find them and gave her the number of the closest mile marker. The 911 operator was grateful for this information which she relayed to the ambulance that was on its way.

The three decided J.D. would stay put at the top of the cliff to wait for the help that was coming, and Matthew and Lilleth would climb down to try to reach Tyler. J.D. was more agile, but Matthew was a doctor who could give Tyler any medical care that might be needed. The two men didn't want Lilleth to climb down, but of course she was not going to wait on the side of the road when Tyler was hurt and lying in a heap somewhere. Lilleth and Matthew scrambled down the steep embankment to get to Tyler. They tried to be careful not to slip and fall. More casualties that had to be rescued would not be good. Matthew was seventy-five. He was an avid tennis player and hunter and in good shape, but he was not a mountain climber. He had to get to his friend, so he somehow found the strength and courage to go over the edge and make the difficult climb down the cliff. It was not an easy descent.

Matthew and Lilleth finally reached Tyler, who was now unconscious. His pulse was rapid and weak, but at least there was a pulse. Tyler was covered with blood, and he had cuts and scratches all over his face and legs. The spandex outfit had protected the rest of his body. His left shoulder and right foot looked all wrong to Dr. Matthew Ritter. He was sure Tyler had some broken bones, including those he could see and those he couldn't.

He wondered how in the world the emergency responders would ever be able to get Tyler safely off the mountain and to the help he desperately needed. Matthew wondered how he and Lilleth were going to get themselves back up the mountain to their bikes. They were both worn out from the climb down to find Tyler and from the stress of seeing their friend in trouble. Matthew Ritter began to wonder if biking at age seventy-five had been a wise choice. Then he rationalized that accidents could happen to people of any age, and they'd been doing fine until the sports car had run into the back of Tyler's bike. Ritter didn't yet know, as no one but Tyler knew at this time, that something disastrous had happened to his bike. The critical failure of the brakes and the steering were what had caused him to lose control.

Lilleth tried to get Tyler to drink some water, but he remained unconscious and couldn't drink. She sat beside him and held his hand. She'd wanted to cradle his head in her lap, but Matthew had urged her not to move him, especially his head and neck, for fear of doing more damage. Matthew felt for Tyler's pulse every couple of minutes, to reassure himself that his friend was still alive. The injured biker was losing blood, but there didn't seem to be an arterial breach. No blood was gushing, and there was no obvious place to put pressure to stop serious bleeding. It seemed as if they waited forever, sitting on the cold, hard, rocky ground. In fact it was less than thirty minutes before help arrived in the form of two young men who quickly and confidently clambered down the mountain to find them.

The two EMTs had brought a body board. This was not their first rodeo. They had rescued people from the side of a mountain before. They quickly assessed Tyler's injuries and stabilized his shoulder and ankle. They braced his neck, strapped him to the body board, and were prepared to carry him up the mountain to the road. A helicopter would meet them there, and Tyler would be on his way to a hospital in Bangor. The two EMTs looked at Lilleth and Matthew, and shrugged their shoulders. These two friends of the injured man were not their problem. They had a patient to take care of. Lilleth and Matthew would have to find their own way back to safety and civilization.

Lilleth wanted to go with Tyler to the hospital, but she wasn't able to climb to the road fast enough. There wasn't really room for her on the small chopper anyway. J.D. got the name of the hospital in Bangor where the helicopter was taking Tyler. He had already called Olivia and Isabelle and told them where to bring two cars, Tyler and Lilleth's rental car and the Carpenters' large SUV. Just the day before, J.D. had, without even being aware of it, noted the size, make and color of each couple's car. That was the way his mind worked. The Carpenters had driven to Maine in their Ford Expedition. J.D. remembered all the rental cars, and he knew the Carpenters' older SUV was the only vehicle in the group with space adequate to hold three people plus carry three bikes in the back. As the owner and manager of a large and successful trucking business, J.D. was a logistical genius and knew what had to happen. Matthew would drive Lilleth in Tyler's rental car to the hospital in Bangor. Olivia would drive Isabelle and J.D., who was by now a bedraggled and exhausted biker, plus the three bikes back to the Inastou Lodge in the Carpenters' SUV. Tyler's bike was long gone, resting at the bottom of Borden Pond.

Text messages were sent and calls were made. The lunch reservation at the Borden Pond House Restaurant was cancelled, and everyone decided to meet in the dining room of the Inastou for lunch and a debriefing about what was happening with Tyler. The popovers helped and so did the delicious bowls of lobster stew and peekytoe crab chowder. Everyone was upset and worried about Tyler's condition. It was the first day of their reunion, and they were already one down. Nothing like this had happened before.

J.D. told the group everything he knew. Then they called Matthew Ritter and put him on speaker phone. "Tyler's going to be all right. He's had some serious injuries, but nothing life-threatening. He has a dislocated shoulder, but it's not broken. He has a trimalleolar fracture of his ankle, and he's in surgery now for that. I checked out the orthopedist, and he's first rate. I told him to take good care of Tyler. Apart from lots of cuts and abrasions and three cracked ribs from the tumble down the mountain, Tyler's okay. He was very lucky. He could have died if he'd gone off the road in a different spot. He could have died falling down the cliff in the spot where he went off the road. He'll be in pain from the broken ribs for a few days. His ankle will be in a cast for a month and then in a boot for another four weeks while he heals from the fracture."

The group had questions, and everyone was thankful that Tyler was going to be all right. Lilleth was staying at the hospital in Bangor. Matthew needed a way to get back to the Inastou. He asked for a volunteer willing to drive to Bangor to pick him up and drive him back to Mount Desert Island. Richard Carpenter volunteered and said he would leave right after lunch. Richard, also a physician, wanted to go to Bangor anyway. He wanted to see Tyler when he came out of surgery and talk to Tyler's doctor. After Matthew Ritter concluded his report, you could almost hear a collective sigh of relief. Everyone ordered dessert, unusual for this crowd that had so many health-conscious members. Almost everyone took a nap that afternoon.

Chapter 4

TYLER MERRIMAN WAS A HIGH SCHOOL FOOTBALL star. The Air Force Academy recruited Tyler to play football, and he played for one year before he was sidelined by a shoulder injury. Tyler stayed on and graduated. He subsequently earned an MBA from Stanford. He became a pilot for the United States Air Force and spent ten years flying military missions for the USA. He never talked about the years he'd spent in the USAF, but his closest friends speculated that he was flying the Lockheed SR-71, "the Blackbird" spy plane that supposedly had the capability to see the numbers and letters on the license plate of a car parked in Red Square. When anyone came right out and asked him if he'd flown the Blackbird, Tyler would hum a few bars of the Beatles' song of the same name and smile his enigmatic smile. If he had flown the Blackbird, he would have been able to see everything and everybody from way up there. But he would never tell.

Tyler had married, briefly, when he was in the military, but his wife was young and somewhat spoiled. She resented the time Tyler spent away from home, and they divorced when they'd been married for less than two years. Tyler moved to Northern California after he left the Air Force. He built a commercial real estate empire and became a wealthy man. Tyler dated well-known and glamorous women — movie actresses, anchorwomen who appeared on national television, and female politicos. He was very good looking and a much sought-after bachelor, but he successfully avoided the altar for decades after his first marriage ended.

Tyler Merriman had been smart and lucky in his business dealings, and he was a consummate athlete. He bought a condominium in Telluride, Colorado so he could ski for several months in the winter. Because he was such a skilled and outstanding performer on the slopes, it wasn't long before he was hired as a ski instructor. His time was his own, and he arranged his schedule so he could spend most of the winter in Telluride. He found he loved teaching others to ski. Tyler had his own plane and flew around the country to check on his commercial real estate empire. He hiked and biked and ran, and he even sometimes played squash, when he couldn't be outdoors. Tyler was a very active guy. He decided he wanted to be closer to his condominium in Telluride and eventually relocated from California to Colorado.

He was in his early seventies when he met the stunning Lilleth Dubois. He first saw her on the ski slopes. Lilleth was skiing The Plunge, the most demanding run on the mountain, with confidence and ease. She was a beautiful and aggressive skier, and her grace and athleticism caught Tyler's attention. He skied close to her and watched her as she turned and handled the difficult moguls and made her way down the slopes. He knew he had to meet her. At the end of the day, he followed her into the ski lodge and wasted no time introducing himself. She did not appear to be with a date, and Tyler moved in to get to know this lovely woman who was at least his equal in the snow.

Lilleth lived in Farmington, New Mexico, and was on vacation in Telluride. Every year, she spent a week of her vacation at a nearby ski resort with demanding runs. She loved the challenge. Lilleth had been married before, but she never talked about her ex-husband. She was not at all interested in a new relationship, but she dated occasionally. When Tyler approached her in the ski lodge, there was something about him that she found intriguing and appealing. She decided to give him a few minutes of her time. As they talked, it became apparent that she and Tyler had much in common in terms of their love of physical activity.

She accepted his invitation to dinner, and they drank a bottle of wine and talked late into the night.

Lilleth was a psychotherapist, and her practice consisted primarily of counseling Native Americans who lived on the Navajo reservations in Northwestern New Mexico. Her job was another challenge she enjoyed. A significant percentage of Native Americans have problems with addictions, and Lilleth spent many client hours dealing with these. Her clients spilled the beans to her about who was embezzling money from the casinos, who was cooking meth on the reservation, who was running the bootleg alcohol business, and other confidences. All psychologists hear people's secrets, but because of the particular circumstances of Lilleth's practice, her clients had more secrets to tell.

Lilleth's patients liked her, and most were grateful for her help. Occasionally, one would go off the wagon, and his or her dark side would take over. He might beat up his wife and children or rob a bank. Anything could happen when the demon rum was let loose. A client who was polite and meek when sober could turn into a deranged lunatic if he or she indulged in too much alcohol.

Once a client had attacked Lilleth when she was getting into her car. The man had been drinking excessively and was wandering around the parking lot of the community center where Lilleth met with her patients. The man had been in trouble before, and that night he pushed Lilleth down when she tried to open her car door. She hit her head, and the resulting gash required several stitches in her jaw. But Lilleth was tough, and she was able to call 911 on her cell phone while she tried to talk the inebriated man down from his anger and confusion. He was threatening her with a knife when the reservation's law enforcement officers showed up to take him into custody.

Lilleth hadn't wanted to testify against him at his trial. Because, on several previous occasions, he had assaulted other people when he'd been drunk, he had to go to prison. Lilleth visited him while he was incarcerated. She was sorry she'd had to participate in sending him to jail. She had forgiven the man for hurting her. Trying to keep her clients away from the bottle was one of the toughest challenges she faced. She wouldn't allow herself to live in constant fear, but she never knew when someone she was treating would go over the edge.

Lilleth and Tyler dated long-distance for many months. Tyler was in love like he had never been in his younger years. Lilleth was even more wary of commitment than he was, but she had grown very fond of Tyler. It was a big step for her when she accepted his invitation to move in with him and live at his house in Bayfield, Colorado.

Tyler had been attending the reunions for years and looked forward to seeing his old friends and their wives and girlfriends. He'd never brought a date or a partner to one of the events. This year, he'd finally convinced Lilleth to accompany him. She was anxious to see Maine, and Tyler had assured her that the group was friendly and would welcome her as if they had known her all their lives. Lilleth was skeptical, but she agreed to go to Bar Harbor. Tyler had planned extra days of hiking, biking, kayaking, and other activities. Lilleth knew he liked to show off his own vigor to his friends. She suspected he also was proud of how strong she was and that she had the stamina to keep up with the men in the group.

Chapter 5

THAT NIGHT, THE GROUP HAD A RESERVATION TO EAT at Gusto, a highly-touted and well-known Italian restaurant that, rumor had it, boasted several stars. They almost canceled because of their distress over Tyler's accident but decided to go ahead and keep their reservation at the pricy eatery. Disheartened that Tyler was in the hospital, they decided, after some discussion, that they needed a really good meal and a few bottles of wine to cheer them up. Tyler would want them to carry on.

The restaurant was in an old farm house, and the concierge had made their reservation for a special table on the second floor. The second floor was the most exclusive and prestigious part of the restaurant. Because there was no elevator or lift to take her to the second floor of Gusto, Elizabeth Carpenter was not going to be able to sit upstairs with the others. She was fine with that. She was independent and urged the concierge to keep the reservation for the rest of the group in the special second-floor room. Elizabeth explained that she was happy to dine alone and did not mind in the least that she would be seated on the first floor while everyone else was eating upstairs. But the group didn't want Elizabeth to sit by herself, so the party was moved to the first floor. The concierge pointed out that, even with two members of the group not able to be there for dinner, the group would be crowded at the downstairs table. The restaurant was completely booked that night, and it was only because of Vanna's connections with the owners that they were able to change their table at the last minute.

Everyone loves Italian food, and the wine flowed. The restaurant made a variety of excellent soups, and the saltimbocca and the pappardelle with duck ragu were the specialties of the house. The conversation, of course, was all about Tyler's accident. Richard Carpenter and Matthew Ritter were the last to make it to Gusto for dinner. They were just back from Bangor and had the latest news about Tyler's surgery.

Dessert arrived and everybody had to try one of Matthew's enormous bowl of zeppole. They were so delicious. It was a toss-up as to which dessert was better, the zeppole or the chocolate bandito which was a warm chocolate cake with chocolate pudding oozing out from the center and crème fraiche on the side. No one had minded that their table had been crowded into a corner. This group had other things to think and talk about.

Richard and Matthew reported that Tyler had been conscious after his surgery and had been able to communicate a few words to his two physician friends. Because he had sustained a bad bruise to his neck when he'd tumbled down the mountain, his voice was raspy and difficult to hear. His words had been almost impossible to understand, but Richard and Matthew had leaned close to the hospital bed so they could hear him. The good news was that Tyler's condition was stable, and he was going to ultimately recover from all of his injuries. What they'd learned from Tyler about his accident had not been good. Even though his voice was weak, his head was clear, and what he had to tell his friends was disturbing.

Tyler insisted that his bike had been sabotaged. He struggled to be able to speak, but he was adamant. He exerted all of his effort to emphasize this important point and get it across to Richard and Matthew. They believed him when Tyler told them that the brakes and the steering on his rented bike had been tampered with. Tyler stated with conviction that he had checked out everything about the bike before he'd agreed to rent it.

Over the years, Tyler had rented countless bikes for biking trips throughout the world. He had check lists he consulted whenever he rented a bike, ski equipment, scuba gear, or a boat. He was compulsive about his safety inspections. This Maine rental had been an almost new bike, and the brakes and steering had worked fine when Tyler had gone over them in the shop. He kept insisting that Matthew and Richard examine the bike. Tyler was sure his assessment, that the brakes and steering had been deliberately damaged, would be corroborated, if someone would just take a look at the bike. Tyler didn't know that his bike had continued on down the mountain after he'd been thrown off and that it was now at the bottom of Borden Pond. He didn't seem to understand that the bike was way beyond anyone's reach. It was gone forever to its resting place in the deep, dark waters of the lake in the Acadia National Park.

On the drive back from Bangor, Richard and Matthew discussed Tyler's resolute account regarding his bike's malfunctioning. They knew their friend and absolutely believed that someone had purposely incapacitated the bike's brakes and steering. His doctor friends had several questions for Tyler that would have to wait a few days. They could not imagine why anyone would want to hurt Tyler. Why would someone purposely damage his bike and cause him to have an accident? He could have sustained a spinal cord injury and been paralyzed for life. He could have died in the fall. He was lucky he'd not sustained an injury more serious than a fractured ankle. Tyler's bike accident was as puzzling as it was upsetting.

Matthew and Richard were able to reassure the group that Tyler was going to be fine. He would be on crutches for several weeks, but in the long run, he would recover completely. On the other hand, their story about Tyler's bike was anything but comforting.

"Could the tampering with the bike have been intended for someone else in the group? There were four of us who rented bikes." Gretchen hadn't been one of the bikers, but she was a problem solver and could figure things out.

"Originally there were eight people who said they were going on the bike ride. I was one of the eight who thought I could do it, but I changed my mind. When I saw a picture of the mountain online and looked at the route you jocks planned to take, I decided I wasn't up to that grueling course. So I called a couple of days ago and cancelled my bike rental." Olivia was athletic but not as athletic as her husband. "I knew J.D. would want to stay with the program. Maybe the bike shop got mixed up. Could the bad bike have been intended for one of us who cancelled?"

"Why would somebody want to hurt any of us, anyway? We're all old, except for a couple of the younger wives and girlfriends. Nobody here in Bar Harbor knows any of us. None of us have ever lived here, and only a few of us have ever been here before. Elizabeth spent a summer in Bar Harbor with her parents when she was eight years old. That was more than sixty-five years ago. Matthew hunted ruffed grouse somewhere in Maine two decades ago. Several years ago, J.D. and Olivia went to Augusta for a few days to a meeting. Bailey has visited Bar Harbor a couple of times in the distant past. Who is going to remember any of that? Why in the world would anybody want to hurt us?" Isabelle was the voice of reason, and no one could disagree with her logic.

"Maybe the rigged bike was intended for another group of bikers, and it got put in with our bikes by mistake?" J.D. had been one of the bikers. His bike had been fine, but he knew first-hand that things at the bike shop that morning had been hectic and confusing. There had been too many people clamoring for the clerks to hurry up and get their bikes ready so they could leave the shop and enjoy the beautiful September morning. In the chaos, bikes could have been mixed up. The others at the table nodded in agreement. This certainly seemed like the best explanation for the bike tampering. No one wanted to believe that someone in their group was a target or that somebody would deliberately want to injure one of them in an accident or a fall down the mountainside.

Tyler's doctors had said he would be released from the hospital late the following afternoon. Several people at the table shook their heads.

In the old days, a person who'd been injured as badly as Tyler had been and who had just undergone surgery for a bad ankle break would spend several days in the hospital. Matthew pointed out that Tyler was lucky they'd kept him at the hospital overnight. If he'd lived in Bangor, they might have sent him home immediately after the surgery. It was still surprising to these older folks that no one was allowed to recover in the hospital any more.

Tyler and Lilleth's room was on the second floor of the Inastou Lodge. When Tyler came home from the hospital, he was going to be using crutches, and climbing up and down the stairs, to and from his second-floor room, was going to be difficult. There was only one handicap room available at the Inastou, and it was not even in the lodge itself. It was across the street and around the corner at Blueberry House, and that room was already occupied — by Elizabeth and Richard Carpenter. When he was able to communicate, Tyler insisted that he would be able to manage the steep steps at the Inastou on his crutches. He'd been an athlete and had experienced injuries and broken bones in the past. He claimed that he was an expert on crutches. Lilleth was skeptical and reminded him he hadn't used crutches in several decades. She used her phone to rent a wheelchair and have it delivered to the Inastou, just in case.

Their room at the Inastou was small, as was the antiquated bathroom. Lilleth explained the situation to the hotel manager, and he did offer to move them to a larger room with a larger bathroom. This would give Tyler more room to move around and maneuver on the crutches. Richard and Matthew would drive back to Bangor the next afternoon to help Lilleth get Tyler into the rental car for their drive back to Bar Harbor. She really wanted to take Tyler all the way home to Colorado, but everyone agreed he needed a few days to rest and get his strength back before he set off on a long and arduous flight with two plane changes.

Tyler had been scheduled to go kayaking with Matthew the next morning. Of course that was out, but they had already paid to reserve the kayak and a guide. Cameron Richardson agreed to take Tyler's place in the two-man kayak, although it had been more than ten years since he'd climbed into one. He was being a good sport, stepping up to take his friend's place so the kayak and the guide didn't go to waste. Sidney rolled her eyes and shook her head when Cameron volunteered to participate in the kayaking adventure. Cameron loved to take risks of all kinds, but he was more a car-racing and motorcycle-racing risk-taker than a water sports enthusiast. Sidney knew better than to argue with her strong-willed husband. She knew he was a good swimmer, but she crossed her fingers, hoping his swimming skills would not be put to the test.

Everyone was exhausted that night from the trauma of the day's unexpected misfortune. They could not know that the calamities had only just begun. Only one person knew what was in store for the group, and their unsuspecting nemesis from long-ago was watching them and waiting while he planned his next surprise.

Chapter 6

They met in New Orleans when he was a fourth-year medical student at Tulane and she was a freshman at Newcomb College. They both had roots in Tennessee, although at different ends of that state. Their first few dates had long-term relationship written all over them. Isabelle Blackstone was considerably younger than Matthew Ritter, but he was committed to being eternally young and worked out every day to stay that way. They made a handsome couple. Isabelle was blonde and beautiful, and Matthew knew she was the one. He was in love, but he wasn't ready to settle down. He had places to go and people to see. He had an internship and a residency to do, and he had signed up to fulfill his obligations to his country by spending two years working for the United States Public Health Service. She had just finished her freshman year in college. Matthew was moving on to California for his internship, the next chapter in the long quest to become a urologist. Would Isabelle go with him or would she stay in New Orleans?

In the end, she decided he was worth it. She would transfer to UCLA and complete her undergraduate studies there. Her parents were not happy when their nineteen-year-old daughter told them she wanted to leave Newcomb College and move to California to complete her degree. But they trusted her and agreed to pay her tuition in California. She was an excellent student and worked hard to graduate with a dual degree in psychology and sociology. Isabelle and Matthew married after Isabelle finished her undergraduate studies, and they moved to the Phoenix area where Matthew served his two years in the Public Health Service, working on what was then called an Indian Reservation. While they lived near Phoenix, Isabelle earned a master's degree in clinical psychology at Arizona State University, and she later opened her own counseling practice in Palm Springs, the same year Matthew joined a thriving urology group in that California city.

The professional corporation Matthew Ritter joined was the leading group of urologists in Southern California. Movie actors and other famous people from Los Angeles drove to Palm Springs for medical care, especially when they had an embarrassing problem they didn't want anyone in L.A. to know about. Matthew was bound by the Hippocratic Oath and the covenant of professional confidentiality not to talk about his patients. And he never did. He kept many confidences about highly-placed people in all walks of life. As well as the Hollywood crowd, he treated wealthy businessmen and politicians, including two governors of Western states, several United States Senators, and assorted Congressmen and judges. His group was known for its medical expertise as well as for its discretion. Matthew knew many scandalous things, secrets quite a few famous people hoped he would carry to his grave. He would, but did they all trust that he would always abide by his commitment to confidentiality?

Isabelle likewise knew her clients' secrets. She was an effective therapist and a warm and caring human being. Her patients loved her. She had a successful practice within a year of hanging out her shingle and had to begin hiring additional counselors to join her. There was a lot of money in Palm Springs. There were also some very large egos in residence, a not unexpected circumstance, as the very successful wanted to live, vacation, and retire in this golf course mecca that was reputed to have more sunny days than any other place in the United States. There was a great deal of infidelity, and many people came to her with problems that were associated with their addictions to drugs and alcohol. There was domestic abuse, and women, who did not want to be seen in public with a black eye or a broken arm, left Beverly Hills to hide out and seek counseling in Palm Springs. Isabelle listened and dispensed advice to the rich and famous.

Isabelle was sometimes called to testify in court, something she hated to do. She didn't like to break a confidence, but she was legally bound to respond to a subpoena to appear in court and to testify honestly when questioned under oath. She had almost been called to testify in the extraordinarily high-profile murder trial that involved a very famous football player and his second wife. Everyone knew the athlete had been beating up his wife on a regular basis. He'd finally killed her and was on trial for murder. Isabelle thankfully hadn't had to testify in that case. But there were other cases where her testimony had resulted in an unstable parent being denied custody of their child or children in a divorce. She had received direct and very personal threats as a result of some of these court cases.

She had struggled to work, at least part-time, while she raised the couple's two children. Isabelle had household and babysitting help, and she spent as much time in her office as she could. She knew she needed the stimulation of doing her own thing while dealing with diaper changes, wiping down counters, making endless peanut butter and jelly sandwiches, and driving her children to their after-school activities and numerous sports events. When her children graduated from high school, Isabelle realized she was burned out being a clinical psychologist, and she began to look for a new and less stressful career.

She found her next identity as an interior designer and owner of an elegant high-end shop that sold European antiques, lamps, and other wonderfully beautiful and expensive accessories for the home. Isabelle's store, *Blackstone White*, immediately became everybody's favorite place to find the perfect piece to make a room both interesting and classy.

What Isabelle had not expected was the extent to which being an interior designer and a store owner would call on her skills as a therapist. People came into the store to talk and sometimes to cry. Her clients had a great deal of money, but they did not always have much happiness or contentment. Isabelle was a good listener. She was patient and kind. People she barely knew poured out their hearts to her. If a husband was laundering money, his wife might express her disgust or her fear about his activities to Isabelle. If a boyfriend was involved in the drug trade, the girlfriend would confide in Isabelle. There were plenty of Mafiosi living in Palm Springs.

Isabelle sometimes helped a client disappear. It started with a woman who was a prolific shopper and regular customer of Isabelle's. The woman came into the store one day, terrified that her husband had sent his henchmen to kill her. She begged Isabelle to allow her to hide in the storage room at the back of *Blackstone White*. Isabell trusted her gut and helped the woman lie down, well-concealed, behind a pallet of oriental rugs. Sure enough, two greasy looking tough guys with tattoos all over their arms, arrived at the store, and without asking, searched high and low for the gangster's wife. Isabelle was frightened, but she was also angry. The mobsters were unable to find Isabelle's client, and as soon as they'd left, Isabelle called the police and reported the two for bursting into her store, turning everything topsy-turvy, and searching her property without her permission. She knew nothing would come of the police report she'd filed, but felt she had done the right thing.

Isabelle hid the frightened woman in her own home for several days and then drove her to Mexico. The woman had a secret bank account in L.A. and hoped to start a new life south of the border. The incident had been terrifying, but Isabelle had found a new calling. She was now an interior designer, store owner, and rescuer of the abused. It was a lot to take on, and Isabelle often asked herself if she had merely traded one stressful job for another even more stressful job.

The interior design part of her business was booming. Isabelle had excellent taste. Everybody wanted her to design the addition to their house; consult with them about the space planning in their new kitchen; and do the paint, curtains, and new furniture in the family room renovation. She had more business than she could handle. She spent a lot of time in clients' homes and often drew on her counseling skills to settle disputes within their families. The husband, who was paying the bill for the redecorating project, didn't like white walls. The wife, who would be spending most of her waking hours in the room, wanted only white walls. He dug in his heels. She refused to talk about it. The interior designer/marriage counselor came to the rescue and brought a compromise and reconciliation. Isabelle often wondered how interior designers without experience in clinical counseling were ever able to accomplish anything.

Isabelle saw and heard many things she never wanted to see or hear. She kept her secrets, but she sometimes wondered if an angry father, who had been denied access to his children because of his mental illness, would remember her court testimony and come after her. She worried that the women she'd helped disappear would be found. Would the assistance Isabelle had given to rescue and hide these victims be exposed? Would an angry abuser come after her?

Chapter 7

The group met the next morning for breakfast. The food at the Inastou was excellent, and the buffet breakfast that came with the exorbitant room fee was not to be missed. Sometimes one or two in the group slept late, but this morning, everyone was present. Even Richard and Elizabeth, who were staying in another building across the road, were there. Whenever they wanted to do something at the main building of the lodge, Richard had to get their car out of the parking lot and drive Elizabeth from Blueberry House, across the street to the Inastou. Then he had to park the car again. It was a lot of trouble.

The ramp that went from the parking area at Blueberry House to the door of their room was made of rotted wood and was in disrepair. A board at the bottom of the ramp had come loose and was sticking up in the air at a dangerous angle. It was an accident awaiting the unsuspecting, and to make matters worse, rusted nails and screws protruded at odd angles from the errant board. Fortunately, the weather was fine. If it had been raining, the ramp would have been impossibly slippery. There were no railings to hang onto as one went up and down the ramp. To remain upright, Elizabeth had to hang onto the structure of the wood-splintered porch supports as she walked on the ramp to her room.

Richard delivered Elizabeth to the Inastou and drove to the back parking lot with the car. Although they had a handicap sticker for their SUV, there were no handicap parking spaces provided near the front door of the Inastou's main building. No disabled people were wanted there!

Elizabeth made it into the lobby, but there was not a single chair available for anyone to sit down in the large and almost empty room. The lobby was an inviting space to look at, but only the desk clerk was allowed to sit down ... behind the registration desk. There was a fireplace that could hold a crackling fire on a cool autumn day. The enormous Persian rug that covered the floor was beautiful and obviously of very fine quality. The wainscoting and woodwork in the room were original to the building. It would have been an appealing trip down memory lane, but no one could ever spend any time in this otherwise lovely room, because there was no place to sit. There was plenty of space for a pair of love seats to be arranged on either side of the fireplace. There was room for a strategically positioned wing chair or two. A few pieces of furniture — something a person could sit down on — would have made this lobby so much more hospitable.

They gathered for breakfast and took their plates to a table on the sunny back porch. The view overlooked Northeast Harbor, and it was a gorgeous day. Both kayakers were dressed to begin their outing on Borden Pond. Cameron and Matthew said goodbye to the others and headed out to meet their guide. Some of those who weren't going boating were a little bit envious of those who would be spending the morning on the water. It would be a fun time, and the weather could not be more perfect. The rest of the group would meet the kayakers at the Borden Pond House Restaurant at noon. They'd managed to reschedule their lunch from yesterday. The popovers at the restaurant were famous, and nobody wanted to miss those.

Matthew had been an expert canoer at Camp Shoemaker, and he'd used his canoeing skills quite a few times in the years since. He and Richard had gone canoeing on the Ouachita River and the White River in Arkansas. Although he'd never been kayaking, Matthew felt that, because of his canoeing experience, he would be fine in the kayak. Cameron had been in a kayak quite a few times, but the last time had been many years ago. Their guide turned out to be a young woman, and she gave them a brief rundown on the safety rules and regulations. The trip was off to an auspicious beginning.

Cameron was in the rear of the kayak, working the rudder, and he began to notice that his feet and his behind were getting wet. They were in the middle of the lake, and it was a calm day. There was no wind, and any kind of danger seemed a million miles away. Their guide was in a one-person kayak, and in addition to Cameron's and Matthew's kayak, she was directing another two-person kayak on the lake. At first the water began to rise slowly around Cameron's legs; then it began to rise more rapidly. Cameron called to their guide, and she paddled over to them.

"Look at this water. I think we've sprung a leak. Do you think we should start back toward the shore?" Cameron was concerned, but the guide wasn't.

"I checked these kayaks out carefully first thing this morning. That's part of my job as a guide, to be sure the kayaks are in good repair and ready for the water. I know there aren't any holes in your kayak. You must be sloshing the water in there. That's why you're getting wet." The guide was not impressed with Cameron's and Matthew's skills as kayakers, but she wasn't paying much attention to them. She was more worried about the lack of skills and the erratic behavior of the two teenagers in the other kayak that was traveling alongside the older men's kayak. "Just relax. You're not going to sink."

A few minutes later, Cameron thought he felt something slither across his thigh. He could not imagine what it was, but it felt like a lot like a snake. The water was rising faster and faster in the kayak. Matthew, in the forward position, became concerned, as it was now obvious that the kayak was sinking. The two men were a long way from the shore, but they both realized they were going to have to extricate themselves from their vessel and swim for it. Cameron knew how to do a wet exit, but Matthew was unfamiliar with how to get out of the kayak in a safe way. He struggled to raise himself out of the kayak and finally realized he would have to wait until the craft had sunk a little more into the water before he would be able to free himself. Finally, the water level was high enough and the kayak was low enough that he was able to safely get out of the kayak and into the water. Both Cameron and Matthew were strong swimmers and they were wearing life jackets, but they were left hanging onto a kayak that was rapidly going down.

Cameron had his hand inside the kayak, trying to hang on, as the two attempted to kick their way to shore. All of a sudden he felt a sharp pain in his hand, and immediately afterwards he felt a sharp pain in his forearm. He'd been bitten. He grasped the thing that had bitten him and pulled it from the sinking kayak. It looked like a water moccasin and was more than a yard long. Cameron told himself not to panic. He had to get to the shore. He had to get help. What if the snake was venomous? He wrestled to hang on to the snake. He was torn between wanting to secure the reptile for a closer examination and flinging it as far away from himself as possible. He kept hold of the snake because he wanted to have it in his possession. He wanted to be able to ask an expert if a bite from the thing could kill him, but he didn't think he could hang on to the snake all the way to shore. He would be lucky if he got to the shore on his own without the snake.

Even as their kayak was disappearing into the water, their guide was paying very little attention to them. She was screaming at the teenagers in the other kayak. They were rocking their kayak back and forth, trying to make it turn over. That behavior was strictly not allowed, and the boys were acting crazy. Matthew wondered if they were on drugs or if they were just brats, determined to do everything the guide had asked them not to do. A two-person kayak is fairly stable, so the two had to go to extremes to make it tip over. In spite of loud admonitions from the guide, they finally succeeded in turning over their kayak. They were both in the water, and they were screaming for help. It turned out that neither one of them was wearing a life jacket and neither one of them knew how to swim.

Cameron and Matthew were both seventy-five years old, but they knew when they had to rise to the occasion. Cameron threw the snake into the water. If it was dangerous, he would deal with that later. The guide was now in the water, trying to grab hold of one of the teenagers, who was thrashing around and fighting her off. She had to slap his face hard to keep him from dragging her under the water. Fortunately, she was a trained water safety instructor and knew what she was doing. Cameron and Matthew had taken a senior lifesaving class at Camp Shoemaker, but that had been a very, very long time ago. The two of them went after the second teenager who had sunk below the surface of the water and disappeared.

It had been a confluence of disasters ... the sinking kayak, the snake, and the rowdy teenagers who were at the very least high on pot. Cameron shed his life jacket and dove down into the water again and again to try to locate the missing non-swimmer. On his fourth or fifth dive, he finally found the limp body. He dragged the young man to the surface and could see he wasn't doing well. He'd probably swallowed and breathed in a lot of the lake water. Matthew and Cameron took turns towing the boy's dead weight to shore. Cameron's hand and arm were bleeding. He had completely forgotten about his encounter with the snake as he attempted to save a life. They finally dragged their charge onto land. Matthew immediately began CPR on the boy. He wasn't conscious, but after a few minutes of regular compressions on his chest, he coughed up a lot of water and began to breathe again.

Matthew and Cameron had saved the young man's life. Borden Pond was very cold. It wasn't meant for swimming, and nobody jumped into the water on purpose. The men who'd rescued the teenager were chilled to the bone. Matthew was shivering. He didn't have an ounce of fat on him and worked hard to keep himself thin. Cameron had a little more meat on his bones and hadn't been affected as much by the cold water. They had not planned on taking a swim. But here they were, sitting on the ground in the cold air in wet clothes. This is not a good idea, even for a person who is twenty years old.

They'd had to swim to the uninhabited side of the lake because it was the closest shore to where their kayak had gone down, but now they were there without any help nearby. Their cell phones were completely ruined. They'd watched as the young female guide struggled with her combative client. She was stronger than she looked, but she had to almost knock the teenager unconscious to get him out of the water. With some help from Cameron, she finally dragged herself and the boy, who was quite a bit taller and heavier than she was, up onto the shore. At least he was breathing and had at last stopped fighting her. The five water-soaked survivors were completely spent. They lay there on the beach on the wrong side of the lake.

Fortunately, there were plenty of people at the Borden Pond House Restaurant who had seen the spectacle of the two kayaks in trouble and the water rescues. Someone had called 911, and a rapidly moving rescue boat was on its way to the opposite shore of the lake. The Camp Shoemaker friends had gathered, expecting to join the kayakers for lunch. They had also witnessed the debacle and then the bravery of the kayak outing.

Sidney and Isabelle were sick with worry. They couldn't see much of anything on the opposite shore. They weren't able to see who had made it onto dry land, who was sitting up, and who was lying down. They had seen their husbands struggle with their own kayak and then struggle to bring a person out of the water. Cell phone service was poor on Mount Desert Island to begin with, and the wives knew there was no point trying to reach their spouses' water-soaked phones. They would have to rely on their patience and wait to find out what had happened.

Several minutes after the initial rapid rescue boat reached the shore across Borden Pond, a helicopter appeared and hovered over the five wet and weary boaters. J.D. Steele had a pair of binoculars in his car, and the watchers passed them around, taking turns, trying to figure out what was happening. The helicopter made several attempts to land before it successfully found itself on the beach. There wasn't much space between the trees and the water for a helicopter to touch down. It was possible to see, through the binoculars, that two people were being loaded onto stretchers and into the helicopter. After what seemed like an eternity, the chopper took off and lingered briefly over the water before making its way toward Bangor. Three figures were seen climbing gingerly into the rescue boat that had been the first on the scene. Those who had witnessed the drama on the water and the precarious helicopter rescue headed down to the dock where they waited for the rescue boat to arrive.

Sidney and Isabelle, two women who were usually willing to step back and wait their turn, did not stand on principle this time. They pushed through the crowd that waited by the pier, telling those who stood in their way that the men who were arriving were their husbands. They'd made their way to the front of the throng of gawkers by the time the boat reached the pier. Both Cameron and Matthew looked terrible. Their clothes were soaked, and they were completely drained of their usual energy. They were bedraggled and pale. The EMTs waiting on land tried to get to them before their wives did, and once Sidney and Isabelle had convinced themselves that Cameron and Matthew were all right, they allowed the EMTs to take over.

"We just want to check them out. I don't think we're going to have to transport them to the hospital. They are cold and exhausted. They're probably hungry and very thirsty. We're concerned about hypothermia right now. Go have lunch while we check them over. Buy some take-out food for them and take them back to wherever you are staying. Hot soup would be good. Make them eat and drink. Be sure they eat dinner tonight. They might want to sleep for hours and skip eating. They may not want to drink all the liquids they need to drink, but they need to be rehydrated. That's the most important thing to remember. Exhaustion and dehydration can lead to worse things. And they've been in very cold water for a long time. Cover them up with lots of blankets and give each of them a heating pad. Let them sleep this afternoon, but wake them up to eat dinner and drink lots of water. Gator Aid would also be a good thing. Their bodies are not really hurt. They just need to get back to normal. Your husbands are not spring chickens, you know."

Sidney laughed a small, nervous laugh, tremendously relieved to hear the news that Cameron and Matthew were going to be okay. "I know that. Spring chickens! Ha!" Sidney said this partly to herself and partly to the EMT.

Isabelle was mostly silent and angry. Why did Matthew always have to prove he was athletic? Why did he always have to go biking and kayaking. He had done this kind of thing all of his life. That had been fine when he really was young and could do all of these things without much effort. But he was now in his mid-seventies, and although he was in excellent physical condition, he was still old. He just couldn't admit it to himself, and he kept trying to act like a man twenty or thirty years younger. Isabelle had had enough of it. She was terribly thankful Matthew was going to be all right, but this was two days' worth of heart-stopping anxiety he had caused her and a lot of other people. She was going to eat lunch. Somebody had to keep their strength up. Somebody had to display some common sense.

They ordered a lot of food at the Borden Pond House Restaurant. They ordered lobster stew, seafood chowder, lobster salad, and the double-stuffed lobster rolls. The waitress who brought the popovers and butter was running back and forth non-stop to the kitchen. Some of the other guests in the restaurant stopped by the table to ask if the men were going to be all right. Did anybody know who the people were who had been taken away in the helicopter? Several diners, who had seen Sidney and Isabelle push to the front of the crowd waiting at the dock, said they hoped their husbands would be okay. It was a boisterous meal, fraught with worry and relief and wondering what in the world would be coming their way.

Cameron and Matthew's kayak had not gone down all the way to the bottom of the lake. It had a certain built-in buoyancy in spite of having almost sunk, and a work boat had hooked it up and towed it back across the pond to the pier. Someone turned it over, and there, on the bottom of the kayak, were gashes where something had knocked holes in the fiberglass. It was obvious the damage had been done intentionally.

Cameron examined the gashes and determined they'd probably been made with an axe. Cameron knew about tools, and it was alarming to him that someone had used a weapon as dangerous as an axe on the kayak. That choice spoke of a significantly angry intent. The workmen who were taking charge of the boat had worried expressions on their faces, and the visitors to the park who saw the gashes when the kayak was turned over gasped in disbelief. Who would do such a thing? Why would anyone want to? It was frightening to see such brutal vandalism used to destroy the kayak. The purposeful destruction could have caused more than one death.

The EMTs were finally finished with the two kayakers. Both Matthew and Cameron were wrapped in warm blankets. They were dead on their feet. Their wives made them drink copious amounts of water. The exhausted heroes seemed to revive a little bit as they began to rehydrate. Their friends had boxes of take-out sandwiches and containers of soup, and the two men were soon devouring everything that was put in front of them. The Inastou Lodge was not very far from the Borden Pond House Restaurant, and everyone was soon safely back in their rooms.

Sidney questioned Cameron about the bandages on his hand and arm.

"I was bitten by a snake." He said it in an off-hand way, but Sidney almost fainted when she heard his answer. "Don't worry. The snake wasn't poisonous. The only thing is, it could get infected. That's what I have to watch out for."

"How could you have been bitten by a snake?" Sidney was incredulous. She thought she'd seen and heard it all that morning, but she still had the snake bite story to look forward to.

"I was bitten by a snake called the 'northern water snake.' According the EMTs, it's Maine's most aquatic snake. It's a very robust and aggressive type. It bit me when I accidentally grabbed hold of it. It delivers a painful bite, but its bite isn't venomous. Did you know there aren't any poisonous snakes in Maine?" Sidney hadn't known that, but she was glad to hear at least one piece of good news.

As he drifted off to sleep, Cameron was thinking of what he hadn't told Sidney about the snake bite. The northern water snake is found only in Southern Maine. So someone had purposely brought the snake to Bar Harbor and placed it in the kayak. Was this some kind of a practical joke, or did someone want to frighten the kayakers? And why? He hadn't told Sidney this part of the story yet. They told each other everything, but he felt she'd had enough to deal with already today. He didn't want to worry her further by telling her he thought someone was out to get one or more of the people in their reunion group.

Chapter 8

CAMERON RICHARDSON HAD ALWAYS LOVED TO build things. From the time he was a child, he'd been taking things apart and putting them back together again. He loved to tinker. He loved to invent. He liked to change something, even just a little bit, to make it work better. That was the way his mind worked. There were stories of the rockets he and a friend had constructed and tried to launch; they were just in junior high school at the time. There were stories of gunpowder explosions in the woods and the resulting craters in the ground. Of course he would study science when he entered the small, exclusive southern college. He transferred to a university with an engineering program for his last two years, and upon graduation, he was immediately recruited by IBM.

Mastering the technology of computers opened up a whole new world to Cameron, and it wasn't long before he was out on his own, inventing and tinkering and making things better. He built an innovative and tremendously successful computer empire. Then he built a second revolutionary electronics enterprise. The man lived to challenge the status quo, and his head was always in the future.

Cameron's businesses dealt with enormous amounts of data, and thanks to computers, this data could be accessed relatively easily. It made him millions. It was inevitable that the U.S. federal government would, from time to time, come asking for help with something.

Cameron was a straight shooter, a good guy. He was an entrepreneur of the first order, but he was also honest, through and through his character and soul. He would not knowingly do something that was illegal or wrong. Sometimes he helped out the feds, and sometimes he didn't. He knew how to say no, even to Uncle Sam. When he said yes, it was never for his own gain but because he felt a patriotic duty to lend his expertise. He helped crack the cell phones that led to the arrests of terrorists. He helped out whenever he felt it was the right thing to do. He didn't want his part in any of these operations to become public, but there were some people who knew he had been instrumental in tracking down and gathering evidence on the bad guys. The question was, did any of the bad guys know that Cameron Richardson had helped to finger them and put them away?

There was no question about it. Cameron had information on everybody and everything. He didn't use it for nefarious purposes, but he did have it. Anybody who knew what his companies were all about knew he had the goods, and the bads. Anyone who has achieved the level of success that Cameron had, and anyone who has made the hard decisions about everything, including personnel, has acquired some enemies along the way. Because Cameron was a fair and benevolent boss, he'd made fewer enemies than most, but he had appropriately fired the dead wood that unfortunately but inevitably turned up, from time to time, among his employees. He'd made some people angry. He was cavalier about his own security, but his second wife Sidney worried about him.

Cameron had married for the first time when he was just out of college, and he'd married a woman several years older than himself. His friends had been puzzled about the union that, to those on the outside, seemed unusual. Were these two well-matched? Did they have anything at all in common? The guys loved their buddy and accepted his marital decision. Sometimes, love is strange. The marriage produced two children but eventually came to an end. The failure of the marriage wasn't anybody's fault.

After being a bachelor for a few years, Cameron met the love of his life. He had made his fortune and his reputation, and he finally had the time to invest in a relationship. Sidney Putnam insisted on it. She let Cameron know that, to make their marriage work, he needed to listen to what was important to her and spend time with her. He was wildly in love with Sidney, but she refused to marry him until he learned that she would be an equal partner in their marriage. She was not a back seat kind of woman.

Sidney's first marriage had also ended in divorce. She had one son, to whom she was devoted, and she'd been able to remain friends with her first husband, her son's father. Most people can't achieve this almost impossible feat, but Sidney had people skills that most people don't. Sidney had been the runner-up in her state's beauty pageant for the Miss America contest. She'd always had the looks, but more importantly, she had the smarts — of all kinds.

Sidney's most outstanding way of being smart was her gift for reading people. Her uncanny ability to know when someone was lying was an asset when she worked as a consultant for the Texas Department of Criminal Justice. She was the prosecutor's secret weapon. She consulted on jury selections and sat in on law enforcement interviews with suspects and witnesses. She was never wrong in her assessments. She didn't necessarily tell the authorities what they wanted to hear. She told the truth. And sometimes, nobody wanted to hear the truth. Sidney demanded that her assistance in criminal cases remain confidential, but she was almost too good to be true. Eventually, what she could do leaked out beyond the walls of the justice department, and she knew being exposed could put her in danger.

Her ability to vet people was invaluable to Sidney when she started her own business. As a single parent, she needed to support herself and her son. With her business, You Are Home, she identified a need that existed and built a business that responded to that need. Her first clients were corporations that frequently moved their employees from place to place. Corporations arranged to move their employee's household goods and paid for the packing and moving and unpacking. The gap in these employee benefits came when the wife, and it usually was the wife back in the day, had to put it all away and set up the new household. The husband, and it usually was the husband back in the day, was off doing his corporate thing, and the wife was at home with the kids, trying to find a place to put their stuff in the new kitchen and the unfamiliar closets.

Sidney's company was hired to come in and put their household goods away where they belonged. Her well-trained employees would organize the kitchen, at the housewife's direction, but with suggestions from the experts about the best kitchen logistics to make it fully functional. They put shelf paper in the drawers and on the shelves. They put away everybody's clothes — organizing, folding, and hanging everything in the most efficient and easy-to-access way. You Are Home would arrange for a room to be painted and would bring in other professionals to position furniture to its best advantage and hang art work. Sidney was good at this, and she taught her carefully-selected employees to be good at it, too. She charged high prices for her services, but there was a huge demand for what she was selling. Her company grew rapidly. She was a very successful entrepreneur in her own right when she literally ran into Cameron Richardson in a restaurant.

It was an expensive steak house in Fort Worth, and Sidney was there having lunch and closing a deal with a corporate client. It was summer, and she was dressed in a stunning white designer linen dress. She had a white cashmere cardigan sweater over her shoulders because the air conditioning was turned up so high in the steak house, to counter the July Texas heat. She got up to go to the ladies' room, and a tall, good-looking man didn't see her making her way through the tables in the dark, wood-paneled restaurant. The man pushed back his chair and stood up from his table with a large glass of iced tea in his hand. He ran straight into Sidney and spilled the entire glass of tea all over her dress, cashmere sweater, and expensive white high-heeled shoes. They were both stunned. He looked into the bright and beautiful eyes of the woman whose clothes he'd just ruined and couldn't turn away. To say it was love at first sight on his part would probably be the truth. She was angry that her outfit had been spoiled, but Cameron Richardson was so gracious about sending a car to drive her home to change her clothes. He insisted on paying for dry cleaning and replaced the clothes that could not be saved. Sidney had to soften her annoyance.

She had no idea who Cameron Richardson was, and they'd had several dates before Sidney fully grasped the extent of Cameron's wealth and success. Sidney was not looking for a relationship of any kind at this point in her life. She had a business to run and a child to raise. She was incredibly busy. But Cameron always went after what he wanted, and he usually got it. He went after Sidney like nothing he'd ever gone after in his life. Cameron pulled out all the stops to court the independent and strong-willed Sidney Putnam. The more she got to know him, the more she realized that Cameron was not only a success. He was also a kind and caring human being. She finally had to admit to herself that she'd fallen in love with the man.

Chapter 9

MATTHEW AND RICHARD PLANNED TO DRIVE to Bangor to help Lilleth get Tyler into their small and sporty rental car. When Tyler had chosen the car, he'd focused on the sporty aspect, never anticipating that he would break his ankle, have his leg in a cast, and be required to climb in and out of the car's passenger seat. Matthew was in no shape to go anywhere after the morning he'd spent on Borden Pond, and he was now sound asleep. Bailey offered to go to Bangor with Richard to help with Tyler. Richard thought he probably could do it alone, but he was happy to have the company on the drive.

Both Richard and Bailey knew how difficult it was going to be for Tyler to maneuver and get into and out of a car with a broken ankle. They knew better than Tyler did. Richard knew because he was a physician and had once had a broken ankle. Bailey knew because he'd done so much work with wounded vets. Tyler claimed he had lots of experience walking with crutches, but his memories were of how he'd handled himself when he was in his twenties and thirties. That had been a long time ago. He was going to need all the help he could get now that he was in his seventies! He just didn't want to admit it.

When they arrived at the hospital, Lillleth and Tyler were waiting for them at the curb. Tyler was sitting in the wheelchair the hospital had provided, and Lilleth went to get their sleek, low-slung, and very impractical rental car. When she arrived to pick up Tyler, the car looked very small to the group who'd assembled to get Tyler comfortably settled inside. They pushed the passenger seat back as far as they could, but Tyler was a tall and lanky guy. It was awkward and difficult to shoehorn him into the seat and get his legs into a position that would be tolerable for the drive back to Bar Harbor. The drive would take more than an hour, and Tyler already looked cramped and uncomfortable. Richard and Bailey were glad they'd come to help out. Even with four people working to get Tyler into the rental car, it had been a herculean feat. Lilleth stated that as soon as she had delivered Tyler to the Inastou Lodge, she was going to switch the sporty rental for a full-size sedan. Even a full-size sedan these days seemed like a small car to those who'd grown up with the enormous gas guzzlers of the 1950s and 60s. Richard and Bailey were going to follow Lilleth back to the Inastou to help her extricate Tyler from the sardine can of a car in which he was now encased.

When they arrived at the lodge in Northeast Harbor, it was another struggle to get their tall friend out of his car. Tyler insisted on using the crutches. Lilleth insisted that he use the wheelchair to get into the lodge. She finally decided to let him have his way, and sure enough, he slipped on the ramp that went up to the front porch of the lodge. He didn't fall all the way down, but caught himself on one of the porch's support columns. He recovered his equilibrium and didn't seem to have hurt himself. But his sheepish grin said it all, and Lilleth's "I told you so" expression said it all and then some. It was going to be a rough few days and weeks for the couple.

Tyler was finally settled on the back porch of the Inastou Lodge. He was in a comfortable chair someone had brought from somewhere else, especially for him to sit in. Comfortable chairs seemed to be in short supply at the Inastou. His foot was propped up on an ottoman that matched the chair. The best view in town was from this porch, and the staff at the lodge had promised to bring Tyler food and water and help him get to the restroom. The restroom situation was a problem at the Inastou. Their only public bathroom, that served its overnight guests as well as those who came to the lodge to have lunch or dinner, was in the basement. There was no bathroom on the main floor. You had to go down some very hazardous, steep steps to get to the bathroom. Tyler had a room in the lodge, and it had its own bathroom, of course. The problem was, that room was on the second floor.

The elevator was not self-serve. Tyler would have to depend on the desk clerk, who was usually tied up with another guest or on the phone or had disappeared into the back office someplace, to operate the elevator for him. All the guests were likewise inconvenienced by always having to wait for someone at the front desk to operate the elevator. Most gave up waiting, unless they had luggage in hand, and used the staircase rather than wait for someone at the desk to put in an appearance to operate the elevator. Tyler had the option of trying to go up and down the main stairs using his crutches, but after his experience on the ramp, he'd decided not to try that. He would have to build up his crutch muscle strength again before he felt confident enough to go up and down the steps. He was still taking a small dose of post-op pain killers which added to his instability.

Elizabeth was sitting with Tyler on the back porch, and Lilleth felt confident leaving Elizabeth in charge of Tyler. Lilleth knew she would summon help if Tyler got in trouble, needed something, or did something stupid. He was always trying to prove what an athletic man he was. Elizabeth could get around pretty well using a cane, but she couldn't do long distances or lots of steps. She rented a wheelchair when she was going to a museum or a hotel. For reasons Elizabeth had never been able to understand, many hotels located their rooms for the handicapped, the rooms that had bathrooms with roll-in showers, as far as possible from the elevators. If the handicap room was a reasonable distance from the elevators, Elizabeth was able to get to a hotel room without a wheelchair. Unfortunately, the more likely scenario was that hotels seemed to want to isolate their rooms for the handicapped and located them as inconveniently as possible.

The group was scheduled to go to Peel's Lobster Pier for dinner that night, and Tyler had been looking forward to this consummate

Maine experience for months. He insisted that he wanted to go to Peel's with the others. Lilleth had reserved a full-size sedan, and she had to exchange the rental cars before time to leave for the lobster pound.

Meanwhile, Darryl and Elena had arrived. They were doing their own thing and had already disappeared, dressed in glow-in-the-dark spandex, to power bike in the Acadia National Park. They had not wanted to hear anything about what had happened to Tyler, and even though Tyler and Darryl were the same age, Darryl and Elena brushed off Tyler's accident as the folly of the inept and the physically frail. Tyler of course was anything but inept or physically frail. His bike had been sabotaged. Darryl and Elena did not pay any attention to that part of the story and said they would be back in time to join the group for the trip to Peel's.

Cameron and Matthew didn't want to miss out on the trip to Peel's either. Even though the two had experienced a harrowing morning, they'd rested all afternoon. They were eager to take on a lobster and some corn on the cob. Cameron looked tired, and Matthew looked pale. But their appetites did not seem to have been harmed in any way by their exploits earlier in the day.

Everyone was excited to eat at the lobster pound. You waited in line to get to the lobster tank. You selected your lobster with the help of the man who did the steaming. He also steamed the corn on the cob and as many dozen clams as you thought you could eat. All the women, except for Elizabeth, ordered lobsters that weighed a pound and a half, and all the guys ordered two-pounders. Elizabeth also wanted a two-pounder, but by the time she got to the head of the line to place her order, Peel's was out of two-pounders. The man who steamed the lobsters asked if she wanted a lobster that was slightly less than two pounds or slightly more than two pounds. Of course, Elizabeth said she wanted one that was slightly more than two pounds. The lobster she ended up with looked as if it weighed considerably more. It was huge and had huge claws. The group found a long picnic table inside the tent that was Peel's dining area, and they carried their lobster stew and beverages to the picnic tables. They sat there with their order numbers displayed on tall metal stands, waiting for the servers to bring their steamed lobsters, clams, and corn.

When the food was delivered, Cameron looked over at Elizabeth's gigantic lobster. Then he looked at his own appreciably smaller lobster with dismay. "What size lobster did you order?" Cameron asked her, thinking there had to have been a mistake of some kind on somebody's part.

"I ordered a two-pounder, but they were out. The man said my lobster would weigh a little more than two pounds."

"A little more than two pounds! Your lobster is twice as big as mine. How can that be? How can they both be two-pounders?"

"I'll be happy to share some of my lobster with you. It's probably more than I can eat."

Cameron refused her offer to share the big lobster, but he kept looking over at it with significant lobster envy. Once he said, "That lobster weighs a heck of a lot more than two pounds. I'll bet it's closer to three pounds." Elizabeth could only laugh, but she did manage to finish eating all the meat from the lobster, whatever it weighed.

The reunion goers were happy to be together again. It was good that Tyler had come along. He had an almost impossible time trying to sit down at the picnic table bench, and the servers at Peel's took pity on him and brought a folding chair so he could sit at the end of the table. He managed to take apart and eat his lobster without any trouble, but by the time dinner was over, he was completely exhausted and had to have some help getting back to the car. Thank goodness this car was bigger than the last one.

Darryl and Elena chose to eat at a different picnic table than the others. Darryl was on his tablet during the entire meal. But it was more than a notion to juggle getting the meat out of a lobster at the same time one was tapping on a touch screen. Elena ended up taking Darryl's lobster apart for him so all he had to do was dip it in the melted butter. He could manage to eat with one hand and still have one hand free for his iPad.

Everyone slept well that night. The only scheduled events for the next day, Saturday, were a sunset cruise, an evening ride on a lobster boat in Southwest Harbor, and dinner afterwards at the famous Down East Café. The day was free for everyone to do their own thing.

Chapter 10

BAILEY MACDERMOTT GRADUATED WITH AN engineering degree from the University of Arkansas. He was hired by IBM directly out of college, and because of his outgoing personality and gift for gab, he quickly became one of Big Blue's best salesmen in his region. But Bailey was an independent guy, and he felt as if he was being smothered in the corporate world. He'd been selling computer systems to the oil industry, to help them with payroll and inventory and to keep track of where their oil was coming from and where it was going. Bailey let a couple of his clients know he was interested in making a change, and within a few weeks he had a job offer from a major oil company. He submitted his resignation at IBM and left his job in Chicago. Houston was calling, and Bailey was ready to conquer the oil business and earn some big money. Soon he was flying back and forth from Houston to the oil-rich kingdoms in the Middle East. Before long, he knew the countries and who the movers and shakers were in the world's wealthiest oil-producing nations.

When the Shah of Iran fell, the world, and especially the Middle East, was turned upside down. Previously ignored actors on the world's political and economic scene were on the march, and a few days after the hostages in Iran were taken, the U.S. Department of Defense was knocking on Bailey's door. He was a patriot and agreed to work with the DIA, one of the pentagon's spy agencies.

At first, he just met with other Americans in Riyadh and other Arab capitals. He carried the packages and papers these agents asked him to take back with him when he flew home to the U.S. Then he was asked to meet with foreign nationals and accompany them to safe houses. Once, in Lebanon, he had to rescue an American who was in desperate shape, running from Hezbollah, and suffering from serious gunshot wounds in his leg and thigh. Bailey drove the man to the airport in his rental car and slipped him aboard the oil company's plane. Bailey's assignments became more and more complex and more and more dangerous. He told himself he was doing all of this because he was helping to fight terrorism, but he also loved the rush he got from taking risks.

After a particularly harrowing mission, Bailey had to take some time off from his regular job with the oil company and from his special work for the DIA. He spent a month recuperating in Paris. He slept late and ate well. He also met and fell in love with an American woman he met at the Rodin Museum. Bailey had gone there to learn more about the sculpture. Marianna Archer was at the museum posing for magazine photographs. She was a gorgeous redhead who earned her living as a highly-paid fashion model. She was doing a photoshoot for an American fashion magazine and was dressed in very tight stretch stirrup pants, enormous earrings, and a sexy faux suede off-the-shoulder top. Bailey stumbled into the room where Marianna had her arms draped around "The Thinker." That day Bailey completely missed seeing Rodin's most famous work of art, but he couldn't take his eyes off Marianna as she pranced and posed around the naked man made out of bronze.

It was the 1980s and Bailey MacDermott decided he had been a bachelor long enough. Marianna was a lonely ex-pat living in France, and she quickly succumbed to Bailey's warm and friendly personality. They spent a lot of time at her apartment getting acquainted, and before Bailey's month of vacation was over, the two were married. It was probably a mistake for them to marry, even under the best of circumstances. The complexity of their work lives and the travel both of their jobs required meant they spent a lot of time apart. Their time together was frenetic, and they never had a chance to really get to know each other.

What Bailey didn't know about Marianna was that she was manic-depressive, a mental illness that has since been renamed "bipolar 1 disorder." If she stayed on her meds, Marianna was mostly fine and a lot of fun. When she went off her meds, all bets were off. When they returned to the U.S., she realized she was pregnant. Bailey and Marianna's son was born in Houston, and Bailey was beside himself with joy. Marianna, on the other hand, lapsed into post-partum depression and a serious depressive phase of her mental illness. She reached the point where she didn't want to get out of bed at all.

Bailey and Marianna eventually divorced. She ceded custody of their son to Bailey, but Bailey was juggling too many things. He told the DoD he wasn't able to work for them anymore, and he quit his job working for the oil company because he didn't want to travel all the time. He began dealing in oil futures and was very successful in this field. He made a lot of money, but the best part of his life at this time was that once he settled down in Dallas, he was able to make a home for himself and his son.

Before he met Gretchen, rumors flew that he had married again in haste twice and then quickly divorced twice! He didn't like to talk about what had happened in his love life during this period, and no one wanted to ask. It was clearly a painful subject for Bailey.

Gretchen Johanssen technically worked in human resources, but she was one of those people who was so competent that, wherever she worked, she eventually took over running much more than the HR department. She was petite and fit, and her good looks and style attracted attention. Once you got to know Gretchen and once you had worked with her for a while, because of her extraordinary competence, you forgot how small she was. Her abilities and her organizational skills belied her size, and she took on a significant presence in any room where she worked or spoke.

Gretchen had married twice and had two wonderful sons. She adopted and raised a foster daughter. Her daughter was still in graduate school, but after her second divorce and after her sons were launched, one into the military and the other to college, Gretchen decided to take a job with an international financial group. She had always wanted to travel and was excited to be sent to run the HR department at her company's office in Zurich.

As always happened when Gretchen arrived on the scene, her ability to get things accomplished was immediately recognized, and she took on more and more responsibilities, above and beyond her HR duties. She always attracted attention at a board meetings. When she made an outstanding presentation to a group of international businessmen, the head of one of Switzerland's wealthiest and most secretive banks noticed her. He wanted to date her and wanted to hire her to work for him. He offered her a salary three times what she was earning in her current job. She agreed to take the lucrative position as his special advisor, but she never mixed business and romance.

The Swiss banker was smart enough to agree to her terms, and Gretchen spent several years making top-level decisions in the arcane world of Swiss banking and international finance. She became fluent in German. She met arms dealers, heads of state, assassins, movie stars, Russians and Saudis, and people she was sure were mafia figures or drug dealers or both. She helped her employers invest their clients' riches. She knew the identities of many who had secret money and needed to conceal it.

When one of her ex-husbands was murdered, Gretchen returned to the United States. Her son, who was a Navy Seal, was involved in an almost-fatal car accident, and Gretchen wanted to spend time with him, helping him heal and boosting his spirits as he recovered. She was an accomplished corporate operator, but she was first and foremost a mother. It was while her son was recovering the use of his legs at a rehabilitation center in Texas that Gretchen met Bailey.

Bailey volunteered at the VA hospital where Gretchen's son was going for physical therapy. Bailey still made deals of all kinds. He had branched out from oil futures into commercial real estate, and it seemed that whatever he touched turned to gold. Volunteering to work with military personnel who were trying to get back on their feet was Bailey's way of giving back. He loved his work, but he loved working with the disabled vets even more. He spent time with Gretchen's son on an almost daily basis, and it was the young Navy Seal who introduced Bailey MacDermott to his mother.

Bailey and Gretchen had both been burned in the marriage department. Neither one was looking for a spouse. Each of them was happy living alone, but as they spent more and more time in each other's company, they realized how much they loved each other and wanted to spend the rest of their lives together.

Gretchen had taken a job with a company in Dallas, and in no time, she had, as she always did, made herself indispensable to her new company. She was the kind of employee who quickly became critical to the organization. When she mentioned the possibility of retirement, she was offered a large bonus to stay on for two more years. At the end of those two years, when the subject of retirement came up again, she was offered an even larger bonus, if she would just stay on a little longer. She might never retire because she was making too much money just by mentioning the word "retirement."

Bailey had moved into doing deals in international real estate, and this new clientele sometimes presented challenges. There were language barriers, although most people involved in the upper echelons of the business world spoke English. There were cultural differences, especially when it came to determining what was legal and ethical and what was not. Most of his clients were legitimate buyers who actually wanted to own a warehouse in Hong Kong or Mexico or an apartment building in Singapore. But a few clients who contacted Bailey were interested in buying real estate for the purposes of laundering money.

The schemes the money-launderers devised were complicated and slick. Bailey found himself involved in a couple of these transactions before he caught on to what was happening. When he realized what these faux buyers were up to, he had to say no. He refused to participate in any money laundering intrigue. More than once, a disappointed money launderer had threatened Bailey's life. Bailey loved the rush and the risk of doing high-flying business transactions, but he definitely did not enjoy having a loaded gun pressed against his head. When one of these crooks tracked him to his home and threatened him, Bailey and Gretchen had to move to a different house. Bailey learned to be more discreet, but it was impossible for him to give up the thrill of making a deal. Now he was always wary when he took on a new client. In his early seventies, he was a vital and busy wheeler-dealer in the financial world.

Chapter 11

ISABELLE, OLIVIA, AND GRETCHEN INTENDED TO spend the morning shopping in the town of Bar Harbor. Richard and Elizabeth were driving Cameron and Sidney on a tour of the Acadia National Park. None of the four wanted to bike or hike up Cadillac Mountain, but they did want to see the magnificent views. Bailey was on the phone, as he frequently was, even when on vacation, talking to somebody in Tokyo or Hong Kong about a deal he was working. He carried three cell phones with him at all times. Gretchen had said more than once that she expected to wake up one morning and see Bailey with a cell phone growing out of his ear. Tyler was taking it easy this morning, and Lilleth would drive him to Bar Harbor to join the others for lunch. Darryl and Elena were traveling to Orono, Maine for the day. They had friends at the University of Maine, and wanted to take the opportunity to get together with their academic colleagues. They didn't want to be included in the lunch reservation at the Bar Harbor Inn's Terrace Grill, the lobster boat ride, or dinner at the Down East Café.

Cameron was a big picture kind of guy, and he was beginning to get nervous about what was happening. He had questioned Tyler in detail about his bike accident and was convinced, as Tyler was convinced, that the bike had been deliberately tampered with. It might have been bad luck that Tyler had ended up riding on the damaged bike, but in combination with the vandalism to the kayak and the deliberate placement of a snake that was not native to the area, Cameron was worried that someone in the reunion group was being targeted. Because he knew about some of the things his friends had done during their working years, Cameron was aware that quite a few of them might have enemies from the past. He knew there were people who had bones to pick with him. But they were now all seventy-five years old. Who would bother or want to take the risk to hurt a guy as old as himself? It was mystifying, and it was disturbing. If there were no more incidents, maybe there was nothing to worry about. Cameron was a man who was always thinking about the future, and he hoped everyone would be careful.

Yellow table umbrellas at the Bar Harbor Inn's outdoor restaurant had been a colorful design choice. They were cheerful and easy to see. Even on a gray or cloudy day, they were the color of sunshine and had the desired effect on the psyches of the diners. They invited you to come and sit down, order a drink and something to eat, and stay awhile. The terrace was located next to the harbor. When you were there, you were at one with the water and the sky. The Terrace Grill was a lovely setting, and the food was delicious. The lobster rolls were some of the best, in a town that offered an infinite variety of those delectable sandwiches served authentically in a square, buttered, toasted hotdog roll. But the star turned out to be the blueberry pie that everyone agreed was the food of the gods.

Bailey MacDermott had actually put down his cell phone long enough to eat lunch, including a piece of blueberry pie that he'd split with Gretchen. In fact, he'd dropped two of his cell phones into Gretchen's carryall. The view at the Terrace Grill was that seductive, and the food was that good. Bailey was going to forget about work for a few minutes and concentrate on the blueberry pie and the ambiance. When he got up to go to the men's room, Bailey left his third cell phone, his personal phone, on the table. He probably hadn't intended to, but he was, for a very rare moment in his life, walking into the Bar Harbor Inn without a cell phone in his pocket. It had to be a first, and it would turn out to be a mistake.

Bailey was on his way back to his table when he thought he recognized someone in the lobby of the Bar Harbor Inn. The man was standing at the reception desk, and all Bailey could see was the back of his head. If Bailey was right and the person was who Bailey thought he was, there was trouble. Sato Nakamura had tried to get Bailey to participate in a money-laundering scheme years earlier. Bailey had not only refused to go along with Nakamura in his illegal real estate transaction; Bailey had called the authorities. The man was arrested and charged, and Bailey testified at his trial. Bailey's testimony had put the criminal behind bars, and Nakamura had threatened Bailey in the court room. Bailey had taken the threats seriously but had counted on the criminal being locked up for many years. Bailey didn't know he'd been released from prison and didn't think he could possibly have served out his sentence. The guy was a very wealthy and connected man in Indonesia. Money talked and was often used to grease more than a few important palms.

Bailey's first reaction was to assume that Nakamura's presence in Bar Harbor was merely a coincidence. Bailey wasn't paranoid about people, even people who had threatened to hurt him. He probably was not as concerned about his own safety and security as he should be. But given what had happened to Tyler and given what had been done to the kayak, Bailey was now more alert to possible trouble. It had not occurred to him that he might be the target of the sabotage. He'd just had a hip replacement and had never thought of signing up for the bike ride. He'd never considered going on the kayaking trip. Now he was beginning to wonder if he could have been the intended victim. Or maybe the man at the front desk wasn't really Nakamura.

Bailey had to hide someplace, somewhere he could see the face of the man at the front desk but the man couldn't see him. There was a small room off the lobby, a room that used to be called a cloak room, although no one in Bailey's lifetime had ever actually worn a cloak. The room had been divided, and the rear part was partitioned off and locked. The locked section was where the bellmen secured the guests' luggage. The front part of the room, Bailey assumed, was still for "cloaks," but it looked like this cloak room had now morphed into being the windbreaker room, the sweater room, and the running shoes room, as well as the lost and found. Bailey would be able to hide there and watch the front desk.

At first, Bailey wondered if he had mistaken Nakamura for another person from Indonesia or some other place in the Far East. After all, it had been a number of years since he'd seen Nakamura, and maybe he'd made a mistake. Bailey was alarmed and disheartened when he realized the man was indeed Nakamura. His interactions with Nakamura had mostly been over the phone, but they had occasionally met in L.A. Nakamura would recognize Bailey. Bar Harbor, Maine was one of the least likely places Bailey ever imagined he would encounter Nakamura. Bailey watched as Nakamura continued to talk with the desk clerk. Nakamura did not appear to have any luggage, and Bailey couldn't tell if the man was checking out or checking in or was doing neither. He tried to eavesdrop on their conversation, but he was able to pick up only a few words of what the man was saying. As he strained to hear the conversation, Bailey heard Nakamura say "Inastou Lodge." A stab of anxiety hit Bailey in the chest when he heard Nakamura utter those words. At that moment, Bailey realized the money launderer could be coming after him. Who else but Bailey could Nakamura possibly know at the Inastou Lodge? The odds and common sense were all against Nakamura knowing anyone but Bailey. Nakamura had to be in Maine for him, and somehow he knew that Bailey was at the Inastou.

Bailey stayed inside the cloak room until Nakamura left the lobby of the Bar Harbor Inn. When he was certain the man was gone, Bailey approached the desk clerk. "Hi, my name is Simpson Dodge. I was supposed to meet a business colleague here this afternoon. His name is Sato Nakamura. I'm a little late, and I'm afraid he might have gotten tired of waiting for me and left. Can you tell me if he has been here and if he's been asking for me?"

"A man was just here, but his name was Nakamura Sato. He didn't seem to be waiting for anyone. He was asking directions to another hotel in the area, the Inastou Lodge, which is not actually in Bar

Harbor. Sometimes people don't realize that the Inastou is actually in the town of Northeast Harbor. We have lots of people stop in here who are lost and want directions."

"Did the man say why he wanted directions to the Inastou?" Bailey knew he was pushing his luck with this question, but he was desperate to know.

"How should I know why he wanted directions to the Inastou? Maybe he made reservations there. He just wasn't able to find the place."

"Thank you. I guess I missed him." It had been a lame misrepresentation on Bailey's part, but he'd gained a couple of pieces of information with his clumsy questions. He suspected that Nakamura might be using a different name here in Maine. Or maybe the name Nakamura had used in his dealings with Bailey years ago had been a fake name. Who knew what the man's real name might be?

What was he going to do now? If Nakamura intended to stay at the Inastou, it would be an impossible situation for Bailey. Bailey could not go back there. It was a small inn, and he and Nakamura would inevitably run into each other. That would happen often, and it would be lunacy for Bailey to take the chance. Even if Nakamura had not come to Bar Harbor hoping to find Bailey to hurt him or kill him, it would never do for Bailey to be staying in the same hotel with the man. Gretchen would be safe there, as long as she didn't mention Bailey's name or her last name. Bailey's brief association with Nakamura and the court case had occurred before Bailey had ever met Gretchen, so the money launderer didn't know what she looked like. Bailey needed to get word to Gretchen not to mention the name MacDermott while she was at the Inastou. He needed to give her some idea about what was going on.

Bailey realized he'd left his cell phone on the table at the Terrace Grill. His other two work phones, a satellite phone for international calls and a regular cell phone for calling clients who lived in the U.S., were both in Gretchen's carryall. He had put them there himself, thinking he wouldn't take any calls about work during lunch. He was afraid to go back to the Terrace Grill. He didn't want to come out of the cloak room until he was certain Nakamura had moved on. The problem was, there were no longer any pay phones around, anywhere. Now everybody had a cell phone, and hardly anybody still had a landline. Pay phones and phone booths had become today's dinosaurs.

Bailey sat in an obscure corner of the lobby at the Bar Harbor Inn, wondering what he should do. He decided he needed to keep as low a profile as possible, and he had no way to communicate with Gretchen or the others to let them know he wasn't coming back to the Inastou. To say he was hiding out sounded melodramatic to Bailey, but in fact that is exactly what he intended to do. He was going to get a room at the Bar Harbor Inn, and he would call Gretchen from his room and tell her where he was. Bailey went to the front desk and asked for a room with a view. The woman at the registration desk informed him that there was only one room of any kind left at the Bar Harbor Inn. It was a two-room suite with a view, and the daily rate was more than Bailey wanted to pay. Bailey took the room. If he was going to have to stay in his room all the time, keeping a low profile, at least he could have a nice room. Thank goodness Bailey had his wallet with his credit cards and his identification.

The registration clerk was more than a little bit suspicious when Bailey said he didn't have any luggage, but after scrutinizing his identification, she let it go. Bailey was a handsome older man and looked prosperous and respectable. And he was all of those things. He was also a man on the run, or at least a man in hiding.

He got to his room and realized he didn't have any pajamas, clean underwear, or even a toothbrush. If he could get in touch with Gretchen, she could bring these things to him. He dialed her cell phone number from the land line in his room and was puzzled when he was informed that the number he'd called was "no longer in service." Then he remembered that his wife had recently changed her cell phone number because she'd been getting too many crank calls. Bailey realized he had no idea what her new cell phone number was. Gretchen had programmed her new number into his cell phone and put all the pertinent information in his "contacts." He did not have a clue how to get in touch with his wife. He could call the Inastou and have them connect him to his room, but he knew, of course, that no one was there now.

Gretchen would be crazy with worry before he was able to let her know where he was. When he didn't return to the table, she would send someone to the men's room to look for him. She would be afraid he'd fallen or become ill. She would be afraid he'd had a heart attack. She might think he'd been taken to the hospital and start to make phone calls, trying to find him. He had to find a way to leave her a message, and he had to do it soon, before she raised the alarm or notified the authorities that he was missing. Since his technology was not available to him, he'd determined the only way to leave her a message was the old fashioned way, to write her a note on a piece of paper.

Chapter 12

J.D. STEELE HAD BEEN AN ATHLETE AND A scholar in high school before he matriculated at the University of Oklahoma. He was handsome and outgoing as well as smart. He joined a fraternity and dated many women, but he also managed to make good grades, at least good enough for him to be admitted to the University of Oklahoma College of Law after he finished his four undergraduate years. After law school, J.D. fulfilled his obligation to Uncle Sam and was stationed in El Paso, Texas with the JAG Corps. J.D. had always wanted to be a prosecutor. He had a strong sense of right and wrong and wanted to help make sure the bad guys were found guilty and put in jail. He would devote twenty-five years of his life to this cause, and he became a legend in Tulsa legal circles. His specialty was trying the most complex and difficult criminal cases, including murder, rape, and drug cases. He was a relentless defender of justice and a dispenser of appropriate punishment. He was always prepared and performed brilliantly in front of the jury. J.D. seemed to thrive on convicting the worst of the worst, and he could count the cases he'd ever lost on one hand!

J.D. and his first wife were married just after they'd finished college. They were both very young, and neither of them was ready for marriage. The two had almost nothing in common, and after less than a year, they realized their union had been a mistake. They had no children and few assets, so their divorce was relatively amicable. They remained friends.

After his divorce, J.D. became one of Tulsa's most eligible bachelors and was quite the man-about-town for a few years until he met Signa Karlsson. It was a love match, and they married and had two children, twins, a boy and a girl. Signa had her pilot's license and loved to fly. Both of their children had graduated from college when Signa was killed in a plane crash. She was a passenger in a friend's private plane. J.D. was devastated and terribly angry. He was convinced that if Signa had been flying the plane, there would not have been an accident. He didn't handle his enormous grief well and vowed never to marry again. He resigned abruptly from his job as an assistant district attorney, abandoned his beautiful Art Deco mansion without even cleaning out the refrigerator, told no one except his grown children goodbye, and left the country for French Polynesia.

This was where J.D.'s life and marital history became murky. Some say he married again on the rebound ... two times! But no one is really sure whether he ever married again at all, or if he did, whether it was once, twice, three or even four times. Rumors flew, and J.D. wasn't talking about it. It didn't matter. J.D. never went back to Tulsa, and his house was sold. He eventually returned to the United States, and with the money he had saved, combined with an inheritance from his now-deceased, well-to-do parents, he bought a trucking company. The company's headquarters were in Missouri, and J.D. bought a condo in St. Louis.

He'd never thought he would enjoy anything as much as he'd enjoyed being a prosecuting attorney, but he found he loved running his own transportation empire. He was good at logistics and good with people, and RRD Trucking made him ten times more money than he'd ever dreamed he would make in his lifetime. He bought a cattle ranch. J.D. liked to travel to Washington, D.C. to lobby his legislators in person about transportation issues. It was on one of these trips to the nation's capital that he met Olivia Barrow Simmons.

Olivia Barrow had been a cheerleader and her high school's

homecoming queen. She was beautiful and outgoing. She was the prettiest and the most popular girl in her school, and she was also very smart. After graduating from the University of North Carolina with a degree in mathematics, Olivia moved to Washington, D.C. where she shared an apartment with three other young women. Olivia had landed a job as a cypher specialist at the National Security Agency, so she wasn't able to talk to anybody about what she did at work.

Because Olivia was so attractive and had such a winsome personality, the NSA quickly identified her as a person who could represent the agency at Congressional hearings and other official public events. She always had all the answers, and although she would rather have been spending her time working on the complicated puzzles, mathematical constructs, and computer coding she loved, she was happy to be the pretty face of the No Such Agency. It was during one of her appearances before the Senate Select Committee on Intelligence that she was introduced to Bradford Simmons, the youngest man ever to be elected to the United States Senate. He was from Colorado, and he had a reputation as a womanizer.

Once he'd laid eyes on Olivia, he had to have her. She was young and vulnerable and flattered that a United States Senator wanted to date her. The women with whom she shared her apartment were envious and urged her to continue going out with Bradford. Olivia was eventually persuaded by the young senator's attentions, and within eighteen months, they were married. Olivia was devoted to her work and insisted on keeping her job at the NSA. Olivia and Bradford had three children, and Olivia chose to stay married to the senator until all three had graduated from college. Then she divorced him and took him for everything she could get in the divorce. Simmons had continued his womanizing behavior all during their miserable marriage, and Olivia had finally had all she could stand of the ridiculously handsome and adulterous cad.

Olivia vowed she would never marry again, and she focused her life on her children, her grandchildren, and the career she loved. Olivia had a very high security clearance and was a valuable employee at the

NSA. Nobody could ever know exactly what she did, but whatever it was, she was very, very good at it. She knew lots of secrets about everything and everybody, but she was a person of the highest integrity. No one ever worried that she would suffer from "loose lips."

Many eligible bachelors in the nation's capital wanted to date her, but she was done with men ... or so she said. Even in her late fifties, she was a beauty. She was a fascinating conversationalist, and everyone, men and women, wanted to sit next to her at dinner. It was at one such dinner party, hosted by her best friend, that Olivia was seated next to J.D. Steele. The two hit it off immediately and were roaring with laughter before the main course was served. The hostess, who had known Olivia for decades, had thought J.D. and Olivia would appreciate each other's company, but she'd greatly underestimated the enormous amount of fun they would have together. For Olivia and for J.D., there was nobody else at the party.

They were inseparable from that night on. J.D. bought a townhouse in Georgetown and courted the woman who had swept him off his feet. He had never expected to fall in love like this so late in life, but he adored Olivia and didn't want to be away from her. Olivia was just as shocked to find herself head over heels in love with J.D. She liked men, but after her disastrous marriage, she wanted nothing more to do with romance. But these two were a match that was destined to be. They had such a good time in one another's company. Each of them had a wonderful sense of humor, and they could always make the other one laugh. Even their very skeptical grown children had to admit it was a beautiful thing to behold.

It was Olivia's idea to move closer to where J.D.'s business had its headquarters. The couple bought a house in St. Louis. She hated to leave her job at the NSA, but it was time to retire. Because Olivia insisted on spending one week out of every month near her children and grandchildren, who all lived in the Northern Virginia, Maryland, D.C. area, she and J.D. kept the townhouse in the District. This was fine with J.D., and he usually came East with her. They traveled and enjoyed their lives. In spite of love and compatibility, Olivia was skeptical about marriage for many years. She didn't see why it was necessary. J.D. finally convinced Olivia that being married would not be the kiss of death, and they ended up tying the knot when they were both in their late 60s.

Chapter 13

$\mathcal{E}$VERY MEMBER OF THE GROUP WAS GETTING nervous, and Gretchen was close to panic. Bailey had left the Terrace Grill to go to the men's room more than forty minutes earlier. The waitress had brought the lunch checks, and it was time to leave. It was after three o'clock in the afternoon. Twenty minutes earlier, when Bailey hadn't come back to the table, Gretchen had sent J.D. and Cameron to scout the men's room. She was worried that Bailey had fallen or was sick and needed help. The two friends reported back that they hadn't seen any sign of Bailey. They'd checked all the stalls in the bathroom, and then they'd looked in all the public rooms at the Bar Harbor Inn. They had even gone to the parking lot to see if Bailey's rental car was gone. The car was still there, in exactly the same spot where Bailey had parked it almost three hours earlier.

Gretchen couldn't sit still any longer. She hurried to the lobby of the Bar Harbor Inn and anxiously waited her turn to talk to the desk clerk. "I was expecting to meet my husband here in the lobby a half hour ago. We must have got the time mixed up, but I know he said he wanted me to meet him here. Has there been anyone around who looked like they were waiting for somebody?" Gretchen started to describe Bailey, but the desk clerk interrupted her.

"I just came on at three o'clock, a few minutes ago. You would have to talk to Gina. She's the one who's been on duty since seven this morning. The trouble is, I think she left early and has already gone home. Do you want to talk to the general manager?"

Gretchen didn't know what to do. She was so worried about Bailey. He'd had a hip replacement a few weeks earlier and had been doing very well with his recovery and physical therapy. It had been important to him to be able to participate in the trip to Maine. Gretchen was worried that he might have fallen someplace. Had he had a heart attack? Bailey was generally in excellent health, but no matter how vigorous someone is, at age seventy-five, there is always a risk that something could go wrong, that something bad could happen. Had he had some kind of stroke and wasn't able to remember where he was? Bailey's mind was sharp as a tack, but there was always the unexpected. Gretchen decided the next thing to do was to check with the hospitals and the local EMTs. If Bailey had been hurt, the local medics would have taken him to an ER.

Gretchen approached the desk clerk with another question. "Has anyone fallen or become ill or had any kind of a medical crisis in the hotel in the past hour?"

"Like I said, I just came on, but I haven't heard about anything like that. If it just happened, I probably would have heard something."

"Thank you. I appreciate your help." Gretchen said to herself that the desk clerk had not been any help at all, but that was not the woman's fault. Gretchen walked back to the park next to the harbor where the rest of the group who'd eaten lunch together were waiting.

"He's nowhere to be found. I can't imagine what's happened to him. He left his phone at the table, but he would have found a pay phone or some other way to call me to let me know where he was and what he was doing."

"Pay phones are scarce as hen's teeth these days." Richard had searched more than once for an elusive and rapidly-disappearing pay phone.

"Maybe he wasn't feeling well and went back to the Inastou. Why don't you call and see if he's there?" Matthew wanted this to be resolved quickly.

"His car is still in the parking lot. We checked again a few minutes ago." J.D. knew Bailey hadn't driven himself back to the Inastou in the rental car.

"Maybe he took a taxi back and left the car for you?" Isabelle was trying, like everybody else, to find a reasonable explanation for Bailey's disappearance.

"He would never just leave on his own and not tell me where he was going. I'm going to call the police and report him missing." Gretchen knew her husband would have left her some kind of message, and she was afraid he was in trouble.

"In most states, the police won't let you file a missing person's report for an adult until the person has been missing for at least twenty-four hours. Some places you can file the report, but they won't consider him or her a missing person or do anything about finding them until this time tomorrow. With children it's different. There's the Amber Alert." J.D. was an attorney and knew the facts about these things.

Nobody had any good ideas. Cameron was quiet, but his mind was racing. He wondered if someone had abducted Bailey. "Bailey doesn't carry a lot of cash with him, does he?"

"No. In fact, when he needs cash, he never has any. He always has to ask me for cash. That doesn't mean somebody hasn't robbed him, but he definitely does not have a wad of cash to flash around."

"I think you should call the Inastou to see if he's there. Then you should file a missing person's report. They will give you a hard time because he's only been gone for a few hours, but if he doesn't turn up, at least you will have started the ball rolling. The police will have all the information they need to begin to search immediately. J.D., you're the lawyer here. You need to go with Gretchen to the police. They will pay more attention to what she says if she has you with her. Two people saying this is uncharacteristic behavior is more convincing than one person, especially a man's wife, saying it." Elizabeth was often the voice of wisdom and summed up what needed to be done.

"That's a plan I can live with. J.D.?" Gretchen was eager to get to the parking lot.

"There's nothing the rest of us can do here. I doubt if anyone feels like shopping anymore, so I think we should go back to the Inastou and wait, unless somebody else has any other suggestions." Isabelle always said something sensible.

"We could search the shops in Bar Harbor." Olivia was an indefatigable shopper. Several of the men groaned. None of them were on board for searching the stores in Bar Harbor. Gretchen called the Inastou, and as she'd expected, Bailey hadn't returned. She and J.D. headed to the car to drive to the police station. Olivia went with them. The rest of the group went their separate ways. The sunset cruise on a lobster boat was planned for that evening. With Bailey missing, no one felt much like cruising on the water, but they'd already paid for the two-hour rental. Somebody ought to show up to take the ride on the lobster boat.

Gretchen, Olivia, and J.D. arrived at the car Bailey and Gretchen had rented at the airport in Bangor. Gretchen had the keys, so she could unlock it and drive it. She was the first to see the piece of paper stuck in the door. It was a note in Bailey's handwriting. She felt an enormous sense of relief before she even had it in her hands: *I'm hiding out from Sato Nakamura. Don't tell anyone, not even our friends. Don't mention your name or mine at the Inastou. Use your maiden name only. Nakamura may be staying there. DO NOT contact law enforcement. I will be in touch when it's safe. ILY.* Gretchen handed the note to J.D. Her hands were shaking with relief and anxiety. Olivia read the note over J.D.'s shoulder.

Even after reading the note, Gretchen was puzzled. She was somewhat reassured, but she was also angry. "What do you think this means? I don't know why in the world he's hiding out from this Nakamura person. That's a guy Bailey testified against years ago, before we met. Nakamura went to jail and should still be in jail." Gretchen could not understand what had come over Bailey, that he would worry her like this. Gretchen thought Bailey's behavior was bizarre, and it was.

J.D. was trying to read the note like a lawyer rather than a friend would read it. "I don't think Bailey wrote this under duress, so it's not like he's been kidnapped or anything. He asks us not to contact law enforcement, and I think we should honor his request not to go to the authorities. But not telling the others in the group that he's okay …. That's going to be a tough request to honor."

"I'll just say I've heard from him and that he was called away on a business emergency. We are the only ones who know the truth. What do you think?"

"I don't think anybody is going to believe you for a minute, but that's just me." Olivia knew the others in the group well, and she was probably right that they wouldn't believe the story Gretchen intended to tell them.

"I'll say I can't talk about it but that he's fine. Of course, I don't really think he is fine. This behavior is very peculiar, and I don't understand it at all."

"You aren't a very good liar, Gretchen. Why don't you let J.D. tell the others what they need to know so they don't worry? Everyone is naturally in a panic about what's happened to Bailey, and they won't stop thinking about it until he's safely back among us." Olivia thought J.D. could pull off the slight-of-hand that was going to be necessary to satisfy the group but not reveal anything Bailey wanted kept confidential. It was a tricky tightrope to walk, but J.D. was good at this.

"Okay, I know what to say." J.D. was already practicing his lines. "We're all going to behave as if nothing has happened. If we aren't fretting, the others won't fret. We're going to take the lobster boat sunset cruise tonight, and then we are all going to the Down East Café for dinner. We can pretend Bailey is there with us."

"I don't know …." Gretchen looked as if she might be losing her resolve.

"You have to put a good face on it, Gretchen. You have to buck up." J.D. knew what had to be done.

"You have to be positive and upbeat. Otherwise everyone will think something terrible has happened to Bailey. It hasn't, and we don't want anyone to think it has." Olivia looked intently at her good friend and tried to be encouraging. "Thank goodness we found the note before we went to the authorities." Olivia wanted this to have a happy ending and for it all to be over soon.

Chapter 14

WHEN ELIZABETH EMERSON WAS A SENIOR at Smith College in Northampton, Massachusetts, the CIA was actively recruiting from the Ivy League men's schools and from the Seven Sisters women's colleges. The spy agency had decided women had good brains after all and made good analysts. The CIA was especially interested in hiring economics majors because they had found that people who understood economics had analytical minds, were able to process information in a systematic way, and could reach conclusions and solve problems. The CIA was not looking for covert operatives when they interviewed the college seniors. They were not hiring women to wear the classic fedora and trench coat spy outfit, lean against a lamppost in rainy, post-war Vienna, and wait for a rendezvous with a Russian double agent. The CIA wanted desk jockeys.

Elizabeth, an economics major, was of the duck-and-cover generation and had lived in the shadow of the Cold War all her life. She was intrigued by the pitch from the CIA and decided to look into what would be required for her to pursue a career with The Agency. She went to the initial meeting on the Smith College campus and then made the trip to Boston with three other women from her college class. In Boston, the four were given a battery of tests, designed to evaluate their abilities to do the work the CIA would require of them. This was the first step in the application process. Those who passed the initial tests would be given more tests, some interviews, and then perhaps the offer of a job in Washington, D.C.

Elizabeth scored "off the charts" in the inductive reasoning part of the testing. Only one other person in CIA recruitment history had ever scored higher than she did in this one very important area, critical to the kind of work the CIA needed doing. Although she had never realized it before, Elizabeth was told she could read and evaluate vast amounts of material in an incredibly short period of time and come up with an accurate analysis and conclusion. The testing people made a big deal over her, and this embarrassed the somewhat introverted Elizabeth. They singled her out, and she didn't like it. Since she'd never known she had this special skill, she wasn't that impressed with herself. She wondered what all the fuss was about.

Elizabeth had been seriously dating a graduate of Princeton who was now a first-year medical student at Tulane. Elizabeth was in love, and she thought Richard Carpenter was, too. It was 1966, and women married young. It was early in the women's liberation movement. Not all women, even very well-educated ones, had careers. Many became housewives and mothers. Elizabeth had always been very independent, but she couldn't imagine her life without Richard. Richard was not enthusiastic about her pursuing a career with the CIA. He didn't really understand that she wouldn't be in any danger, sitting in an office in Langley, Virginia, reading newspapers and looking at data sets. He wanted her with him in New Orleans, although he'd not yet asked her to marry him.

When he did pop the question, Elizabeth said yes. They would be married that summer. The CIA was disappointed when Elizabeth turned down their offer of a position as an analyst. They pulled out all the stops and harassed her mercilessly for the remainder of her senior year. They played the "serving your country" card and everything else they could think of. Elizabeth did not waiver, and she and Richard were married in August. She got a job teaching in the New Orleans public schools, and the CIA became a distant memory. But the CIA kept its eyes on her, and years later when she decided to change careers, they welcomed her with open arms.

After she left New Orleans, Elizabeth went to graduate school. After spending two years on the faculty at the University of Texas at El Paso, she took a position teaching economics and economic history at a small college in Maryland. She was pressured to change a grade so that a failing student could become a "C" student. The student, who had not put forth any effort whatsoever in her class, had to have a "C" in order to maintain his eligibility to play basketball for the college team. The academic dean leaned on and threatened Elizabeth. Because Elizabeth was only a part-time professor, the dean told her she could easily be fired from her position, if she didn't do as she was told and change the grade. Elizabeth refused to knuckle under to the threats and gave the student a "D." He had barely made the "D" and had just escaped failing her class by the skin of his teeth. After she'd turned in her grades, someone went to the registrar's office and changed the student's grade to a "C." The young man never missed a step or a dribble on the basketball court because of his failing academic work. Learning and getting an education had proven to be an afterthought, or given no thought at all, when it came to qualifying for a sports team.

Elizabeth thought she could hang on to her job, but she decided she did not want to be a part of the rotten system any more. She'd always known academia was fraught with politics, corrupted by competition to get ahead of one's colleagues, and filled with bloated and narcissistic egos. She decided life was short, and she didn't have to play the stupid games required to succeed in the university arena. She didn't want to be around the grasping and ambitious meanies any more.

She made some phone calls and began the difficult task of hiring babysitters, drivers, and a housekeeper. She made complicated arrangements for her duties at home to be taken care of when she was gone. She began to build her cover story, that she was taking a research position at the Wharton School in Philadelphia. It was a three hour commute one-way to her new job, and she would be away from home a couple of nights a week, sometimes more. It was a big commitment, but her new boss was willing to work with her to maintain the illusion of the imaginary job she supposedly had at the University of Pennsylvania. She was a valuable commodity, and the CIA helped her manage her home duties and her fictitious position in Philadelphia, as she committed to the more dangerous job she'd really been hired to do.

Most of her work was in Virginia, using the skills she'd demonstrated when the CIA had wanted to hire her years earlier. Occasionally she had to make trips overseas. None of her family or friends ever doubted for a minute that she was working at the Wharton School. They thought it was odd that she was gone from home so much, but by now, two of her children were away at boarding school in New England. Only one daughter was still at home. No one, not even Richard Carpenter, was allowed to know what Elizabeth did when she was out of town.

It was a rocky period in the Carpenters' marriage. Richard was consumed with his work as head of the surgical pathology department and clinical laboratory at the local hospital. He participated in the children's activities whenever he could, but he was pretty much oblivious to Elizabeth's needs at this time in their lives. He was angry that she wasn't around all the time, as she had always been before, but he was so preoccupied with his own career, he only noticed she wasn't there when something went wrong.

Richard Carpenter had risen to the top of his career and was the main partner in his pathology group, Richard Carpenter, M.D., P.A. He had done his internship and residency at the University of Pennsylvania, and during those years he'd had the opportunity to work with Philadelphia's medical examiner. In addition to spending his days accompanying the chief medical examiner on his rounds, Richard did moonlighting for the medical examiner's office to earn extra money. The young doctor became a skilled and convincing expert witness. He was a favorite with prosecutors because juries loved his boyish looks and earnest, honest voice. When he was on the witness stand, members of the jury believed everything Richard Carpenter, M.D. had to say. If he gave evidence against someone in a murder trial, that person was always convicted. Vance Stillinger, M.D. was Philadelphia's chief medical examiner, and Richard Carpenter M.D. became his golden boy.

Carpenter's testimony had sent a number of very bad guys to prison. The child molesters, murderers, drug dealers, and drivers who had committed serial DUIs all should have known it was their own behavior that had caused them to be convicted. But bad boys and girls always want to find someone other than themselves to blame. Carpenter became a lightning rod for their anger, and some wanted to blame the blonde, cherub-faced scientist who had so convincingly swayed the juries that had convicted them. Occasionally, a defendant would shake his fist at Carpenter when he was on the witness stand.

Once a man stood up and shouted threats at Carpenter after he'd given his expert witness testimony. The defendant, who had been resoundingly drunk when he'd crossed the highway's median strip and run headlong into a van full of children, said Carpenter had misrepresented his blood alcohol level. The driver of the van and four of the children had died, and the defendant was sent to prison. The drunk vowed that when he got out of jail, he would hunt down Carpenter and kill him and his family.

Elizabeth Carpenter had just come home from the hospital after giving birth to the Carpenters' second daughter. Law enforcement took the threats against Carpenter and his family seriously, and until the convicted criminal was sentenced and safely locked away, the police kept a guard on Carpenter's rented house in the Philadelphia suburbs. Elizabeth wondered who would be there in a few years to watch out for her family when the man was released from prison.

Stillinger tried to convince his protégé to stay in Philadelphia and become a forensic pathologist, but Carpenter owed Uncle Sam two years of his life, serving in the U.S. Army. Furthermore, Carpenter had educational debts and needed and wanted to earn some money. He wanted more income than the salary of an urban medical examiner would pay him, and he didn't want to live in a city. The Army sent Carpenter to William Beaumont Army Medical Center in Texas for two years, and from there, Carpenter took a position at a hospital in a small town in Maryland where he built a successful pathology practice. He still testified as an expert witness, but the threats that had come his way when he was at the Philadelphia Medical Examiner's Office were long-forgotten. The question was, had the men he'd helped send to prison forgotten him?

Chapter 15

SEVERAL MEMBERS OF THE GROUP WERE SITTING on the back porch of the Inastou with Tyler and Lilleth when J.D. approached with news.

"Did you file the police report?" Richard asked J.D. Richard wanted to hear that something constructive had been done.

"We didn't have to. We found a note from Bailey that he'd stuck in the door of his rental car." J.D. was determined to sell this story to his friends, but he knew he couldn't tell the whole truth. "He had some kind of a business emergency. He would have let Gretchen know, but he'd left this cell phone at the table and was unable to find a pay phone. He left the car for Gretchen and took a cab to Bangor. It must have cost him a fortune, but he said he had to leave in a hurry."

"That doesn't make any sense. How could he have had a business emergency when he didn't have a cell phone?" Matthew wasn't buying the story as it had been told so far.

"He didn't go into details in his note, but I think he ran into somebody he knew in the lobby of the Bar Harbor Inn. He had to leave suddenly, but he left the note stuck in the car door so Gretchen would know he was all right. He specifically said not to go to the authorities, that he's fine."

"I don't believe it for a minute. I'm not saying you're lying to us, J.D., but I am saying you're not telling us the whole story." Sidney could always tell when someone wasn't telling the truth. It was not a good idea to try to lie to Sidney.

"We have to be at the pier in Southwest Harbor at five thirty this evening for the lobster boat ride. That's less than an hour from now, and everybody needs to be sure they arrive at the pier on time." Matthew had made the arrangements for the sunset cruise, and he wanted to be sure no one was late.

"Do you think I can make it onto the boat? I would really love to go. I've been looking forward to this." Tyler didn't want to miss anything, but he still wasn't very good at getting around on his crutches.

Matthew was skeptical. He looked at Tyler, and he looked at Elizabeth. "I haven't seen the boat or the pier, so I can't tell you ahead of time if either one of you will be able to get down to the pier or get on the boat. The concierge set this up, and even though I told her about Elizabeth, I don't think it quite registered with her what having a disability means exactly. I don't know to what extent she took into consideration that anyone has disabilities, and now we have two people with disabilities."

In the end, neither Tyler nor Elizabeth was able to make it to the boat. The extremely steep gangway, that went from the parking lot down to the pier where the boat came in, presented the problem. The gangway was set at more than a forty-five degree angle to get to the pier. It was difficult, even for those with strong and sturdy legs, to make it down the steep walkway to get to the lobster boat. Getting onto the boat itself was not difficult, but getting to the pier to get to the boat turned out to be impossible for Tyler and Elizabeth. Tyler was bummed, but he told Lilleth to go on the boat ride without him. The two members of the group who were staying behind sat on a bench above the harbor and watched the beautiful sunset from there. As the rest of the group left the dock in the lobster boat, they waved to their friends who waited on the land.

"I've been wanting to ask you some more specific questions about your bike accident." Elizabeth was inquisitive, and she was determined to figure out what had happened to Tyler's bike. "I know you well enough to know you checked everything out completely before you agreed to take the bike, but for some reason, in spite of your efforts, the bike's brakes and steering failed when you were on the road. Are you absolutely certain the bike you ended up riding was the same bike you'd checked out?"

"Yes. I know it was. It was an almost-new bike, but it had a long scratch on the front fender. I know the bike I rode was the same bike I'd gone over so carefully."

"Was the bike ever out of your sight after you went over it?"

"Only when they took it around to the back of the shop to check the tire pressure and put more air in the tires. They did that with all the bikes. The bike was in the back for about ten or fifteen minutes, I think. That's the only time it was out of my sight."

"It took ten or fifteen minutes to put air in the tires? That seems like a lot of time, but maybe not for four bikes. Did they take all four bikes to the back at once?"

"They were really busy at the bike shop, and it was pretty confusing. Everybody who'd rented bikes for the day was there first thing in the morning to pick them up. All four of us got exactly the bikes we'd specified when we called to reserve them. The shop was pretty efficient about that. The guy who gave us our bikes was annoyed with me because I spent so much time checking everything out. And then of course I had to check out Lilleth's bike, too. The rental place runs a pretty good operation. Their bikes were in good shape, and it seemed like they were getting everybody, not just us, the bikes they'd reserved. They were just busy. I had the feeling they have more employees to handle the customers and the bikes in the summer. In September, all the college kids are back in school, so I think the shop was shorthanded. Their people are overworked. The guy we were dealing with just wanted me to hurry up, hand him my credit card, and get out of there, so he could get on to the next customer."

"You said the bikes were in the back for ten or fifteen minutes, having the tires checked and the air put in? That's how long they were out of your sight, so that's when the tampering with the brakes and the steering had to have happened."

"It wasn't more than fifteen minutes. I'm sure of that, even though it seemed like they were taking forever with the tire check and the air. We'd arrived early and were at the head of the line. Whoever messed with the brakes and the steering didn't have much time to do it. They wouldn't have had time to tamper with more than one of our four bikes. I was the unlucky one."

"Do you know why your bike might have been singled out? Is there any reason anyone would want you to have an accident. Or was it so chaotic in the shop that no one could have been certain the bike they were damaging was yours?"

"I don't know. It was pretty chaotic. I don't think I have any enemies here in Maine. At least I don't know of any. I've never been to Maine before. I have to admit I've made a few enemies in my life. Not many, but a couple. Commercial real estate is sometimes a cutthroat business. It isn't for the faint of heart. But I don't know anybody who lives in Maine. I've never done a business deal here. I'm a west of the Mississippi guy, always have been."

"I know you were in the U.S. Air Force when you were younger. Is there anything that happened back then that could have made anybody really angry? Angry enough to want to hurt you?"

"That was such a long time ago. And you know I'm not allowed to talk about what I did. But I will tell you that I spied on and saw many things, such that, if anybody knew what I'd seen them doing, they might want to kill me. But I would never talk about any of those things. Part of my job was to keep secrets."

"What if somebody knows you know these things and doesn't trust you to keep those secrets forever."

"Believe me, that idea is barking up the wrong tree, for sure. All the people in the world who once knew what I did and what I know ... they're all dead. My commanding officers ... all gone long ago. There's nobody left who knows what I know, except me, and I'm not talking."

"I guess we just have to write it off to a random evil prankster, and you were the unlucky person who happened to get the bike he sabotaged."

"That's my best explanation, too. Except for the fact that somebody deliberately hacked the crap out of Matt's and Cameron's kayak the very next day. And put a snake in it. It seems somebody has our little band of warriors in their sights, although why they would target our group is as puzzling to me as why they would target me personally. Thank goodness somebody knows where Bailey is. I was beginning to worry that he'd been kidnapped or something worse had happened to him. Paranoia is in danger of taking over, and we can't let that happen."

The others returned from the boat ride with tales of how to measure lobsters to be sure they were large enough to qualify as "keepers" and what the fines would be if a lobsterman kept an illegal lobster he found in his trap. The sunset had been beautiful. There hadn't been any cocktails or hors d'oeuvres served on the boat. The two who'd had to stay behind had not missed much.

They all proceeded in various cars to the Down East Café, an iconic area restaurant that served Maine specialties. The café's menu offered Lobster Newberg, Lobster Thermidor, and other lobster dishes. Clams were prepared in a variety of ways, and the menu included quite a few non-seafood dishes. Some people were "lobstered out" and ordered steaks or the vegetarian special. Others couldn't get enough of Homarus americanus and ordered the Shore Dinner that had made the restaurant famous. The Shore Dinner consisted of a bowl of clam chowder, one or two dozen steamed clams with a container of clam broth and a container of butter, and one or two steamed lobsters with more butter, corn, and boiled potatoes.

The Down East Café was built out over the water on pilings, and customers could look down through the gaps in the old wooden floor boards and see the tide coming in. It was rustic, and because it wasn't heated, most of the restaurant was closed off during the colder months. The structure had been added on to over the years and was built on several levels. It was almost impossible for Tyler and Elizabeth to get to the table, but they were both determined to have a shore dinner and managed, against all odds, to maneuver themselves into their chairs … she with her cane and he with his crutches.

Everybody was too stuffed to eat dessert, and as they were finishing their meal, Sidney motioned to the people sitting on either side of her to look at the table by the door. There was something familiar about the woman who was sitting there. She was very tall and had on a very fake-looking long blonde wig. She was wearing a dress, and that was the oddest thing about the woman who was seated alone at a table for two. Hardly anybody ever wore a dress anywhere anymore, and even fewer wore dresses in Maine. Nobody wore a dress to the Down East Café, so this woman stood out like a sore thumb. Sidney knew immediately who the woman was and began to laugh. She caught Gretchen's eye and nodded her head in the direction of the unusual diner. When Gretchen looked where Sidney was motioning, a look of embarrassment and horror spread across her face.

Gretchen got up from the table and knocked over her chair. If she'd hoped to remain inconspicuous, she was not off to a good start. She stomped over to the table where "the woman" was sitting. Gretchen stood facing the table with her hands on her hips. Anyone who was watching Gretchen's angry stance from the back could tell she was furious and was giving the woman a stern lecture. Finally, Gretchen grabbed the woman's arm and marched her out of the Down East Café and into the parking lot.

Sidney said in a hushed voice to the others at the table, "It's Bailey. He's in a disguise." She collapsed with laughter. "It's not a very good one either."

They asked for the bill and waited for Gretchen to return. She finally came back to the table and threw her credit card down. She refused to sit, and she looked sheepish and furious at the same time. "I don't want to talk about it." She said. "He's impossible! What in the world does he think he's doing? He's impossible! I don't want to talk about it. Can somebody please drive me home?"

"Home to Dallas?" Somebody asked her.

"I wish!" Gretchen answered. She had a piece of paper in her hand. "He wants his phone, his clothes, his briefcase, his toothbrush, and God knows what else …. He's hiding out, except when he isn't. And he's dressed up like a looney toon and making a fool of himself. He won't tell me where he's hiding, but he said he didn't want to miss out on the Lobster Newberg. He's been here before and loves the place. He knew we were coming tonight and thought this would be the perfect time to give me the list of things he needs. I told him just to come back with me to the Inastou. He said that's the last place in the world he can be right now. But, of course, he refuses to tell me why that is. I don't want to talk about it!"

"Is he all right?" Somebody asked.

"No, he isn't all right. He's stark raving mad." Gretchen was at her wits' end. Everyone laughed and waved to Bailey as he reappeared from the parking lot and returned to his table to finish his Lobster Newberg. His friends made an obvious and wide berth around him as they exited the Down East Café. The group had needed a good laugh, and Bailey had certainly provided that.

Chapter 16

THE SCUTTLEBUTT ABOUT DARRYL HARCOMB WAS that he had read the entire World Book Encyclopedia when he was in junior high school. Some people said he'd even memorized it. Even if he'd just read the thing all the way through and hadn't memorized anything, it would have been a prodigious undertaking. No one doubted that Darryl was brilliant. It was inevitable that he would graduate summa cum laude from college and eventually earn a PhD in something. History was his chosen field, but he knew a great deal about many things. He loved to read, and he loved to write. Darryl's intelligence and agility with words allowed him to rise rapidly through the ranks of academia.

He was a married associate professor at a university in the northern Middle West when he was seduced by one of his students, Elena Petrovich. They began meeting because they both enjoyed biking, but the relationship quickly proceeded on to more vigorous activities. Darryl left his wife and moved in with the much younger woman. Darryl published books and scholarly articles, and eventually he became the editor of the university's history magazine.

Elena Petrovich was Russian. She had a past about which she refused to speak. Her English was excellent, and only when she became angry or excited did her speech reveal the slightest foreign accent. Elena was working on her PhD in history. She had chosen to write her dissertation on some technical point surrounding the 1917 Russian Revolution. Some argued that she belonged in the Slavic Studies program or even in Political Science, but she had the chairman on her side. She stayed in the History Department.

Elena was not as young as Darryl thought she was. She was not as young as she had led everyone else to believe. She looked young, and she was very pretty. Her light brown hair fell in soft waves around her heart-shaped face. Her high cheek bones, flawless skin, and large, wide, innocent eyes cast her as an ingénue, an innocent. She had an almost childlike appearance and demeanor, but in fact, she was anything but naive. At this stage in her life, it was not a stretch to believe her when she claimed that she was seven years younger than her real biological age. If you are a well-preserved and young-looking thirty-three, people can easily believe you are only twenty-six. It was what she had done with those seven years that she was afraid Darryl and others might find out.

Her passport and all of her papers were forgeries. Elena had spent her teens and part of her twenties in Moscow. She had been trained as an active agent of the SVR, Russia's external intelligence agency, an organization comparable to the CIA. After her training, she had been sent to the USA as a sleeper spy where she successfully melded into American society and spied on the country that had taken her in.

After several years working as a spy in the United States, she had become romantically involved with a U.S. citizen. She'd told the SVR she would no longer work for them. She genuinely loved Darryl Harcomb and had decided she wanted nothing more to do with spying and nothing more to do with Russia. She was going to become a U.S. citizen and marry Darryl. Whatever Elena set out to do, she almost always accomplished. Seducing her history professor had been easy compared to some of the assignments Elena had taken on. She now wanted to put her Russian past behind her. Was the SVR going to allow her to opt out so easily, because she said she wanted to? She had been schooled to be a spy, and she had sworn an oath to Mother Russia. She was one of Vladimir Putin's highly-trained operatives. Could she realistically hope to escape that world and her own involvement in it, just because she loved Darryl Harcomb?

Darryl liked to participate in the reunions and enjoyed seeing his friends from the past. He sometimes had a bit of a superior attitude, and a few of his old buddies thought he regarded his career and his life as more erudite and on a higher plane than their own. Darryl was very intellectual, and he tended to ignore the more mundane things of life. But he felt a certain affection for and loyalty toward his childhood chums. The time he spent with them took him away from the high-stress academic life that frequently caused his blood pressure to soar.

Elena, on the other hand, didn't especially like Darryl's old friends. Elena had grown up in a different culture, and she didn't understand Darryl's desire to stay in touch with people he'd known in the past. She didn't appreciate his attachment to these boys he'd grown up with. Elena thought only about the future and about her career. She wanted nothing to do with the past, anyone's past, especially her own. Because his friends were not in the academic world, she thought they were somewhat beneath her and Darryl. Even though the men were all leaders in their professions and all had been very successful, accomplishment in academia was the only realm for which Elena had any respect.

She liked the women in the group even less. They'd all had successful careers and raised families while working, either full-time or part-time. Elena felt she had nothing in common with these women she regarded as domesticated minions. Elena had never had a child. She felt that being a mother was beneath her. Because these women were not teaching at a university, Elena thought they were intellectually inferior.

She discouraged Darryl from attending the yearly reunions, and she wouldn't allow him to go by himself. He'd once proposed going to the reunion alone, and Elena had let him know in no uncertain terms that he was not going to be allowed to go anywhere without her. Elena was a beautiful, intelligent, and accomplished woman, but in spite of her position and achievements, she was insanely jealous. She wouldn't let Darryl out of her sight. She was especially jealous of the students

Darryl taught. She had once been the seductive young undergraduate, and she knew only too well how the wiles of the fresh and nubile could twist and turn an older man into a blob of jelly.

Once in a while Elena agreed to attend the reunions. If she knew the trip was going to be to an interesting place, she might agree to let Darryl go, and she always went with him. Elena had never been to Maine. She knew there were some excellent art museums and art galleries in Rockport and Bar Harbor, and she loved lobster. She decided she could put up with Darryl's friends for a day or two. She would ignore the women completely, and she would turn on her considerable charm with some of the men. She wasn't really interested in any of the old guys; she just wanted to make their wives jealous of her youth and beauty.

They made their plans to go to Maine. They would not be there for the first night. Elena liked to show up unexpectedly and always late. They wouldn't tell anyone their definite flight or arrival plans. "Keep them guessing" was her mantra. She and Darryl were too important and too in demand to spend as much time away from work as those who were retired wanted to spend on these long weekends. Elena always implied that they could barely get away from their high-level positions to join the others. Their university would surely perish from the earth if Darryl and Elena were not in residence.

They'd heard that a reservation had been made at a Cuban restaurant for Sunday night. Because they were fans of the Castro brothers and the socialist paradise they'd built in the Caribbean, Elena wanted to be sure they made it to the dinner at Cuba Libre. Never mind that the owner of the restaurant had been forced to leave Cuba many years earlier because of the Castro brothers, and she hated them to the core of her being.

Chapter 17

*T*HAT NIGHT, AFTER THEY RETURNED FROM THE Down East Café, the group decided to sit on the back porch at the Inastou and have a nightcap. Everyone would be in Maine for only one more day. Their time together was precious, and they wanted to make the most of it. They were sitting on the porch watching the magnificent full moon rise, when they heard a loud argument in the parking lot below.

That morning, Elena and Darryl had made it clear they intended to drive to Orono, and no one had seen them all day. Tonight, however, everyone could see Elena in the parking lot, yelling at a man they didn't know. Where was Darryl? Elena was very angry, and when the man tried to grab her arm, she pulled an amazing karate move and twisted his arm behind his back. She held him in that position while she got in his face, giving it to him in rapidly spoken Russian.

Tyler's chair and ottoman were set up on the side of the porch that overlooked the parking lot, so he had the best view of the two who were arguing. Gretchen, who was still agitated by her encounter with Bailey at the Down East Café, was like a cat on a hot tin roof and couldn't sit still. She was pacing. She walked to the edge of the porch and leaned over to see what was going on. A couple of the others were also curious. They'd never heard Elena speak Russian and wondered who in the world she was taking apart in her native language. Although they recognized the language Elena was speaking, no one in the group understood Russian. They could only judge how the argument was going by the tone of the screaming and the body language. Darryl was nowhere to be seen.

There was almost no lighting in the Inastou's rear parking lot, and it was difficult to make out the face of the man Elena was arguing with. He was trying to stay in the shadows, and he kept his head down. When Gretchen was able to focus on what was happening, she almost fainted when she realized she recognized the man who was standing there with Elena. Gretchen hadn't seen the man for more than a decade. The last time she'd seen him had been in a very private office in a very private bank in Zurich. She had met with this Russian and had assisted in a huge transfer of funds, a transaction of more than five billion dollars, to several separate bank accounts around the world. She'd been sworn to secrecy about the deal and about the people who were involved.

But she knew who this man was. She knew he was one of Vladimir Putin's "special assistants." He was a kind of high-level gofer, one of the men who hid the money and took care of the dirty details the dictator didn't want anybody to know about. Gretchen had imagined he was one of the men who arranged for the assassinations and disappearances of those who wouldn't go along with what Bad Vlad wanted. Having to deal with people like this man had helped her make the decision to leave her job at the Swiss bank. She was not able to remember the man's name, if she had ever heard it. He'd probably traveled to Zurich using a false identity anyway. Whatever his name was, Gretchen knew he was very bad news, and if Elena was tangling with this extremely dangerous guy, she was in very big trouble. Gretchen was frightened. She should have kept her mouth shut, but the words slipped out before she could stop herself.

"I know that man."

Tyler, who had also been closely watching the interaction in the parking lot below, spoke quietly so that only Gretchen could hear him. "So do I. So do I."

Gretchen was stunned that she knew the man and that he was in Bar Harbor. What in the world would ever bring him to this remote part of the USA? When she heard Tyler say he also knew the Russian, she was doubly shocked. How could Tyler possibly know who this man was? Gretchen knew that, in the past, Putin's buddy hardly left the Motherland. He would never travel to the U.S. Gretchen stared at Tyler, and Tyler stared at Gretchen. They knew they had to talk, and it had to be a private discussion, without the others. They were both afraid for Elena, although she seemed to be getting the better of the argument. Sidney and Olivia didn't hear what Gretchen and Tyler had said out loud, but they'd seen the looks that had passed between the two, and the women's radar went on high alert.

Cameron was watching Sidney. He always knew when something important had caught her attention. She had a certain tilt to her head and a certain set to her mouth when she was working hard on unraveling a puzzle. She would tell him about it later, but he couldn't help wondering what was up. He knew his wife was smart. All the women in the group were smart. Cameron made a bet with himself that it would be the women who finally figured out what the heck had been going on with the dirty tricks someone was playing on them.

One by one and two by two, they drifted off to their rooms. Gretchen stayed behind to talk with Tyler, who told Lilleth he wasn't tired yet and could get up to their room on his own. Lilleth had gone on the lobster boat ride and had been taking care of Tyler for two days. She was exhausted and ready to sleep. Sidney and Cameron were in the lobby when Elena burst through the front door of the Inastou and ran up the stairs, presumably to her room. They were relieved to see she'd survived her encounter with the mystery man.

Gretchen and Tyler were finally alone.

"I don't know his name, but he was a client at the Swiss bank where I worked in Zurich. He's one of Vladimir Putin's close personal friends or administrative assistants or bagmen, or something. I know what I did for him, but I certainly don't know everything he does for Putin. And I don't want to know. Working with people like that Russian man was one of the reasons I left a very high-paying and powerful position. I couldn't stomach it any more. That's how I know him, even though I don't really know him. I can't imagine what he's doing here, talking to Elena. I know she's Russian, but how would she ever know an important person like that? There is obviously much more to Elena than meets the eye. Now it's your turn."

"I can't really tell you how I know what I know, but I will tell you that this man is a former KGB thug. That's not a big secret. Vladimir Putin is also a former KGB thug. The U.S. kept a very close eye on both Putin and this friend of Elena's for years, up until the fall of the Soviet Union." Tyler pointed to where the man in the parking lot had been standing. "He was a money man for the KGB. In his younger days, he carried the actual cash to banks and people all over the world. Then it became easier to transfer the money electronically, and he pretty much stayed close to the Kremlin. He has to be sixty years old or older by now, much too old to be running around fighting with a hot tamale like Elena. I cannot begin to imagine what those two could possibly have to say to each other. I wonder if Darryl has any idea about their meeting tonight. But then he never takes his eyes off his tablet long enough to notice much of anything." Tyler had a brief pang of conscience about disclosing even these few pieces of information about the mysterious Russian.

"Do you think we need to tell anybody about what we know?"

"What do we know, really, and what is there to tell? I say we keep what we know to ourselves. Elena may have a past she doesn't want anybody to know about. I don't think her argument with the former KGB guy has anything to do with the accidents that have been happening. Do you?" Tyler knew what a very, very bad guy the man was. Tyler wanted as few people as possible to know as little as possible about the Russian. He hadn't told Gretchen a fraction of what he knew about the dangerous operative, but he was quite concerned about Elena's involvement with him.

"I agree, we don't need to tell anybody about this. I caught a glimpse of Elena going up the stairs to her room, so I know she's all right and not in danger … for right now." Gretchen was relieved to be able to tell Tyler that Elena was now safely inside and upstairs and no longer hanging out in the parking lot.

"What I've just told you is all highly classified information, and I know what you have told me is also confidential. I have to say I was beyond being shocked when I saw that man here at the Inastou. I would love to know what brought him to Bar Harbor, but I'm sure we will never know." Because of the unique circumstances, Tyler had said things to Gretchen tonight he would never have thought of saying to anyone.

"Maybe it's best we don't know." Gretchen was tired.

Tyler wanted to change the subject. "See you tomorrow. The Sunday brunch at the Island Morning Restaurant is supposed to be fabulous. The blueberry pancakes are like crepes, thin and crispy. I'm having a stack." Tyler struggled with his crutches to climb the steps. As usual, the desk clerk was nowhere around to operate the elevator for him.

Gretchen was exhausted from the activities of the day and from worry. She would have loved to go immediately up to her room and go to sleep. Instead, she went to her room, packed a bag for Bailey, and left the lodge to get her car. She had to drive to meet Bailey at the entrance to the Acadia National Park and take him the things he'd asked for on his list. She hoped the Russian agent would be long gone from the parking lot. If he were still there, she hoped he wouldn't see her or recognize her from their one encounter, long ago in Switzerland.

The next morning they all met at Island Morning, and the blueberry pancakes and the rest of the food offered at the brunch was just as wonderful as had been advertised. The lobster omelet was in contention with the blueberry pancakes for most favorite brunch item. The Lobster Thermidor in puff pastry was also a big contender for the breakfast prize. Everyone ate too much, and all were ready for a nap when they arrived back at the Inastou.

Before their cars had reached the lodge, they could see that something was very wrong. The front driveway was full of law enforcement vehicles, flashing red and blue lights, and a van that said "Office of the Hancock County Medical Examiner" on the side. This was trouble of a whole new order. Somebody was dead.

Chapter 18

THE FRONT DRIVEWAY AND THE REAR PARKING LOT were both blocked off with yellow crime scene tape, so they left their cars along the road and walked to the front door of the Inastou. Nobody was there to keep them from entering the lobby. Whatever bad thing had happened, it had happened outside. The group moved instinctively to the back porch. A few of the Inastou's other guests were already there, leaning over the porch railing and trying to see what was taking place below on the ground level. The previously-longed-for naps were put on the back burner, and everyone's attention was focused on the excitement in the Inastou Lodge's rear parking lot. A tent had been set up, and everything of importance was happening inside the tent. The curious onlookers were unable to see much of anything except a lot of official-looking people coming and going.

Tyler's chair and ottoman were in the best position to observe the activity, and he motioned to his friends that something was happening. A few of the group moved closer to the edge of the porch to see what Tyler had alerted them about. Sure enough, there was the van from the medical examiner's office. It had moved from the driveway in front of the Inastou to the back. The gurney, a narrow stretcher on wheels, sat on the concrete. The gurney had a black body bag on it. There was definitely something inside the body bag, but it was zipped closed. They would have to depend on Richard to find out who was in the bag.

A very long time ago, Dr. Richard Carpenter had worked for the Philadelphia Medical Examiner's Office. He knew about dead bodies and crime scenes. He knew how to talk to these official people and would be able to find out what had happened. When they'd arrived back at the lodge after brunch, Carpenter had made his way to the rear parking lot and located the man in charge. He was easy to identify because he wore a windbreaker that said "Coroner" on the back. Richard Carpenter was an outgoing, friendly guy, and he just walked up to the medical examiner and introduced himself. It was that easy.

"Hi. Dr. Richard Carpenter." Richard put out his hand, and the coroner politely shook it. "I'm a retired pathologist and used to be with the Philadelphia Medical Examiner's Office. Right now, I'm a guest at the Inastou. I'm on vacation, and I have to say, I wasn't expecting to see the medical examiner's office here today."

"Benjamin Mahoney, M.D., Hancock County Medical Examiner. I work full-time as a pathologist at a hospital in Bangor, but when Hancock County needs me, I'm the ME. We haven't had a murder here on Mount Desert Island in more than seven years. It just isn't that kind of place. I'm usually called when there's a car accident or an unattended death. It's always pretty obvious what's happened, and I just pronounce somebody. No intrigue and no mystery. Just died in a car crash or died of a heart attack. So, I have to admit, I may be in over my head with this one. Unfortunately, it's a murder. Two gunshot wounds to the head and one to the chest, and the guy doesn't have any identification on him. No wallet, so we have to think of robbery." Mahoney looked depressed, like he wished he were anywhere but in the parking lot of the Inastou Lodge.

"I worked with Vance Stillinger in Philadelphia, and he taught me a lot. I used to testify for the medical examiner's office in court. I put that all behind me when I went to work at a rural hospital in Maryland. More money and less stress. There were always way too many murders in Philly, and I don't know how Stillinger could get up every morning and go to work." Richard didn't want to interfere with Mahoney's case, but he wanted to let the other doctor know he knew his way around a crime scene.

"Vance Stillinger is a legend. He wrote several books on forensic pathology. I've read a few of them. You were lucky you had the chance to work with him."

"Yes, I was. I considered taking a job with Stillinger after I'd finished my years in the Army, but being a medical examiner in Philadelphia was too depressing. The suicides got to me more than the homicides did. And when a child died, I just couldn't deal with that."

"The cause of death here is pretty obvious, but of course I'll send the body to Augusta for the post. I don't do criminal cases. The CSI team that's here is out of Bangor, too. They have more experience with murder cases there. There aren't any criminalists in Bar Harbor. Bar Harbor has the county sheriff and some deputies, and the town has a good, but very small, police force. Neither has any criminal investigators, not even a detective. I don't know who will have jurisdiction in this case."

Carpenter wondered if he should tell Mahoney anything about the mysterious Russian man who had been hanging around in the parking lot the night before. Although he knew he might live to regret it, Richard took the leap and made the decision to become involved. "There was a Russian guy hanging around here late last night. Our reunion group was having a nightcap on the back porch, and we saw him in the parking lot. It was dark, and the lighting back here is terrible, one light for the entire lot. It's very treacherous to try to park your car here after dark. Not because of lurking criminals but because of the condition of the parking lot's pavement and the lack of lighting. The pot holes in the black top and the tree roots are dangerous enough, without worrying about being murdered. The Russian was having a loud argument with someone, and we could hear more than we could see. Although no one in our group speaks Russian, a couple of us recognized that the man was shouting in Russian. We couldn't understand what he was saying, but he was very angry. Of course, the dead man may not be the same man we saw hanging around. I just mention it because the guy didn't fit in here. He wasn't the usual tourist who stays at the Inastou Lodge or comes to Bar Harbor on vacation."

Carpenter wanted to be very careful about implicating Elena in any way. He thought she was rude and didn't like her very much, but he wasn't going to mention her in connection with a murder.

"Did you get a good look at this Russian guy? Do you think you would recognize him if you saw him again?" Mahoney was moving toward the gurney and the body. He unzipped the body bag and revealed the pallid face of a very dead man who had two distinct bullet holes in his forehead. He'd been shot at very close range. Richard could see the stippling, the powder burns on his face. If the man had been shot from the rear, the exit wounds in his face would have made him unrecognizable, even to his nearest and dearest. As it was, Richard Carpenter easily recognized the corpse as the same man who'd been arguing with Elena.

"Yes, that's the man who was screaming in Russian in the parking lot last night. How long has he been dead, do you think?"

"Are you sure he was speaking Russian? And are you certain this is the same man? He's been dead about twelve hours. Nobody found him until ten this morning."

"Yes and yes. It's the same guy. I don't know if he's a Russian national, but he was definitely speaking Russian last night."

"What time did you see him?"

"I saw him here at the edge of the parking lot at about ten thirty last night."

"This is very helpful information, Doc, and I'm grateful. I now know when he was most likely last seen alive, and your information confirms my estimated time of death. I also know he was involved in some kind of an altercation. But the most important thing you've told me, from my point of view at least, is that he was speaking Russian. That means I will be able to call the FBI and hand this whole mess over to them. They can sort out his identity and figure out what the heck he was doing in Bar Harbor. You've been a big help to me. I owe you." Mahoney gave Carpenter his business card and promised to contact Carpenter if he found out the dead man's name.

"The FBI is sometimes very proprietary with their investigations, and they don't want to give out information. You know this, I'm sure. They want to know everything you know, but they don't want to tell you anything. So keep me in the loop. I want to know where this investigation goes." Richard Carpenter handed Ben Mahoney a piece of paper with his name and cell phone number on it.

"I'm going to have to give your name and number to the FBI. Sorry about that, but you and your friends may be the last people to have seen the guy alive … except for the killer, of course. So, I have to give you up as a witness. I hate to do it, but the FBI will be calling you." Mahoney sounded as if he really was sorry.

"It's okay. I know what to do. I've dealt with the FBI before." The two pathologists shook hands and said their goodbyes.

Richard wanted to share as much as he could with the others in the group, but he was worried because of Elena's involvement. He knew that when the FBI questioned him, he was going to have to tell them that Elena was the person who had been arguing with the Russian man the night before. Richard didn't want to involve her unnecessarily in a murder investigation.

Richard made his way slowly around to the front of the Inastou and walked through the lobby to the back porch. He wondered if he should try to talk to Elena before he said anything to the others. He knew Elena didn't like him, and she probably wouldn't be willing to talk to him about anything. The eager faces of his friends greeted him. They'd been watching him have a long and intense conversation with the Hancock County Medical Examiner, and they were expecting to hear all the details. They would be surprised to learn, when Carpenter gave them his report, that he had actually given more information to the medical examiner than the medical examiner had given to him.

"Has anyone seen Elena? I need to talk to her." Carpenter asked the group that was gathered on the back porch.

"No one has seen Elena or Darryl this morning. We knew they weren't going to brunch with us, but they say they're definitely going to dinner at Cuba Libre tonight." Matthew was keeping track of the restaurant reservations.

Considering Elena's argument with the Russian the night before, she and Darryl might have changed their plans and decided to leave Maine early. They never wanted anybody to know exactly what their plans were. Richard Carpenter realized he wasn't going to be able to talk to Elena before he had to tell his friends everything he knew about the body in the bag. Some of them might be contacted by the FBI and asked to give witness statements, and no one would be happy about that. Carpenter decided not to mention that part of his discussion with Ben Mahoney until he absolutely had to.

Later that afternoon, Matthew Ritter brought out some old photographs he'd saved all these years and lovingly brought to Maine to share with his friends. Matthew was more than a little bit compulsive about some things, and although he hadn't saved his childhood photos in a scrapbook, he had carefully filed them away so he could easily put his hands on them. The photos from their early years at Camp Shoemaker were in black and white, and they were in excellent condition. A few of the photos were candid shots taken with a Brownie camera and developed by Kodak. Each print had a date on the back. The 8" X 10" photos were posed shots. Camp Shoemaker had hired a professional to take formal photographs of the campers, lined up in rows in front of their cabins. Each boy was given a glossy copy of the photo at the end of the camp session. The photos of the boys when they were older were in color, and those unfortunately had faded over the years. Candid shots from these later years had been taken with an Instamatic camera. They had also been developed by Kodak and had the date stamped on the back. It was a wonderful gift to have these photos dated for posterity.

The group took over a long table in the dining room of the Inastou. It would be hours before the staff had to set up for dinner. They spread the old photographs out over the table and poured over them. The wives and girlfriends had never before had a chance to view these prized pieces of memorabilia, and they loved seeing the men as young boys. Everyone marveled at how handsome they'd been and how they'd grown from year to year. Stories were told and retold, and the trip down memory lane was nostalgic and fun.

There was also sorrow in the recollections because one of their group had died two years earlier, after a long battle with Parkinson's Disease and non-Hodgkin's lymphoma. All were diminished by his loss. Another member of the group had stopped attending the reunions a few years ago. He and his second wife had divorced, and after he had fallen several times, he'd accepted that he was no longer able to live alone. He had moved into an assisted living facility in Little Rock, and although he missed participating in the yearly trips, he was not able to travel any more. His friends visited him when they could and often went out of their way to plan trips to see him in Arkansas.

Isabelle was curious about the younger boy who seemed to sneak into the camp photographs over the years. In one photo, he was sitting cross legged on the ground in the center of their posed cabin photo, almost like a mascot. In a photo taken a few years later, he was half-way hidden behind the back row of campers, peeking around the side of the group. He wasn't always in the pictures, but he was there often enough to be noticed.

"Why is this boy in several of your photographs? He seems to get his little face in there pretty often. He's much younger than you guys, so he wouldn't have been in your cabin." Isabelle thought the boy's eyes looked dark and sad, in spite of his big grin. She was a psychologist and noticed things like that, even in a photograph.

"I remember that kid. He was always hanging around with us, and we were always telling him to get lost. I don't know why he picked us out to be his friends, but we thought he was a pain in the neck." J.D. remembered the little kid and how annoying he'd been.

Matthew remembered him, too. "His mother worked at the camp. That's why he was always around. He wasn't ever a camper, but he did like to hassle us. He always wanted to know what we were doing, and he always wanted to go with us. I don't know what it was about us. I don't think he bothered any of the other campers like he did our group."

"His mother was a cook in the dining hall. I remember he sometimes brought us cookies. They weren't that good. The cookies were from a box, not homemade. He wanted us to include him in everything we did. He couldn't seem to understand that he wasn't a camper to begin with and was too young to go with us on our adventures. He was a little "off," I think. Not retarded really, but he was just not all there in the appropriateness department. He must have been lonely. There weren't any other kids his age at the camp for him to play with. We weren't exactly mean to him, but he was always underfoot. We didn't like him. I can't remember what his name was." Richard Carpenter remembered the kid. He'd felt kind of sorry for him at the time, but the kid had really made a pest of himself. At one point, Richard thought they'd complained to their cabin counselor or the camp director or somebody about the little boy who wouldn't leave them alone.

The chef of the Inastou appeared beside the table. His body language indicated that he was angry, but because of his large mustaches and beard, it was hard to tell. "Whatever you are doing, you will have to wrap it up now. It's time for us to set the tables for dinner." The chef was tactless and abrupt, even rude, with them and stomped out of the dining room back to his kitchen.

"Whoa, I guess we ticked off the chef. What was that all about? We weren't harming anything, just sitting at one of his precious tables." Tyler didn't understand why the chef had gone off on them.

"It's a good thing we aren't going to eat any more meals here, except for breakfast tomorrow. He clearly doesn't like us much, or at all. What did we ever do to get under his skin? That was very weird." Cameron was right, and he was also concerned. The chef's interaction with them had been strange and totally uncalled-for.

Isabelle was impressed with how inappropriate the chef's comments had been. She'd noticed something she didn't think anyone else had seen. The chef had been watching them through the round window in the swinging door that went from the dining room into the kitchen. Isabelle had seen his fat face at the window and wondered why he was so interested in what they were doing. Then he'd come into the dining room and watched them from a distance as they poured over the camp photographs. He'd been standing near the wall, close enough to listen to what they were saying. He was eavesdropping. Finally he'd approached and angrily told them to pack up their photographs and get out. His attitude perplexed and worried Isabelle. Lilleth, who was also a psychologist, likewise found the chef's behavior disturbing. The others, not professionally trained to identify the signs of mental illness, were just offended … and glad they weren't eating at the Inastou again, except for breakfast.

Chapter 19

SUNDAY NIGHT WAS THEIR LAST DINNER TOGETHER, and the Cuba Libre restaurant was supposed to be something special. Everyone except Bailey was there, and even Elena and Darryl were on time. A table for their group had been set up in The Wine Room. The room was not in a cellar at all, but a part of the first floor. The restaurant served Cuban food, which had evoked mixed reactions among the members of the group, but it was known for its wine selection. They were in Maine, after all, and some would have preferred a restaurant with a more Down East focus, rather than an eatery that specialized in the cuisine of an island in the Caribbean. On the other hand, they'd gorged on lobster, so maybe it was time for something different. Elizabeth's experience with Cuban food had been mostly at the airport in Miami, and although Richard had loved the greasy, overstuffed pork, ham, and cheese sandwich, it wasn't his wife's favorite. She was willing to give it another chance, but after looking at the menu her skepticism returned.

Matthew ordered several bottles of wine for the table, both white and red. Some people ordered mojitos, which was Cuba's national drink. Elena was seated on the same side of the table as Richard that night. She'd been glancing sideways and staring at him since they'd arrived at the restaurant. He hadn't tried to talk to her about his encounter with the Hancock County Medical Examiner, but she might have seen him talking with Ben Mahoney in the Inastou parking lot. If she'd seen the two talking, Elena didn't bring it up with Richard. She didn't say a single word, just kept looking at him. Ordinarily a very cool customer, always superior and always in control, tonight Elena looked stressed and anything but composed. Her agitation was obvious to everyone. No one believed she'd had anything to do with the Russian man's murder, but something was bothering her and had upset her in a way no one in the reunion group had ever seen before. Was the Russian man who'd died someone from her past, someone she'd feared? Did she think her own life was in danger? Was she afraid, because the man had been murdered, that she might be next? Was her former life catching up with her?

Elizabeth had read a review of the Cuban eatery and ordered an appetizer of mushroom spring rolls, which online diners all agreed were outstanding. Almost exclusively associated with Asian cuisine, spring rolls seemed to be a peculiar offering in a Cuban restaurant. But when the mushroom spring rolls arrived, Elizabeth burst out laughing. The spring rolls had been deep fried to a rich dark brown color, and each one was exactly the length and diameter of a cigar. She had in front of her a plate of spring rolls that looked more like cigars than cigars themselves looked. One spring roll was standing up vertically as if the edible cigar had just been stubbed out, extinguished on the bed of arugula that covered the plate. The other three "cigars" were scattered randomly over the greens. Elizabeth realized the restaurant had a delightful sense of humor. She split the order of spring rolls with Olivia. Elizabeth scoured the menu for other humorous foods.

Elena ordered the pork loin which had been rubbed with Old Bay seasoning, another curious culinary combination, in Elizabeth's opinion. Did they even have Old Bay in Cuba? Most people associated the spicy seasoning with seafood, specifically with Atlantic blue crabs and crab cakes. The plate of roast pork was garnished with cubes of smoky bacon and a multitude of fresh bay leaves. It was certainly a very odd combination of flavors, but Elizabeth didn't have to think very long before she "got it." This was a dish that evoked the disastrous, failed Bay of Pigs invasion of Cuba that had occurred during President

John Kennedy's administration. Elizabeth wondered if Elena realized what she had ordered.

Elena was drinking way too much wine, and she was drinking it very fast. She didn't usually get drunk, but tonight she was well on her way. Before the group ordered dessert, Elena was talking in a very loud and unpleasant tone of voice. She wasn't really speaking to anybody in particular, just generally pontificating about politics and Cuba and random other subjects. People at nearby tables were staring at her. She wasn't making much sense, and Darryl repeatedly told her to hold it down. Of course, she paid no attention to him. She just got louder and louder. Finally, she stood up on her chair and sang *The Internationale*, the Communist/Socialist workers-of-the-world unite Marxist theme song. The song had been the first national anthem of the former Soviet Union. It was a totally bizarre display and humiliating for the entire group. Everyone in the restaurant was now looking at their table and at the woman who was completely out of control. More than a few people wondered if she was on drugs.

Sidney was sitting directly across the table from Elena. Sidney tried to look around and past the drunk woman, anywhere but at the embarrassing spectacle Elena was making of herself. The display was just too painful and pathetic to watch. Seated with her back to the rest of the restaurant, Sidney was facing a huge, ornately carved wooden mirror that hung on the wall behind Elena. The mirror had been brushed with gilt paint, and Sidney, who knew about these things, guessed that it was a very old and very valuable Cuban antique. The reflecting surface of the mirror itself needed to be re-silvered, and it was difficult to see anything in it. The reflection was blurred, and the mirror was obviously intended to be an art object rather than a way to check one's makeup.

Because of where she was seated, Sidney couldn't help but look in the mirror. Trying to focus on anything but Elena, Sidney was forced to watch the hazy reflection of the woman who was standing at the back of the restaurant. Because of the condition of the mirror, Sidney wasn't able to see the woman very clearly, but the woman was obviously somebody important here, maybe the owner or the owner's mother.

The woman in the mirror was strikingly beautiful. She could be anywhere between the ages of fifty and seventy. She had black shiny hair twisted into a complicated chignon that rested at the base of her neck. She wore large gold earrings and a heavy necklace of old gold links that lay on her chest against a black silk caftan. The woman was tall and robustly built, and she had dark, piercing eyes. She was watching Elena's performance with an expression on her face that made chills run down Sidney's spine. Sidney was sure the Rubenesque woman was going to come over to their table at any minute and ask them all to leave. But the woman never moved, just stood there, as still as a statue, staring at Elena, mesmerized. Sidney would not realize for several days what she had accidentally observed through the foggy and faded antique mirror.

Almost everyone ordered dessert, even the exceedingly drunk Elena. Darryl wanted to take her home, and told her she didn't need to have dessert. Elena ignored him and ordered the blueberry and strawberry cake. She insisted that the waiter refill her wine glass. The evening had gone completely downhill and was headed for a disastrous bottom.

The desserts arrived. Several people had ordered the cake, and Elizabeth recognized the beautiful arrangement of colorful red and blue fruits with the white cake and icing on the plate as a creative and quite accurate representation of the Cuban flag. Elena's cake arrived first, and she began to eat before the other desserts were served. Elizabeth was just about to point out to the others at the table how the cake had been made to resemble the Cuban flag, when Elena clutched at her throat and began to scream. She stood up and tried to get away from the table, but she was unable to move. She continued to scream and tear at her blouse. She finally collapsed back down into her chair. Her head fell forward, and her face landed squarely in the plate of cake. Richard and Matthew jumped from their seats and rushed to help. They cleared her airway and tried to do whatever they could to save her.

The room was in chaos. Someone called 911 and yelled that the paramedics were on their way. A man and woman from the next table came over, pulled Elena out of her chair, laid her on the floor, and began doing CPR. Except for the two physicians who had come to her aid, the others at the reunion table were shell-shocked into silence and immobility. Unable to do anything to help and unable to speak, they sat and stared and waited, numb with horror. Darryl was hysterical. He shook Elena's body, as if trying to wake her up. The two people who were doing CPR kept pushing him out of the way. Richard and Matthew restrained him to keep him from attacking the two good Samaritans who were ministering to Elena, determined to continue their useless efforts to revive her.

When the EMTs arrived, the couple finally halted their attempts to revive Elena. The EMTs used the defibrillator heart paddles on her repeatedly to try to restart her heart. Darryl was clawing at her and pleading with her to talk to him. He kept telling her she wasn't dead and that it was time for her to look him in the eyes. His grief was palpable and raw. The EMTs wouldn't let Darryl in the ambulance because he was such a basket case. Matthew and Richard agreed to drive Darryl to Mount Desert Island Hospital, the twenty-five bed facility in Bar Harbor that was just a couple of minutes away from Cuba Libre. Everyone except Darryl realized that Elena was beyond help. No amount of CPR or defibrillation was ever going to bring her back to life.

At the hospital Elena was pronounced dead and her body was taken to the morgue. Because hers had been a suspicious death, the autopsy would be done in Augusta at the office of the state's chief medical examiner. Because of the way she had died, a full range of toxicology analyses would be done, including tests for obscure drugs and poisons.

Darryl Harcomb's two doctor friends drove him to the hospital and stayed with him in the emergency room. While Matthew waited with Darryl, Richard Carpenter stepped outside the hospital's doors and called his new friend Dr. Benjamin Mahoney. Richard told him that Elena Petrovich was dead, probably from some kind of drug or poison. Richard told the medical examiner that Elena had been the person the murdered Russian man had argued with the night before in the parking lot of the Inastou Lodge. He told Mahoney that Elena was a Russian national and that her background was probably worth looking into. Richard suggested that Elena's Russian past might have something to do with the homicide of the mystery man at the Inastou and with her own death. He didn't know exactly how all the pieces fit together, but he suspected the deaths were connected.

While Richard Carpenter was on the phone with Mahoney, he insisted that Elena's post mortem be "the full monty." Something very strange had occurred at Cuba Libre. Elena Petrovich was a relatively young woman in excellent health, and she had not died from natural causes. Everyone would be demanding an explanation about her violent death. Ben assured Richard they would do every possible test, even the most obscure ones, and they would get to the bottom of what had happened to Elena.

Darryl was so distraught and his sobbing was so convulsive, he was unable to sit up in a chair at the ER. He had to lie down. When he'd arrived at the ER, his blood pressure had been through the roof. The ER doctor who examined Darryl was concerned for his life. The doctor explained to Richard and Matthew that he was afraid Darryl might have suffered a small stroke. Darryl was sedated and admitted to the hospital overnight for observation. In spite of living with a much younger woman and in spite of working out every day to remain youthful and fit, Darryl was not a youngster. The new widower was clearly in emotional extremis, and the prudent course was to keep him tranquilized. The doctor who admitted Darryl assured Richard and Matthew that he would keep their friend in the hospital until he was certain Darryl was no longer in any physical danger. Apparently, Darryl was Elena's only family. Whatever family she'd once had in Russia, they were no longer in the picture.

The reunion group had experienced two murders in one day. The first shock had been finding out about the shooting death of a mysterious man they didn't know. The second shock had been the inexplicable and sudden death of the partner of one of their own. It had happened right in front of their eyes, and it had happened in a public place. These violent and distinctly rare circumstances were devastating and considerably more than the elderly and respectable group of retired professionals had ever had to deal with. It was unprecedented, and they were paralyzed by shock and disbelief.

Aside from the physicians who were at the hospital with Darryl, Cameron seemed to be the most able to cope with the tragic circumstances of the night. He was used to functioning in very high stress situations and was able to compartmentalize his emotions. He paid the bill at Cuba Libre and made sure all drivers in the group were sober and not too distressed to make the ten mile drive back to the Inastou. He sent one couple back in a taxi. Neither spouse was in any condition to drive, and they could pick up their car in the morning.

Cameron realized that no law enforcement officials had turned up at Cuba Libre that night. Bar Harbor was a small town with a small police force. It was possible that no one had even called the police about Elena's death, but he wondered why a police car had not accompanied the ambulance. Elena had been taken to the hospital, and there would be an autopsy. At some point, the local police or the county sheriff's office would become involved. They would want to question everyone who knew Elena, everyone who had been seated at their table for dinner. The authorities would have to question the other people in the restaurant who had witnessed Elena's death.

The members of the reunion group were moving in a daze as they entered the Inastou lobby and made their way up the stairs to their rooms. The desk clerk had turned in for the night, and she was, as usual, not available to operate the elevator for anybody. Even Tyler on crutches had to stagger and stumble his way up the staircase.

When they were able to get away from the hospital, Matthew drove Richard back to Northeast Harbor and delivered him to Blueberry House. Richard was anxious to get to his room. Elizabeth had driven the Carpenter's SUV back to the Inastou. Richard was concerned about Elizabeth and hoped she'd been able to make it from the parking lot to the building without any problems. He was worried because the single small light bulb on the side of the house, the only lighting at the rear of the building, wasn't on. He knew Elizabeth would have left it on for him.

There were no lights at all in the parking lot of Blueberry House. After the sun went down, there was no ambient light behind Blueberry house, for parking or for walking. It was impossible to see anything other than the occasional skunk or raccoon that streaked across the gravel. There was one very small light on the wall near the door to their room at the back of the building, and Elizabeth always remembered to turn the light on before they left to go to dinner. If she didn't turn on the light by the door, when they got back, they would have to negotiate both the dark parking lot and the dark back porch to get to their room.

Chapter 20

EVERYONE ON THE SECOND FLOOR OF THE INASTOU Lodge was awakened when they heard screaming. Sidney came running out of the room in her pajamas, all color drained from her face.

"I don't know much about snakes, but this one was very aggressive. It was big and mean and smelled bad. Cameron said it looked like a water moccasin. I'm not spending one more night in this place. In fact, I'm not spending any more of this night in this place."

"What are you talking about? What snake?" Olivia could see Sidney was upset, and hardly anything ever upset Sidney. "What happened?"

"Somebody put a big fat snake in our bed. At first I thought it was Cameron's leg. I kept telling him to stop moving, that I had to go to sleep. Then I looked over at him, and he was sound asleep and not moving a hair. I reached down to see what was climbing around my ankles, and it was a snake. Cameron is in there with it now, getting it out of the bed. It's not like the snake he found in the kayak. He thinks this one is poisonous. I am out of here … now!"

Cameron came to the door, and the others who were gathered in the hall were surprised to see him also look shaken. Cameron was very angry. He slammed the door behind him and didn't say a word. He headed for the stairs. Somebody was going to have it handed to them tonight. It was almost midnight, and there wouldn't be anybody at the desk in the lobby. But Cameron would hunt them down and find them, wherever they were. He had that kind of look on his face.

Isabelle hurried down the hall to speak with Sidney. "We had a snake in our bed, too. When I got back to our room tonight, I smelled something vile, like an animal or a bird had died in there. I knew I wouldn't be able to sleep with that smell, so I went down to the lobby to try to find somebody to talk to about giving us another room. Of course nobody was there. They never are, after about nine o'clock. When Matthew got back here from the hospital and I told him why I was sitting in the lobby, he told me I was imagining things. But after he went to our room, he knew I hadn't imagined anything. The minute he opened the bedroom door, he recognized the smell of a cottonmouth snake. The snake was in our bed … under the sheets! Matthew used the tongs from the fireplace in the room and was able to get the snake out of the bed and into the bathtub. He closed the bathroom door and came back down to the lobby. He got somebody over here from wherever the desk people hide at night, and they gave us a new room. We packed up our stuff and moved. The kid who gave us the new room didn't seem to be fazed at all by the fact that somebody had put a snake in our bed. Matt was furious and yelled at him. The kid just shrugged his shoulders, said, 'Whatever,' and handed us the keys to our new room. I guess nothing gets the 'whatever' generation flustered."

Matt came up behind Isabelle and finished the story. "I asked him if he was going to get the snake out of the bathtub, and he told me that would be housekeeping's problem in the morning. I told him I thought it was a poisonous snake. He just shrugged his shoulders again. Unbelievable! Thank goodness we're leaving tomorrow. Is anybody else, other than Richard and Elizabeth, staying here Monday night?"

Sidney was still pretty shaken. "We decided to take a walk in the Japanese garden before we went up to bed. We probably shouldn't have been walking outside that late at night, especially considering everything that's happened, but we were so rattled over Elena's death, we didn't think we could sleep. We didn't go up to our room until about twenty minutes ago. The room always smells musty to me, and I leave all the widows open to air it out when we aren't there. I thought it smelled worse last night when we went in, but the smell of the Pine-Sol they use to clean the bathroom is so overwhelming, it's sometimes hard to smell anything else in there. I leave the bathroom window open, too, when we're out, to get rid of the Pine-Sol smell. By the time we made it up to the room, we were both exhausted and just fell into bed. Cameron went right to sleep, and I thought what I kept feeling was him moving his leg. I told him to stay still and not move around so much, until I realized he wasn't the one who was moving. I reached down and actually touched the thing." Sidney shuddered as she remembered her encounter with the cold and squirming creature. "I'm not moving to another room. I'm moving to another hotel. Somebody did this on purpose. Water moccasins aren't found in Maine. Somebody brought these poisonous snakes here. Someone is intentionally harassing us and trying to harm us. Why would anyone want to do that? It had to be somebody who works at the Inastou. Otherwise how could they get into the rooms? What did we do to piss off somebody so badly? None of us are ever here. We're gone all day."

"Lock picks have been known to allow a person to break into rooms as old as these. Lock picks don't work on electronic locks, like most newer hotels have these days, but a good lock picker could get into any one of these rooms at the Inastou in less than a minute." J.D. seemed to know a lot about how to break into a room.

"How do you know so much about picking locks?" Olivia was asking. This was a side of her husband she didn't know anything about. She looked skeptical and suspicious.

"Remember, once upon a time, I was a prosecutor. A suspect in a robbery showed me how he picked a lock. I bought my own set of lock picks and practiced. It was kind of fun. I told myself I needed to develop the skill to better try my cases. But the real reason I learned to pick locks is because it was exciting … and I like to know how to do stuff like that."

"So we don't know for sure that it's someone with a key to the rooms that put the snakes in the beds. It might have been J.D. or some other expert lock picker." Isabelle's room had been violated, and she wanted to find out who had done it.

"Why did they put snakes in our two rooms and not in any of the other rooms?" Sidney was beginning to get some color back in her face.

"Matthew and Cameron had the snake in their kayak. That one wasn't a dangerous snake; it was just meant to scare them. Whoever is doing this has raised the stakes. He went after two of us in the kayak. Now he's upped the ante with poisonous snakes. And he's put them in our beds!" It was obvious to Isabelle what was happening. She just didn't know who the evildoer was behind these very dangerous practical jokes, if that's what they were meant to be.

"Nobody has done anything to me or Olivia. Or to Richard and Elizabeth, as far as we know. Why do you think we've been spared? Or spared so far? If this mischief-maker is going to do anything to the rest of us he'd better hurry up. We're leaving tomorrow. Of course, poor Darryl. Somebody killed his wife." J.D. put his arm around Olivia and hugged her when he said this.

"We don't know that these things are related at all, although I agree it seems a stretch to believe that two different people would have it in for us and want to hurt us. I can't believe even one person wants to hurt us, but it's pretty obvious somebody does." Olivia hated snakes and was so thankful no one had put one in her bed. She was sorry for what had happened to her friends, but she was relieved that it hadn't been her room and her bed.

The sound of loud yelling from below reached the group that was gathered in the second floor hall. It was Cameron, giving it to whatever member of the hotel staff he'd been able to roust at this time of night. No one could hear exactly what he was saying, just a word or two here and there. "Worst hotel experience …," "… irresponsible …," "… dangerous and potentially deadly …," "… terrible service …," "… antiquated bathrooms…," "… dirty tricks …," "… windows rattle…," "… musty, bad odor…," "… disgusting …," "… cover it up with Pine-Sol …," and other words and phrases occasionally floated up the stairway from the lobby.

Cameron came running up the steps. He was livid. "I don't know about the rest of you, but I have had it with this place. My car is out front, and I've got a room at the Bar Harbor Inn. Sidney and I are out of here. I suggest the rest of you get out, too." Cameron stormed into his bedroom, and there was a lot of noise that sounded as if he was throwing things around the room. Sidney and the others who were gathered in the hall just stood there and wondered what would happen next. Cameron appeared at the door pulling two suitcases. Clothes were hanging out the sides of the luggage. He was juggling two carryall bags and a briefcase. He handed the carryalls to Sidney, grabbed her hand, and dragged her down the hall.

"I have on my pajamas. I can't go anywhere in my pajamas," she protested as he propelled her down the stairs and through the lobby.

"I have on my pajamas, too. It doesn't matter. I'm not spending one more minute in this miserable place." Cameron was a logical, reasonable man, and he was slow to anger. But if you crossed him one too many times, you were in trouble, and the Inastou had definitely crossed him one too many times.

The group in the second floor hall heard car doors slam and a car lay rubber as it squealed out of the driveway of the Inastou Lodge. Nobody wanted to go back to their rooms. They all wanted to leave and go to the Bar Harbor Inn with Sidney and Cameron. Realizing that this would be their final night at the hotel, they drifted back to their rooms to try to get some sleep. Morning could not come soon enough for this exhausted group, but Monday morning would bring more trouble than a whole barrel of snakes.

❋

Chapter 21

BREAKFAST WAS A SOLEMN EVENT. ELIZABETH didn't show up at all, and Richard came in later than usual. No one felt like talking. They ate in silence.

Richard, who'd heard nothing about the snakes because he and Elizabeth were staying in Blueberry House, across the road, finally spoke. "Elizabeth fell last night. She's okay. Didn't break a hip or anything."

J.D., who was very solicitous of Elizabeth and was always there to help her into the car and go for her wheelchair when she needed it, was quite concerned. "I knew somebody should have ridden with her and helped her park the car last night. We were all so rattled about Elena, and we were just trying to get ourselves back here in one piece. I'm sorry, Richard. Somebody should have helped her get safely to her room."

"No, J.D., it wouldn't have helped to have anybody drive back with her. She made out fine getting to Blueberry House, and she was able to park the car. She even made it through the ruts and potholes in the dark parking lot without a problem. It was the ramp … and the light by our door."

"I knew that ramp was trouble. It has to be a hundred years old, and the plywood it's made out of is rotted. At least it wasn't raining last night. How did she fall?" Gretchen had seen the old wooden ramp and thought it looked like an accident waiting to happen, even in the daylight. Because of her job, she was very aware of compliance with federal regulations of all kinds, and she wanted to know the details.

"Elizabeth always turns on the light by our back door before we go to dinner each night. There isn't any lighting at all in the Blueberry House parking lot, and the only light back there is a tiny bulb on the wall beside the door to our room. I know she turned it on last night before we left for Cuba Libre because we talked about it. We wondered if the Inastou could possibly find a lower wattage lightbulb to put in the light fixture. So the light was definitely on when we left. But when she got back, the light was out. She's very, very careful, as you all know, especially when conditions are hazardous. There are no railings to hang on to, going up the ramp back there. You have to hang on to the side of the building or the side of the porch. The porch supports need painting, and the raw wood is full of splinters. You have to be careful when you hold on to that side, the porch side. Anyway, she's gotten used to all of that. What she couldn't see in the dark was that someone had hacked holes in the ramp. They used an axe. Because the light was out, she wasn't able to see the holes. She tripped and fell into one of them. She could easily have broken a hip or her leg, but thank God she didn't. She has some pretty serious bumps and bruises, though. "

"That's it. I'm reporting this place to somebody. I don't know who I'm going to report it to, but this has now gone beyond absurd." J.D. was loaded for bear.

But Richard wasn't finished with his story. "While we were at dinner, somebody took the light bulb out of the light fixture so it would be completely dark back by our room. And, they left the axe lying right there next to the door, the axe they'd used to chop holes in the ramp. Someone deliberately tried to hurt her. They booby trapped the back porch of Blueberry House and left the axe there, almost as if to gloat about the damage they'd done. Elizabeth was able, with great difficulty, to get herself out of the hole in the ramp and stand up. Getting out of the hole in that ramp wouldn't have been easy for a person who wasn't disabled, and it was almost impossible for her. She was able to get the room key out of her purse and finally made it inside. And that's not all. There's a little vestibule between our bedroom door and the bathroom door. When Elizabeth finally unlocked the door, there was a skunk closed in the hallway. Somebody purposely put the critter in our room."

"Snakes, and now skunks?" J.D.'s face was bright red with anger.

"Fortunately, the skunk ran out as soon as Elizabeth opened the door, and he didn't spray. It would have been impossible for us to sleep there last night, if the skunk had sprayed its scent all over the place. The skunk had been in the vestibule for a while, so the room smelled bad enough as it was. Elizabeth took a shower and cleaned the dirt and blood off her legs and arms. We put bandages on her scrapes and scratches. She's still working to remove all the splinters from her hands. My guess is she has a couple of bruised ribs, but I don't think anything is broken. Whoever wants to hurt me knows the best way to do that is to do something to hurt Elizabeth. But she's a tough old bird. I love that about her." Richard was half-way making a joke, but he had tears in his eyes when he talked about somebody trying to hurt his wife of more than fifty years.

The others wanted to know what they could do for Elizabeth, and Richard told them not to mention that she had fallen or ask her about it, unless she brought it up first. He didn't want her to have to go over the whole unpleasant event again. Matthew and Isabelle told him about the snakes that had been left in their room and in Cameron's and Sidney's room. Richard was horrified. J.D. was becoming more and more agitated and looked like he was ready to jump out of his chair or out of his skin or both.

Matthew and Richard had planned to drive together to the hospital to see how Darryl was doing, but Richard said he needed to help Elizabeth pack. They'd decided to check out of the Inastou and move to a motel on the highway for the night. The ramp outside their room was full of holes and much too hazardous to walk on. The entire ramp would have to be replaced before anyone could safely use the room again. Because of her sore ribs, Richard said Elizabeth wasn't able to bend over and pick things up. Even walking was more difficult for her this morning. As independent as she wanted to be, Elizabeth needed Richard's help today. Matthew would have to go to the hospital alone.

The word was that Sidney and Cameron had called their pilot at five o'clock that morning and told him to meet them at the airport. Gretchen reported they'd flown out of Bar Harbor on their private plane about seven. Everyone else was wishing they had a private plane that could whisk them away from the Inastou.

They'd had some great times together in Bar Harbor and eaten some wonderful meals, but there had been too much tragedy and near tragedy. Something very sick was happening here at the Inastou Lodge. J.D. announced that he was going to seek out the general manager and have a "come to Jesus" talk with the man. J.D. was a lawyer, and he knew how to phrase a threat about a lawsuit in the nicest and most polite language possible. The GM would get the point, and he might or might not realize right away that J.D. had laid down the law to him.

Richard went to see about Elizabeth, and the others went to their rooms to get ready to check out of the Inastou. Something was nagging at the back of Isabelle's mind. She had a great visual memory. Her job demanded it. She could remember colors and always knew whether or not a piece of furniture would fit into a certain spot in a client's home.

On the wall in the dining room there was an attractive arrangement of photographs of the Inastou's food services staff. The photos had been professionally done and nicely framed. Someone had gone to considerable trouble to honor the people who ran the restaurant at the lodge. Once again, it occurred to Isabelle that the food services must be run by a different group than whoever managed the guest rooms and the facility in general. The food was excellent, and the wait staff was several cuts above the others who worked at the Inastou.

Isabelle studied the photos on the wall, and she looked for a long time at Chef Eugene Bonier's photograph in particular. Bonier was the head chef at the Inastou. Viewing the photos more closely confirmed the suspicion that had been growing in her mind. She was almost certain. She asked one of the busboys who was clearing the breakfast dishes what time Chef Bonier came in on Monday. The busboy said he thought the chef came in about 10:30. That was only twenty minutes from now, and Isabelle decided she would wait. Her bags were packed, and she and Matthew were leaving to drive to Camden, Maine after lunch. They planned to spend Monday night in Camden, visit LL Bean on Tuesday, and fly out of Portland back to the west coast early Wednesday morning.

J.D. returned from a very frank discussion with the General Manager of the Inastou. J.D. had laid out all the things that had happened to the reunion group during their stay. When he came to the dining room to get his mid-morning cup of coffee, J.D. found Isabelle sitting at a table studying the photo display on the wall. He sat down with her to drink his coffee, and she shared with him what she had figured out just a few minutes earlier. He was astounded that she had been able to recognize the chef as he looked today from the photographs of when he was a little boy.

"I don't think he looks anything like the skinny little kid from the 1950s. That guy in the chef's hat must weigh more than three hundred pounds. And with the moustaches and beard, how could you possibly know who he was and put it all together?"

"It was yesterday, when we were all in here, looking at the camp pictures. He was watching us through that little round window in the swinging door that goes to the kitchen. Then he came in here and stood over in the corner and eavesdropped on what we were saying. Then he got angry and scolded us and shooed us out of the dining room. That behavior was all wrong and put him on my radar screen. Something about him has been bugging me ever since, and I finally figured out it was his sad eyes. In spite of his big smile, he had those sad eyes in the photographs from decades ago. He has the same sad eyes today. And the eyes aren't just sad, they are also mean. Mean little eyes. The eyes are what really put me onto him."

"I would never have seen all those things, but now that you mention it, I think you are absolutely right. Nobody could remember that kid's name yesterday, but the name Eugene rings a bell for me. I'm pretty sure that was the boy's first name. We used to tease him and call him 'Genie.' You know, like he had a girl's name. He was such a pest." J.D. paused, remembering things from a long time ago. He continued. "But the name Bonier doesn't sound right. That wasn't the last name of the little boy who followed us around all the time. I can't remember what his name was, but it wasn't Bonier. Maybe he's changed his name. Bonier sounds French, like a chef's name."

"Even if he turns out to be the little tagalong from Camp Shoemaker, we don't know for sure that he's the one who's been doing all these rotten, malicious things to us. But, I think it's a good possibility. He may have recognized one of you guys when you showed up here. Or more likely, he recognized Matt's name when Matt initially called to see if there were enough rooms for all of us to stay at the Inastou." Isabelle was figuring it out.

"Are you going to talk to him?"

"Yes, I am. The first thing I'm going to ask him is if he's the little boy from Camp Shoemaker. Then I'm going to ask him if he's behind the accidents — the snakes and the skunk and all of it. I don't know if he will tell me the truth, but if he did do it, I think he might actually want to confess. I think at some level he wants us to know what he's done and why he's done it. That's the psychologist in me talking, I guess."

"Does Matt know about your theory?"

"No. I just confirmed the theory in my own mind a few minutes before you sat down. Matt left forty-five minutes ago to see Darryl at the hospital. He's going to pick me up here, and we're going back to the Borden Pond House Restaurant for lunch before we drive down to Camden. Matt has to have another bowl of that seafood chowder. He had a take-out container of the chowder from the restaurant and loved it. He missed having lunch there because of the kayak accident. He keeps talking about it and wants to eat there before we leave."

"I'll go with you to talk to Chef Bonier. You were never at Camp Shoemaker, but I spent many summers there. I can ask Bonier specific questions about the camp. I'll be able to tell if he's the same little kid we think he used to be."

J.D. and Isabelle decided Chef Eugene Bonier was probably in his kitchen by now, and they walked through the swinging door to confront the man.

Chapter 22

"CHEF BONIER, I THINK WE KNOW EACH OTHER. I wish you'd introduced yourself to me and the others." J.D. had decided to start the conversation off on a positive note. "This is Isabelle Ritter, Matthew Ritter's wife. She recognized you by comparing some old photographs from Camp Shoemaker with your photograph that's hanging on the wall in the dining room. You used to spend your summers at Camp Shoemaker in the Ozarks, didn't you?"

"I don't know what you're talking about. I'm busy. Get out of my kitchen. I know you all are leaving today, so just leave." No one was in the kitchen except the chef. They had the place to themselves.

"We want to know if you are responsible for the dirty tricks that somebody has been playing on us since we arrived in Maine." Isabelle went right to the question she wanted Bonier to answer.

"I told you, I don't have any idea what you're talking about. Just get out."

"It won't be hard to find out all about your past. You know, in today's electronic world, there are no more secrets. Everybody knows everything about everybody. I know that, and I know you know that. Did you recognize our names when we called for our room reservations? Did you Google us to find out what we've been up to since we were all together at Camp Shoemaker? Why didn't you say something to us and tell us who you were?" J.D. was a former camper, and the chef had known him well.

Chef Bonier glared at J.D. and Isabelle. They glared right back.

"We know you've tried to hurt us. Is that because you felt left out when the big boys wouldn't pay attention to you? It was such a very long time ago." Isabelle was trying to provoke him into talking. "Why would you want to do these mean things, all these years later? You are obviously very successful. We've loved the food at the Inastou. You're the head chef here. What could you possibly hope to gain by your malicious behavior?" Isabelle tried both shaming and praising him, but nothing seemed to be working with this guy.

The man remained silent.

"You know very well that I'm a lawyer and used to be a prosecutor. I know all about criminals who threaten people, and I know how to prove who did it. Don't try to mess with me, Genie. I know all the ropes around the legal process."

Calling the chef "Genie" was the final straw that got to him. He began to bellow. "You pretty boys always called me that, and I hated it. You mocked me and made fun of me, and I hated you for that. All I wanted was to be a part of your group, but you weren't letting anybody else in. You were all so perfect and so smart. You didn't have time for a little kid who looked up to you. You didn't want anything to do with me, and you were mean to me."

"You were three years younger than we were, Eugene. You weren't even a camper at Camp Shoemaker. How could you possibly think we would have wanted to hang out with you? We had our own activities. You were too young to do anything with us. You just didn't get it, that it wasn't appropriate for you to be included as part of our group of friends. You didn't get it back then, and you don't get it now." J.D. was trying to offer a rational explanation to a person who was anything but rational.

"You made me feel inferior. You shunned me. You never included me. I just wanted you to pay attention to me and let me do things with you." The man had a high voice, even as an adult. As he regressed more and more into his childhood memories, his voice grew higher and shriller. He began to sound more and more like the child he had been at Camp Shoemaker.

Then he began to cry. Isabelle momentarily felt sorry for him. J.D. was just angry. He was annoyed that the guy still was not able to understand why he hadn't been welcomed by the group of boys who were three years older than he was. They'd been campers, and Eugene wasn't a camper. The group had probably been somewhat uncaring toward him. They had definitely rejected him, at every possible opportunity. He was a nuisance. They wanted nothing to do with him, and they probably had made fun of him. They shouldn't have called him "Genie," but they'd just been kids themselves at the time. How could anyone harbor a grudge about something that had happened more than sixty years ago? Because he'd been a part of the criminal justice system for so many years, J.D. was logical and analytical.

Isabelle was a psychologist and had more insight into mental illness and the fact that Eugene was not at all rational. She knew he was mentally ill, that a part of him had never grown up. In some ways, Eugene continued to be the little kid who was left out, the boy who wasn't wanted by the bigger boys. The rejection had festered over the years and had taken on a larger than life importance for Eugene. A more normal person with a stable mental state would have been able to leave their childhood traumas behind and move on to form healthy adult relationships. Isabelle doubted if Eugene had ever had a significant other.

Isabelle knew that Eugene had been a troubled child. Something was already "off" about him when he'd been the needy, desperate boy without any friends at Camp Shoemaker. Most kids would have understood they were too young to hang out with the older boys and would eventually have given up harassing them and trying to get them to accept him into their group, year after year. But Eugene had never understood any of that. Instead, he had remembered and dwelled on the slights from his summers as a boy, the slights that had actually occurred as well as those he might have exaggerated in his mind or even imagined entirely. Seeing the boys from Camp Shoemaker again had triggered his obsession and his anger.

"When you saw our names on the reservations list, it all came back to you, didn't it, Eugene? You saw your chance, finally after all these years, to pay us back for not wanting you as part of our group. You saw your chance to punish us, to hurt us." J.D. understood revenge and retribution, and he could see how strong Eugene's motivation had been to inflict pain on the members of their group. Eugene would finally be the one in control; he would finally be the big boy. He was now the one who was being mean and rejecting the others.

J.D. and Isabelle were trying to figure out what to say or do next. It was hopeless to try to reason with this mentally disturbed person. They didn't feel especially threatened or in danger as they sat at the table in the Inastou kitchen, but while they were talking and as Chef Bonier puttered around his domain, he had been preparing more than the lunchtime soup.

All of a sudden he turned around and looked at them with a menacing look on his face. He had a hypodermic needle in his hand and stabbed it into J.D.'s arm. J.D. slumped over in his chair, unconscious. Isabelle got up out of her chair and tried to run, but she wasn't able to get away fast enough from the maniacal Eugene. He had another hypodermic needle ready for her, and soon she was unconscious on the floor, slumped against the legs of the chef's table. No one else was in the kitchen to see what he'd done. No one would see what he did next.

A Gator was parked just outside the kitchen, and Eugene had no trouble lifting the very light-weight Isabelle into his arms and carrying her out through the kitchen door. He dumped her in the rear of the Gator and went back inside for J.D. J.D.'s dose of whatever Eugene had put in the hypodermic had not been powerful enough to keep J.D. knocked out. J.D. put up a fight and began to punch and scratch the chef's face. But the chef outweighed J.D. by more than a hundred pounds, and J.D. finally went down again when Eugene pumped another dose of sedatives into him. Eugene dragged J.D. out the door and down the steps, and pulled him into the passenger seat of the Gator.

Eugene made a fast getaway and drove the vehicle pell mell down the hill behind the Inastou to a shed in the woods. The shed was no longer used, except by resident critters and insects. It had been scheduled for demolition years ago. There were holes in the roof, and the shingle siding had mostly fallen off. It had a dirt floor and was full of cobwebs and raccoon poop. It had been an eyesore at the edge of the woods. The vegetation growth of several years had overtaken it, and it had disappeared into the woods. It could no longer be seen, unless one was looking for it. Hardly anybody remembered the shed was there, and nobody would ever come looking inside.

Eugene dragged his prisoners into the shed. He had plenty of rope in the Gator, and he bound the two with more than enough to keep them immobilized. He stuffed gags in their mouths and wound yards of duct tape over and around their heads to hold the gags in place. He lay Isabelle and J.D. down on the dirt inside the shed. He hadn't expected to have any of the group in his clutches, so he hadn't yet decided what to do with his captives, his prizes.

His rage and instability were escalating. Seeing the men who had once been boys at Camp Shoemaker had provoked his anger. He had long fantasized about what he would do to these fiends, if he ever found them again and had the chance. A few months ago, an opportunity had miraculously presented itself. He could scarcely believe his luck when he realized reservations at the Inastou had been made by the people he most hated and wanted to retaliate against. He saw the Camp Shoemaker reunion in September, the coming together of the group of old friends, as an omen and a sign that he was meant to strike back and avenge his childhood hurts.

He hadn't counted on being able to take two hostages, but he had prepared his hypodermic needles just in case. Initially, he hadn't wanted to hurt anybody really badly, but the more "tricks" he played on them, the more he realized he enjoyed it. It gave him a thrill. Revenge had turned out to be very sweet for this boy-man who had suffered all of his life with severe mental illness. As he reveled more and more in his evil deeds, he'd begun to wonder what it would be like to kill them. He became obsessed with the idea. This morning two of them had wandered into his kitchen. Eugene saw this as another omen, and he was trying to figure out what to do about it.

He made sure his victims were unconscious and tightly bound. He put more duct tape around their mouths. No one would ever hear them yell from way out here in the woods anyway, but he wanted to guarantee that no one ever found his hostages. He needed time to think about what to do with them and exactly how he wanted to torture them. His excitement mounted as he contemplated the possibilities.

He remembered he had to finish his soup. It was almost lunchtime. He climbed on his Gator and drove back to the kitchen. He had taken both Isabelle's and J.D.'s cell phones. He found his largest chopping knife and hacked each phone into two pieces. Then he fed the remains of the phones down the sink's commercial-strength disposal. He resumed chopping vegetables. It was as if nothing at all out of the ordinary had happened that morning.

Chapter 23

"Has anyone seen Isabelle? She was supposed to meet me here in the lobby at noon." Matthew had just returned from visiting Darryl at the hospital and was anxious to get to the Borden Pond House Restaurant for lunch. Richard and Elizabeth were having one last lobster roll at the Inastou before moving to the Hampton Inn for the night. Matthew was distressed when he saw Elizabeth's injuries. It was obvious she was in a lot of pain because of the way she lifted the lobster roll to her mouth and the way she held her fork. She was very quiet and was missing her usual spunk.

Richard answered his question. "We haven't seen her or anybody else except Olivia. She and J.D. were going to join us for lunch, but J.D. didn't show up. Olivia has gone to look for him. The last she knew he was heading to the Inastou General Manager's office to have a talk with him. That was this morning. J.D. intended to give the manager a piece of his mind about all the things that have been going on around here. When Olivia checked with the GM, he said J.D. left his office nearly two hours ago."

"Isabelle is always on time, and she never gets confused about the plans. You know her; she's the most responsible and efficient person there is. If there's a screw up between the two of us, I'm it. She told me she'd make sure our bags were down in the lobby by eleven thirty, so we could leave as soon as I got back from the hospital. When I went up to our room, the luggage was all still there in a pile in the middle of the floor. Our lunch reservation is at noon, and Isabelle knows that. This is so out of character for her. I'm not angry yet, but I am beginning to get worried."

"What could have happened to her? She was here in the dining room when I left to go back to Blueberry House after breakfast. That was around ten o'clock." Richard could see how concerned his friend was. He knew Isabelle and knew how responsible she was. She was never late for anything.

"What was she doing when you saw her here in the dining room? Was she with anybody or talking to anybody?"

"She was looking at the pictures on the wall over there. She was all alone. She looked fine, just like herself. I didn't say anything to her when I left."

"I don't know what to do. She can't have disappeared into thin air. She hasn't sent me a text or an email or tried to call me. I've tried to call her on her cell phone, but it goes right to voice mail every time. I've sent her multiple texts, but she hasn't answered any of them. We're already late for our lunch reservation. She knows how much I wanted to go to the Borden Pond House Restaurant. She wanted to go back there, too. I've got the luggage in the car, and I'm parked in the driveway, waiting for her. I guess I'll have to put the car in the parking lot again. It can't stay here. You know how they like to scold you, if your car is parked out front for too long."

"Do you want to eat lunch with us?"

"No! I want to eat lunch with Isabelle at the Borden Pond House Restaurant!" Matthew was not a happy man. He stomped out of the dining room to move his car from the driveway of the Inastou.

When Matthew reached the front door of the lodge, two large policemen were walking into the lobby. They stopped Mathew and asked him his name. They referred to the list they had on a clipboard and told him they were going to have to take a statement from him. They told him they needed to interview him in connection with Elena

Petrovich's death at the Cuba Libre Restaurant the night before, Sunday night. Matthew groaned and told the policemen he had to move his car. He said he'd be right back. He knew he was never going to see another bowl of seafood chowder now, even if Isabelle showed up in time.

The policemen went to the front desk and had a brief conversation with the desk clerk. They were upset to receive the news that everyone on their list, including Matthew Ritter, had already officially checked out of the Inastou. The woman at the desk said she didn't think everyone on their list had left the lodge yet, and she directed the officers to the dining room where she told them they could find Richard and Elizabeth Carpenter eating lunch.

The state policemen approached the only couple that was sitting in the dining room. "Dr. and Mrs. Carpenter? I apologize for interrupting, but before you leave the lodge, we need to talk to both of you. You were witnesses to a homicide last night, and we are taking statements from everybody who was at the restaurant. I'm Captain Dryden Trimper of the Maine State Police, and this is Detective Creighton Laurence. We're investigating Elena Petrovich's death."

"I've been wondering if anybody was going to show up to ask me about last night. As soon as we've finished our lunch, my wife and I will be happy to answer your questions. There isn't any place to sit down in the lobby, but if you check with the desk clerk, there's a small reception room next to the bar that has some chairs in it. We can all sit down in there. The chef is very touchy. He's grouchy about his dining room and doesn't like anything but dining to go on in here."

When Elizabeth and Richard appeared at the door to the reception room for their interviews, Matthew Ritter was already there being grilled by the state police. Trimper had said they wanted to question each person separately, so the Carpenters went to the bar to sit and wait their turns. The only place Elizabeth was able to sit down in the entire bar was on the bench of the spinet piano. All the tables in the bar were impossibly tall, and all the bar stools were designed to be used at the impossibly tall tables. There was not one table or one chair at regular table height. Because of her arthritis, Elizabeth would have had a difficult time climbing up into one of these bar-height stools under normal circumstances. Because she had fallen the night before, her arms and legs were sore and her ribs were bruised. She was even less likely to be able to make it up onto one of those beasts today.

There was nowhere she could sit down in this ultra-modern, enoteca-style bar, except on the piano bench. She wondered if anyone besides herself knew the words to *The Battle Hymn of the Republic*. It was the only piano piece she still knew how to play from memory. Elizabeth chuckled to herself as she imagined what the reaction would be if she actually played that patriotic and religious song in this bar. The décor screamed for hip hop or rap music or something sad and soulful sung in French or Portuguese. The ambiance of the bar seemed to Elizabeth like a set from an episode of *Saturday Night Live*. It was very out of place with the historic, some might say dated, décor of the rest of the Inastou Lodge.

When it was Richard's turn to be interviewed, he met Matthew in the lobby as he was coming out of his talk with the state police. Richard wanted to know how his friend had done with the questions from law enforcement. Richard knew how upset Matthew was about Isabelle. "How did it go? Did they ask you anything you couldn't answer?"

"Not really. It was pretty straightforward, at least the part about what happened with Elena. Their questions about Darryl … well, that was a different story. I guess the number one suspect in a homicide is always the spouse, but they totally grilled me about poor Darryl, about their relationship, about why he's in the hospital now, and about everything else you could possibly think of. Can they really think he might have murdered her? I told them they were nuts, if they thought Darryl killed Elena. They didn't like hearing that. They also can't understand why I don't know where to find my wife. I think they might suspect *me* of some kind of foul play. I told them exactly what I told you. They want to know why I haven't raised the alarm, if I'm that worried about her. I told them I would have raised the alarm if they hadn't interrupted me and demanded that I talk to them first."

The state policeman stepped out of the reception room and told Richard Carpenter they were ready for him. Richard told the investigators that when he had been a pathology resident many years ago, he'd spent some time working with the Philadelphia Medical Examiner's Office. Because of this, Trimper and Laurence granted him more respect and credibility than they might have given to a civilian witness. Richard's account of what had happened at the restaurant was comprehensive. He told them that Elena had drunk too much wine and made a fool of herself by being loud and standing up on her chair and singing. He listed the major points he thought they would want to know, like who had touched the body and what he'd observed about a possible cause of death. He told them about the CPR and the EMTs. He had purposely made a note of the moment Elena's face had fallen into her plate of cake, and the investigators were visibly pleased to have an exact time of death. They would be disappointed when they realized that nothing else about this case would be as exact as Richard Carpenter's witness statement.

Then they asked him when he'd last seen Isabelle Ritter. Did he have any ideas about what had happened to her? They asked him where everybody else was. Richard knew that Cameron and Sidney had left Bar Harbor that morning in their private plane, but he honestly didn't know where anybody else was. Trimper told him that he and Elizabeth weren't to leave the area until he gave them permission to do so. The captain stressed that this was a murder investigation, and everyone involved was going to have to give statements and make themselves available for further questioning. Captain Trimper told Richard that Sidney and Cameron had been contacted and were on their way back to Maine. When Richard heard that, he knew things were serious. Were any of them really murder suspects? That was hard to believe, but the state police were looking at everything from their own point of view.

Elizabeth was next. Richard had told the officers his wife had fallen the night before and injured her ribs. He helped her into the interview room. She was able to walk with her cane, but her pain was obvious. She gave a cogent and complete description of what had happened at

Cuba Libre. The policemen were pleased with her account. The doctor had given the facts, but his wife had given them some insight into the players involved in the terrible restaurant drama. They didn't ask Elizabeth about her fall.

While Elizabeth was speaking with the law enforcement officials, she'd heard loud voices in the lobby. She tried to concentrate on what she was saying, but the shouting in the next room was distracting. She knew it was Olivia who was arguing with somebody. Had she found J.D., and were they having a knock-down-drag-out?

Olivia stormed into the reception room. She was more upset than Elizabeth had ever seen her. "I've just been informed that I'm a witness in a murder investigation and that I have to stay in Bar Harbor until you people say I can leave. Just let me tell you that your murder investigation is the least of my worries right now. My husband J.D. Steele has disappeared, and I have no idea where he is. He was supposed to meet me for lunch, and I have looked everywhere he could possibly be. I want to report a missing person, and I expect you to look for him and find him. I want the search for him to take precedence over the murder of a Russian bimbo."

"What is it with your group of friends, Mrs. Steele? It seems that almost everyone has disappeared. Are you saying that your husband is also missing?" Captain Trimper was more than a little bit curious now.

"Do I need to call the sheriff's office or the FBI to report him missing? I can tell you two aren't going to do anything to find him."

"I'm sure you know that as an adult, your husband has to be missing for twenty-four hours before we can declare him officially a missing person."

"I don't give a rat's ass about that. He's a former prosecutor, and he put away some very, very bad dudes in his day. He never lost a case, by the way. Quite a few of the people he convicted threatened him in court. They said that when they got out of prison, they were going to come after him and kill him. A couple of them said there was no place he could hide that they wouldn't be able to track him down and get to him. One bad guy threated to cut him up alive and put him in a barrel of acid. He takes that very seriously, and so do I. With prison overcrowding and the court system not wanting to hurt anybody's feelings these days by keeping them in jail, there's no telling who could be out of prison and hunting for J.D. He could be kidnapped and killed before your twenty-four hour time limit kicks in. I intend to hire a private detective to look for him. I know you aren't going to do anything about it."

"Ma'am, you are free to do whatever you want to do about your missing husband. Just be aware that hundreds of them disappear every day, many into the arms of much younger women. So be careful what you wish for in terms of finding your J.D. Studley."

"It's Steele! J.D. Steele! And how dare you. If you think I'm going to cooperate with you on your investigation, you have another thing coming. If you aren't going to do anything for me; I'm not going to do anything for you."

"You are going to have to stay in Bar Harbor, or at least in Maine, until we say you can leave. You are required by law to make yourself available to us during our investigation into Elena Petrovich's murder."

"Why don't you ask the KGB about her? She's a Russian, and she probably killed that Russian guy who was shot in the parking lot a couple of days ago. And furthermore, I don't have any place to stay tonight. The Inastou is full and the Bar Harbor Inn is full, and you are telling me I have to stay here indefinitely. Where am I supposed to go? I don't have a place to sleep, and I don't have a husband." Olivia stomped out of the reception room and out of the Inastou.

"Are you finished with me, Captain? I need to go and talk to my friend. She's usually the sweetest person in the world. Right now, she's very, very worried about J.D. I might be able to talk to her and calm her down." Elizabeth was worried about Olivia, and she was worried about J.D. It was not at all a good thing that both J.D. and Isabelle were missing. And she hadn't seen Gretchen since yesterday. Where was everybody?

Elizabeth caught up with Olivia on the front porch. "Olivia, can we talk? I'm very worried, as you are, about J.D. Did you know that

Isabelle is also missing? So many frightening things have happened. I think you are entirely right to be upset, and I don't think you are overreacting. I support your idea of hiring a private detective. I'll bet Matthew will want to hire a private detective, too. He's quite beside himself that Isabelle is nowhere to be found."

Olivia had collapsed into one of the porch chairs and when she saw Elizabeth, she began to cry. Elizabeth sat down next to her and held her hand.

Chapter 24

After she'd had a good cry, Olivia seemed to get control of herself. She began to tell Elizabeth everything she was doing to try to find J.D. "I've already called a private investigator. He's highly recommended, and he's coming from Portland. I have friends there, and they know this guy. He found their daughter in Oregon when she ran away from home and joined a cult. That was years ago, but they say he's the best. The next thing is, I don't have any place to stay tonight. You heard me whining about that to the state police. But I'm working on that, too. Where are you staying tonight?"

"We have a reservation at the Hampton Inn, but because we called at the last minute, they don't have a room available for a handicapped person. So I'll be taking a sponge bath tonight. That's fine. I'm too stiff and sore to take a real shower anyway."

"As it happens, I've just called a friend of mine who lives in Fort Worth. Her mother has a house in Maine, near here someplace, maybe even in Bar Harbor. I'm trying to get her to rent it to me for a week. I've never seen it, but I think it's a pretty big house. I know it's a really nice house. If my friend's mother agrees to rent the place to me, will you and Richard stay there with me, at least for tonight? I don't want to stay in a strange place by myself. You'd be doing me a favor. I told her I need it as of tonight and for the rest of the week. If J.D. doesn't turn up soon, who knows how long I will have to be up here?" Olivia's eyes filled with tears again.

"Of course, we would be happy to stay with you at your friend's house. But as you know, I have to stay on the first floor. I can't go up and down the stairs without an elevator. Do you know if there's a bedroom on the main floor or if there's an elevator?"

"I don't know for sure, but I think it's a one-story house. Patty, my friend whose mother owns the house, will give me all the details when I talk to her the next time. She's going to call me at three o'clock Eastern Daylight Time. She's in Fort Worth, and that's Central Time. Her mother and father built the house years ago in the 1940s, and the family's always spent the summers there. Even though they call it Indigo Cottage, I don't think it's that small. Patty's father died a few years ago, and her mother recently went into an assisted living facility. She's in her nineties and doesn't come up to Maine anymore, but there are four kids in the family. When I say kids, I mean kids who are a little younger than we are. And there are tons of grandkids and even a couple of great grandkids. Indigo Cottage is supposed to be a real show place, but kind of rustic, too. It's been redone with a modern kitchen and up-to-date bathrooms, unlike the miserable bathrooms here at the Inastou Lodge. I hope she'll let us stay there. I told Gretchen that she and Bailey could stay there, too, if Bailey gets his act together and comes out of hiding … whatever that's all about. You know, the police told me we have to make ourselves available to them until they tell us we are free to leave the state. That may be days from now. Who knows? The Inastou and the Bar Harbor Inn and every other place in town are all full. All the rooms in the area are taken because leaf-peepers' season happens earlier this far north. Everybody thinks it starts on Columbus Day in New England, but here in the Bar Harbor area, it begins the last week in September. That's why we had to have the reunion when we did. All the reservations before and afterwards were taken. There is literally no room at the inn from today on through the next two weeks. You ran into that with the Hampton Inn not having a bedroom with a bathroom to accommodate the handicapped."

Olivia was better now that she was thinking about practical matters. She was an excellent planner and could figure out how to make things happen. Elizabeth hoped Olivia's PI was as good as she thought he was and that he would be able to find J.D. before too much time went by. As long as Olivia could focus on doing useful things, in terms of finding J.D. and finding a place to stay, the less likely she would be to yell at the law enforcement people and give them a bad time. Olivia really was the sweetest person you could ever hope to know, but Captain Trimper probably didn't believe that right now.

"Try to stay calm when you give your statement to the officers. They're just doing their jobs, and as much as I hate to say it, they are right about the twenty-four hour wait to begin looking for a missing adult. You heard J.D. explain that to Gretchen when Bailey went missing." Elizabeth was trying to lend some rationality to the situation and remind Olivia that the state police had some valid points.

"Of course, I know about all of that. It just makes me mad that they are so worked up about Elena. I know the woman used to be a spy for Russia, and maybe she still is. I'm not going to tell you how I know that's true, but it is. I don't know why Darryl ever married her. Well, I do know why he married her, but that's beside the point. They need to be looking at her background, from before she ever met Darryl, not at Darryl. The poor guy is completely destroyed. Did you hear they think he might have had a stroke? I guess he was so upset, his blood pressure spiked, and he stroked out. I don't think it was a serious stroke, but there isn't any stroke that's a good thing."

"It doesn't help anything to refer to her as a Russian bimbo." Elizabeth tried not to be critical.

"I said that, didn't I? That was bad. I shouldn't have said that, even though it's true." Olivia was trying very hard to sound sorry. "I was upset. I am upset. I'm frantic with worry about J.D. I'll tell them I'm sorry I said that about her, although really, I'm not sorry. She's hated me from the first time she met me, but I decided not to take it personally because I think she hates, hated, all of us. I have to say I'm not sorry she's dead. I'm sorry for Darryl, but she was a … rhymes with witch. Oops, gotta go. Here comes The Captain. Where's Tennille? That really dates me, doesn't it? I promise I will behave myself and be polite and helpful, if you promise to talk Richard into giving up the room at the Hampton Inn. I want you both to stay with me at Indigo Cottage."

Elizabeth hadn't been able to sleep much the night before, and she dozed off while she sat on the Inastou's front porch. If she and Richard were going to the Hampton Inn, they needed to get going. If they were going to cancel their reservation, they needed to do it soon. It had been an upsetting day. What could have happened to Isabelle and J.D.? Elizabeth hated to think their disappearances had anything to do with the other bad things that had happened on this trip, but she had a sick feeling in the pit of her stomach that they were related. She was trying to figure out why somebody wanted to hurt this group of nice people, and they were very nice people. It was difficult for Elizabeth to travel, but she made the effort every year to take this special trip because she liked the group of friends so much.

But Elena's murder? That didn't feel like the other prankish, mean and dangerous things that had been done to the group. Elizabeth realized she was thinking too much about all of it and trying too hard to figure it out. She knew if she thought about something else for a while, the solution might eventually come to her. She hoped Olivia could make the rental house idea work out for them. Elizabeth would much rather stay with friends than go to an impersonal Hampton Inn, but she always worried about accessibility issues in an unknown place. She briefly wondered where Richard had gone. She thought he was helping Matthew search for Isabelle.

Olivia hurried out to the porch to find Elizabeth. She'd heard from her friend in Fort Worth. "I have a little bit of good news, although unfortunately, it's a long way from being the good news I wish I had to tell you. J.D. is still nowhere to be found. But we have the house. Patty said her mother would be delighted for us to use it. J.D. was always one of her favorites. I told Patty that J.D. was missing, but she didn't have the heart to tell her mother. Patty's mom, Lorraine Ryan, is ninety-seven and still has all of her marbles. Lorraine doesn't want us to pay her any rent. She said we can pay the utilities for the time we're there, and we can pay the housekeeper and the cleaning people. When the family comes for the summer, they hire a staff to take care of the house — cook, clean, take care of the yard, do the laundry, and do everything else. There are so many people here, she says it's just easier to bring in help to do it all. She's sending some of the staff to take care of us, and we are to pay them. There will be a housekeeper who will do whatever cooking we want her to do, and there will be two cleaning people. One of them will do laundry, too. I told her that would be all we'd need, and we'd be happy to pay them. Patty said they'll be thrilled to have the extra work and the extra money. Summers are short here. There's plenty of work for three or four months. When September ends, it's a long, lean winter, without many visitors. Most of the summer houses are closed up. Anyway, let's go out there and take a look at it. Can you give Richard and Matthew the address and tell them to meet us there? I don't know if Matthew wants to come, but I do know he doesn't have a place to stay tonight in Bar Harbor. He and Isabelle were going to spend the night in Camden, but ...."

"I need to check out the house before we cancel our reservations at the Hampton Inn. If there aren't any downstairs bedrooms or if there are too many stairs to get in the door, I can't stay there, no matter how wonderful it is. Sorry, Olivia, but that's my reality."

"Oh, that's the other good news. Patty's dad, Cabbott Ryan, was in a wheelchair for several years before he died, and the family completely renovated the house to make it more wheelchair-friendly for him. The main living area is very open, and there are four bedrooms on the main floor. Each bedroom has its own bathroom, and one of the bathrooms has a roll-in shower. That will be your room. So how about that? Problem solved. There's a ramp that goes up from the parking area to the back door, and it's supposedly very easy to get inside that way. No worries. Tell Richard to meet us there."

Elizabeth called Richard and explained what was going on. She was disappointed he didn't have any news about Isabelle, and she didn't have anything to report about J.D. Elizabeth asked Richard to cancel the Hampton Inn reservation and find out if Matthew wanted to come to Indigo Cottage. Richard got the address and said he would arrive later with the luggage. He was still helping Matthew search the Inastou grounds for Isabelle, and they hadn't turned up anything. Richard sounded down and discouraged.

Olivia and Elizabeth drove by the entrance to the house twice before they realized which one it was. Both women had been looking for either a blue house or a house with blue shutters or blue trim because of the name, Indigo Cottage. Nothing on the house had ever been blue, or the shingles had faded. The sprawling gray-shingled cottage with white trim had been added onto over the years, and it was much larger than Olivia had expected it to be. The center section of the house had two stories, and it was on several acres of property with wonderful views. There were two guest houses and a swimming pool in the back yard.

Unfortunately, the weather report wasn't good. The tail end of a hurricane that had ripped through Florida was scheduled to bring record-breaking rain and coastal flooding to the Bar Harbor area. The group had lucked out weather-wise during their long weekend, but the rain and wind were supposed to start on Tuesday and continue for days. Elizabeth could already feel the barometer dropping.

They parked in the back and went up the ramp. The back door was unlocked, and there was someone in the kitchen unloading bags of groceries. Vivian Jordan was the housekeeper who came with the house, and she was already on the job. She introduced herself and went back to work. She was welcoming, but she was no nonsense. She had work to do. "Go look around and see if everything is suitable for you. Then I want to talk to you about dinner tonight and how many people there will be."

Oliva and Elizabeth walked through the kitchen that opened directly into the great room. The entire living area had been made into one large space. There were two huge fireplaces, one at the kitchen end of the room and one at the opposite end of the room where the library was located. Large folding wooden doors could close off the kitchen, if necessary. Another matching set of folding doors could be closed to make the library into a quiet and private spot. Right now it was all open, a welcoming and comfortably furnished living room. A covered porch ran the length of the front of the house and looked out over the ocean. It was still sunny and not too cold, but the surf pounded furiously on the rocks. Clouds were gathering on the horizon. A storm was coming.

"I've laid a fire in both fireplaces, and I can light them for you when you're settled. I took the liberty of shopping for groceries for tonight's dinner. I figured you would be arriving at different times, and everyone would be tired. You can tell me what to buy for meals in the future. For tonight I have steaks from the butcher shop the Ryans always use. The butcher cuts the steaks especially thick for us. A pot of homemade tomato basil soup is on the stove and will be ready by six. Sliced cold lobster out of the shell with a mustard sauce, baked potatoes with everything on them, green beans, and a tossed salad with lots of local tomatoes should keep everybody happy. I bought a big chocolate cake at Costco, because I didn't have time to make anything myself."

"It sounds perfect. I can't imagine how you were able to go to the store and make soup and put all of this together in the time you had. I just heard that we were going to be staying here a little over an hour ago. How did you do it?" Elizabeth knew about food, and she knew this woman was a food magician.

"The Ryans, especially Mr. Ryan when he was still flying his own plane, used to call me and say they'd be arriving at the house in thirty minutes. He always wanted steaks and baked potatoes and cold lobster with my special mustard sauce on his first night here at Indigo Cottage, so I'm very good at getting that meal together quickly. I just did for you what I used to do for him and Mrs. Ryan. It's become a first night tradition for the next generation, too. Mr. Ryan loved his food. He was no vegan. He loved lobster, but he also loved steaks. Mrs. Ryan used to tease her husband that he was fonder of their butcher than he was of her. It did seem sometimes as if he paid more attention to the butcher than he did to Mrs. Ryan."

"How far do you have to drive to get here from your home, or do you live on the grounds?"

"That's another one of my secrets as to how I pulled all of this together for you in such a short period of time. I live next door. Also, the butcher shop and the grocery store both deliver."

Olivia took a tour of the rest of the house. She showed Elizabeth the bedroom and bathroom that had been built for Mr. Ryan when he was in a wheelchair. The room was spacious with a wonderful view of the ocean. It had a king-sized bed, and the bathroom was huge. The shower had two tiled benches, plenty of grab bars, and no doors. It was ideal for Elizabeth. She wanted to collapse on the bed right then, but she rallied and returned to the great room. Fires were roaring in both fireplaces. Indigo Cottage had the ambiance the Inastou Lodge should have had. Guests felt welcome here from the minute they walked in the door.

"I need a glass of wine. How about you?" Olivia was already opening a bottle and had two glasses out on the low table in front of the fire. Elizabeth could see that, after her burst of energy and being busy arranging for the house, Olivia was having a sinking spell. Now she had to sit down and think again about the fact that J.D. was missing. It wasn't any wonder she felt like a glass of wine. It would be a rough time for Olivia and for Matthew going forward, until their loved ones were found. And poor Darryl. Elizabeth couldn't even think about that sad man and what he had to deal with. A glass of wine was the last thing Elizabeth wanted right now. A nap sounded much more enticing, but she decided Olivia needed somebody to keep her company.

"Sure. I'll have a glass, if it's red. Let's drink to J.D. and Isabelle walking through that door, and soon."

Chapter 25

But J.D. and Isabelle were not going to be walking anywhere, anytime soon. They were both still unconscious from the sedatives Chef Eugene had injected into them. It was dark when Isabelle woke up. She had no idea where she was. Her mouth was dry, and her brain was foggy. She couldn't move, and at first she wasn't able to remember why her legs were tied together and her mouth was taped closed. She drifted back into unconsciousness. The next thing she knew, something or somebody was hitting against her leg. She tried to tell whoever it was to stop, but she wasn't able to speak. She made some noises in her throat to try to communicate with whoever was kicking her.

J.D. took longer to regain consciousness, but once he did, he remembered everything that had happened and who had put a hypodermic needle in his arm. He had no idea what time it was, and he had no idea where he was. It was dark inside, and he thought it was probably also dark outside. He hoped Isabelle had been able to escape Eugene's needles. But as his eyes became accustomed to the dark, he could make out what he thought was a silent form lying on the ground against the wall, a short distance from where he was tied up. J.D. guessed it was Isabelle. If it was a person, who else would it be? Eugene had done a good job of trussing up the two of them. He'd wound the duct tape so tightly around J.D.'s mouth and head, J.D. was almost unable to breathe.

J.D. had been in the military, and although it had been many years ago, he still remembered a few basics about how to extricate himself from a situation like this. At the very least, he thought he ought to be able to get the duct tape away from his mouth so he could breathe better. He looked over at the small, still form lying against a wall of the dark space with the dirt floor. J.D. worried that, if it was Isabelle, the duct tape might have cut off her air supply. He also worried that the dose of sedatives Eugene had used on her had been too much. Isabelle was very small and very thin, and Eugene could easily have overdosed her. If it was Isabelle who was lying against the wall, she was much too still. She wasn't moving at all. J.D. wanted to be sure she was alive and able to breathe.

He tried to move his body over toward the motionless form, but his feet were bound together. It took him a long time to roll toward Isabelle. Wherever they were being held captive, the space was full of junk, old garden equipment, and bugs. There were too many obstacles in the way, and it wasn't easily to roll across the dirt floor. J.D. figured they were in some kind of an old shed. It didn't feel like a basement. He finally made his way over to the still and silent form against the wall, close enough to the motionless body to be able to kick it. He kicked with both his feet and made contact with something. He wanted to try to wake her up, and this was the best he could do.

When he first began to kick what he thought was a person, there was no response, no sound and no movement. He was almost certain it was Isabelle, and he was panicked that her lack of any reaction at all meant she was dead. Finally, he heard a small whimper, and the whimper came from the motionless form lying close to his feet. He kept kicking, but he didn't want to hurt her. He just wanted to rouse her. At last, there was a louder noise that J.D. thought came from her throat. It was a sound of protest, an objection, probably, to his constant kicking. He stopped kicking, and then he lay back and rested, relieved that Isabelle was alive and able to at least make a faint guttural sound. The effort to make his way across the floor of the shed to reach Isabelle had worn him out, and he had not entirely shaken the effects of the sedative drugs. He fell asleep again.

Isabelle was now more awake and began to remember what had happened and how she had come to find herself in her current predicament. She recalled that she and J.D. had confronted Chef Eugene in the kitchen at the Inastou. The chef had pretty much admitted he was the one who had been playing the dirty and dangerous tricks on the members of the reunion group. Isabelle remembered Eugene ranting and raving about the boys at Camp Shoemaker. She hadn't realized how seriously mentally ill the man was until he'd gone on the unexpected and unhinged tirade. If she'd had any idea he was so consumed by his delusions, she never would have confronted him. She would have called the police to question him, instead of attempting to question him with J.D. She was angry with herself for having been foolish enough to go after Eugene, and she was feeling guilty that she'd involved J.D. He had volunteered and in fact had insisted on coming with her to question the chef. But she was the one who had put it all together and figured out who Chef Eugene really was.

Isabelle remembered that Eugene had stabbed J.D. with a hypodermic needle and that she'd tried to get away from the mad man. But she hadn't moved fast enough, and here she was, someplace where Eugene had brought her, tied her up, and left her. She was facing a wall and wasn't able to roll over and look into the room. Something was blocking her, and she wasn't able to move. She figured out it was an old riding mower that was keeping her pressed against the wall. She was bound and gagged and trapped against the wall of a smelly shed with a dirt floor. She wondered if it had been J.D. who'd been kicking at her leg. He must be in here with her. Who else would it be? Isabelle figured he had been trying to communicate by kicking her. She twisted her body and her head around to try to see who and what was here in the shed with her. She caught a glimpse of a pile of clothes that could be a person, but it wasn't moving. If it was J.D., he was unconscious. She hoped against hope he wasn't dead. Isabelle wondered what drug Eugene had given them. She felt groggy and had a terrible headache, but at least she was alive.

She concentrated on trying to loosen the duct tape that was wound tightly around her mouth and head. If she could breathe more easily and get more air into her lungs, she might have more energy to try to get out of the yards and yards of rope that bound her legs and arms.

Isabelle realized she was in a very bad situation. She knew that people like Eugene tended to get worse and decompensate. His irrational behavior could be expected to escalate. Eugene was paranoid, and he could go downhill rapidly. The success of taking two captives and keeping them in a secret place would give him a thrill and a tremendous sense of power. Holding hostages, over whom he had total control, would be an indication to Eugene that it was possible for him to achieve his goal of finally getting back at the boys from Camp Shoemaker.

Isabelle knew there was an angry little boy inside the body of a very sick man. He might even decide to kill her and J.D. She was frightened that Eugene would find the idea of destroying the two of them too tempting to resist. Supreme control, after all, is the ability to decide who lives and who dies. That kind of ultimate achievement would be his crowning moment. She didn't know how much time they had, but she knew that in order to save their lives, they needed to get out of Eugene's clutches as soon as possible.

All she could hope for was that Matthew or somebody would be able to find them, wherever they were, or that they would be able to free themselves and get out of this mess. She would use all of her energy to try to escape, before Eugene reached his homicidal tipping point. She knew Matthew and Olivia and the others would be doing everything they could to find her and J.D.

She scolded herself again for being so eager to confront Eugene. She'd not had any idea he was going to be violent enough to take them hostage. She had misread how deeply disturbed the man really was. Taking prisoners and hiding them away was not a good sign. It meant Eugene was building very fast toward a catastrophic end.

Tyler and Lilleth moved their luggage to Indigo Cottage, and they took another one of the first floor bedrooms. With practice, Tyler had become much more adept with his crutches, but it would be easier for him if he didn't have to negotiate the stairs.

Gretchen had accepted Olivia's invitation to stay with the group. When Gretchen had last heard from Bailey, he'd said he had a crazy story to tell her. He texted that he had been successful in whatever he'd been working on. He told her that he and some federal agents were just about to do something big. It was a hastily written text, and Gretchen was just as confused after reading it as she'd been before he'd sent it. She had no idea what Bailey had been up to for the past three days. He said he didn't want to tell her anything about what he was doing because he didn't wanted to put her at risk … whatever that meant. She was worried about him and angry that he'd gone off on a wild hair. She was reassured because he did make contact every once in a while with his short, confusing text messages. She trusted that the communications were really from Bailey. Who else could possibly get himself into such a goofy situation, and who else would write these cryptic, whacky notes to her. It could only be Bailey. She hadn't told him that J.D. and Isabelle were missing. She figured if he was in the middle of something that involved federal agents, he didn't need any distractions. J.D. and Bailey were close, and Bailey would be consumed with worry when he learned about J.D.'s disappearance. Because Bailey had recently had a hip replacement, if and when he ever showed up again, he and Gretchen would also have a first floor bedroom.

No one knew exactly when Cameron and Sidney would be arriving. Cameron wasn't happy to have to return to Bar Harbor, but he'd known when he left town Monday morning that he and Sidney would be required to give the police or the FBI or somebody an official statement. They were witnesses to Elena's death and would have to tell the authorities what they had seen.

Cameron had scheduled an important conference for Monday afternoon. He had to attend because he was the boss and was running the meeting. He couldn't miss it, and he'd left town early Monday morning, before anyone in law enforcement could tell him not to leave. He'd known that he and Sidney would have to come back to Maine, but he'd hoped they would have a few days at home before the law caught up with them. At least he'd been able to make it to his meeting.

Olivia knew that Sidney and Cameron were coming back, and she'd sent them a text to invite them to stay at Indigo Cottage. Sidney had texted back that they would have their pilot with them. They always put their pilot up in a hotel when they were traveling, but there weren't any rooms to be had in any hotels or motels in the area for the next two weeks. Sidney wanted to know if there was room for their pilot at the cottage. Olivia consulted with Vivian and learned that one of the guest houses in the back yard was a sizeable two-bedroom, two-bathroom unit. It would work for the Richardsons and their pilot. She let Sidney know they had room. Sidney texted back that they would be arriving sometime late Tuesday, weather permitting.

Olivia had opted for the luxurious master bedroom on the second floor. It was a two-room suite and had once been Lorraine and Cabbott Ryan's domain. When Cabbott could no longer go up to the second floor, a first floor addition had been added to the house, especially to meet his needs. One of the Ryan's married children had then taken over the second floor master bedroom. Elizabeth suspected that one reason Olivia wanted a room on the second floor, away from everybody else, was that she didn't want any of her friends to hear her crying herself to sleep at night. Olivia put on a brave face when she was around the others, but Elizabeth knew that inwardly she was frantic about J.D. Olivia was a strong woman who always looked on the positive side of life. Those who knew her realized she grieved alone when no one else was around to feel sorry for her. There were other bedrooms and bathrooms and a large bunkroom for grandkids on the second floor. If Matthew ever took a break from his search for Isabelle and came to his senses, there was room for him at Indigo Cottage, too.

Richard arrived and moved his and Elizabeth's luggage into their first floor bedroom. He reported that Matthew intended to look all night for Isabelle. The man was understandably determined to find his wife. Richard had tried without success to talk his friend out of continuing the search after dark, but Matthew was adamant that he would not give up until he found Isabelle. Richard had taken sandwiches and bottled water to Matthew and tried to make him drink and eat. Matthew wouldn't take time to eat or drink anything and was, in Richard's opinion, acting irrationally. Richard finally left him with the address of Indigo Cottage and given him a last stern warning that he was putting himself in danger by stumbling around the Inastou grounds in the dark. Who knew what Matthew would decide to do?

There was plenty of room for everybody in the Ryan's beautifully rustic house. Vivian Jordan had warmed up to the reunion group, and they were singing her praises and were in her debt. By the time she served dinner, she was everybody's new best friend forever. The long dining table could seat eighteen, and the housekeeper had set the table for six. Was it possible that their group had shrunk to just six?

Vivian put the food she'd prepared out on the large serving island in the kitchen. Everyone helped themselves to her wonderful tomato soup directly from the pot on the stove. Vivian had prepared food for many more than six people. She said it would be available if anyone came in later, and it all made great leftovers. Bottles of wine were opened, and everyone tried to enjoy the meal and put a good face on their anxieties.

Olivia broke down a couple of times during dinner, but she was trying hard to be hopeful. She looked exhausted, but she had to stay awake. Her private investigator was driving in from Portland to talk with her tonight. She told herself she had to stay sharp to be able to tell him what he needed to know to find J.D. Olivia was putting all of her eggs in the PI basket.

When tragedy strikes and people are under great stress, everyone reacts differently and uniquely. Some people stop eating altogether. Others seek solace in food and can't get enough to eat. Lots of people deal with stress by drinking more alcohol than usual. Some people can't go to sleep when they are worried. Others retreat into sleep and want to sleep all the time. Some cry. Others become stoic and hold it all inside. Some become angry and lash out. The reunion group manifested all of these various and varied human reactions to the events of the past few days.

Elizabeth went directly to her room from the dinner table. She was overtired and knew she could get sick if she didn't rest. Richard was also exhausted, but he decided to go back to the Inastou to try, one last time, to talk Matthew into giving up the search for the night. He was taking a box of food that Vivian had prepared, and he hoped he could talk Matthew into eating something. Elizabeth sent an email to a friend, took a shower in the wonderfully accessible Indigo Cottage bathroom, and went to sleep.

Elizabeth woke up briefly when she heard the water running in the bathroom. The clock said two in the morning. She knew Richard was back from the Inastou, and she made herself stay awake until he came to bed.

"Did you convince Matthew to stop his search for the night and come back with you?"

"He was wandering around the grounds of the Inastou, aimlessly, going in circles. When I found him, he'd collapsed on the grass behind the main building. It was exhaustion. He was dehydrated and chilled to the bone. He hadn't eaten anything and wouldn't drink anything. He was hallucinating and babbling incoherently. I figured he must have a fever." Richard sighed, sad that his good friend was in such bad shape. "He had fallen or collapsed on the ground, and then the sprinkler system came on. They water the grounds after dark. I'm sure they don't expect anybody to be wandering around out there at night. So, Matthew's clothes were soaking wet. I had to roust somebody from the lodge to help me get him to the car. It was quite a trek. We finally got him into the passenger seat of the Expedition. He started to warm up, and I made him drink water and eat some of the food Vivian had sent. He came around a little bit, but he was still pretty much out of his head. I told him that, if he didn't straighten up, he would be the next one to have a stroke, like Darryl had. That didn't get through to him. Nothing did, really. He is a desperate man. I told him we would organize a search party and hire a private detective on Tuesday, but no rational idea was going to make it through his emotional fog. He went to asleep or passed out in the car before I finished explaining to him what today's plan would be. I turned up the heat full blast and drove him back here. It was almost impossible to get him into the house. I didn't want to wake anybody up, but Olivia heard us and came down to help me. I don't think she'd been asleep. I know she'd been crying. There was no way we were going to get him up the stairs, so we put him in the empty bedroom on this floor. We just let him collapse on top of the bed. I got him out of his soaking wet clothes. That wasn't easy, let me tell you. He hadn't even bothered to put on a sweater or a warm coat, if he had one. He was still shivering when we got back here, even after being in the warm car. It was damp out there, even before the sprinklers came on. After the sun went down, the temperature dropped considerably. He'd been lying on the ground for I don't know how long and was chilled through and through. He was coughing when I found him, and he's continued to cough. I know he's running a fever, but I don't know where to find a thermometer. He's pretty sick, Elizabeth. We piled blankets on top of him in the bed to try to keep him warm, but I'm afraid he's coming down with pneumonia."

There was nothing Elizabeth could say, except to tell Richard to get some sleep.

There was a special bond between Richard and Matthew. They had been roommates for a year during medical school. Many years ago, Matthew had been a groomsman at Elizabeth's and Richard's wedding. Richard and Matthew still hunted together in the Arizona desert. Matthew loved to hunt quail, and when he'd been stationed in Phoenix with the U.S. Public Health service, he'd bought a small, primitive hunting cabin on a few acres of land near Sonoita, Arizona. He stayed in the cabin and hunted quail in the area whenever he had a chance.

He'd kept his hunting cabin after he and Isabelle moved to Palm Springs. He flew to Tucson and then drove to Sonoita for long weekends during the quail hunting season. The flight to Tucson was just an hour from Los Angeles, and Matthew lived for his days tracking birds in the environs of Santa Cruz County and Cochise County. When Elizabeth and Richard bought a winter home in southern Arizona, Richard joined Matthew in Willcox or Sonoita almost every time he hunted there. Since Matthew had retired from his urology practice, he'd been able to spend more and more of the quail season at his cabin. The two physicians had become close and even owned a hunting dog together. Richard would go more than the extra mile for Matthew.

Chapter 26

The friend to whom Elizabeth had sent the email the night before was another member of the Camp Shoemaker reunion group, Theodore "Teddy" Sullivan. Teddy was still working full time. He traveled a great deal, and he wasn't able to participate in most of the yearly reunion trips. Last year he'd been in the Czech Republic, and he hadn't been able to make it again this year. Elizabeth missed him. Teddy was an architect and city planner, and Elizabeth had done work in both of these fields. They both loved music. Elizabeth was very fond of Teddy and didn't see enough of him.

She'd sent Teddy an email to let him know what was happening at the reunion. She told him specifically that Elena Petrovich had been murdered and that Darryl was in the hospital. Elena and Darryl didn't participate in most of the reunion trips either, and Elizabeth didn't think Teddy had actually ever met Elena. In her email, Elizabeth told Teddy about the various incidents that had occurred and, most importantly, that J.D. and Isabelle were missing. She knew Teddy was off on a job someplace and wasn't able to do a thing about any of what was happening to the rest of them. She felt a little guilty about sending him a message filled with bad news, but it made her feel better once she'd sent it.

As a well-known and much sought-after architect and urban planner, Teddy traveled to work with clients all over the world. His expertise in the field of historic preservation was prized by cities and countries everywhere. His home base was Charleston, South Carolina, but he was so busy, he was hardly ever there. Even those who knew him best often wondered whether his frequent trips abroad were just to look at old buildings and old neighborhoods. Elizabeth suspected that he went to some of these dangerous and exotic places for reasons other than purposes of historic preservation. He might disappear for weeks or even months at a time, and then he didn't want to talk about where he'd been or what he'd been doing. Underneath his charming exterior, Elizabeth and others suspected there was another dimension, another purpose, to Teddy's jet-setting, international life style.

Teddy was funny and smart, and everybody loved this handsome, gay man. It wasn't important to his group of friends that Teddy was gay. If he'd come out at Camp Shoemaker, when they'd all been young and unsophisticated and chasing girls, revelations about his having a different sexual preference would have caused a stir. But all these years later and with all the changes that had happened in the world, no one thought much about it anymore. Everybody, male and female, was drawn to Teddy's magnetic personality. He was delightful company, and everyone always had more fun when Teddy was around. The guys loved their old friend, exactly as he was.

Chapter 27

J.D. was able to push the gag out from between his teeth and loosen the duct tape over his mouth. He was afraid he might have swallowed some little pieces of the nasty black tape he'd managed to chew away, but that was the least of his worries right now. He was breathing more easily, but he'd expended a lot of energy to gain a better airway. He had to rest. He was thirsty and hungry, and he was also still feeling the effects of the sedative injection. He hoped to try to speak to Isabelle, to reassure her. More importantly, he wanted to tell her how he'd been able to achieve some success getting around the duct tape to get more air. He couldn't see much of anything, but he was almost certain Eugene had bound Isabelle in the same way he'd tied him up. There was little movement from Isabelle, who faced the outside wall of the shed, and J.D. continued to be worried about her.

He tried to speak, "Isabelle, Isabelle, are you over there? Are you all right?"

He thought he heard a sound and hoped it was a "yes" sound. "Isabelle, if you are over there against the wall, make that noise again in your throat, once for 'yes' and twice for 'no.' Make a noise, any kind of noise, as loud as you can, so I can hear it." He heard one growl, louder than the previous noise she'd made. So now at least he knew it was Isabelle. She was alive, and she could hear him.

"Are you able to breathe? Answer once for yes and twice for no." He heard one weak growl, which he took to mean she was having difficulty.

"Are you having difficulty breathing?" The answer was one vigorous growl from Isabelle's throat.

"I was having trouble breathing too, so I'm going to tell you how to get more air. If Eugene stuffed a gag in your mouth, you can push that out of the way with your tongue. Then you will have to chew through the duct tape a little at a time. You might swallow a few little bits and pieces of it. But you need more air, and once you get more air, you will eventually be able to work the tape loose enough that you will be able to talk. Do you want me to tell you how I got the gag out of my mouth and chewed the tape?" Again, she answered with a vigorous growl, a yes.

J.D. gave instructions and guided Isabelle through the process. Remembering his military training had paid off for him, and it looked as if it was going to pay off for Isabelle, too. She eventually did get more air and was able to begin to speak.

"How are we going to get out of this? My hands are tied so tightly behind me, I can't feel my fingers at all. I think my circulation has been completely cut off." Isabelle sounded more angry than frightened.

"I'm working on getting my hands free, but Eugene did a heck of a job tying us up. My hands aren't numb, but I'm not making much progress. I'm worn out, and without any water, I know I'm getting dehydrated. We have to watch out for that." J.D. knew dehydration was a real threat to their survival.

"I need to rest. I'm way past being out of steam. Do you think anyone will be able to find us? I know Matthew is looking and won't give up until he finds me or he's dead. We have to hurry. Eugene has gone over the edge, and I think our lives are in danger. I'm saying that as my professional opinion, as a psychologist. The sooner we can get out of his clutches, the more chance we will have to live." Isabelle didn't think she was overreacting. She had to let J.D. know she felt Eugene was a homicidal threat.

"Do you really think he's that dangerous? Why would he want to kill us?"

Isabelle began to explain, but realized J.D. had dozed off again. They didn't know it, but they had worked all night long, just to find a way to breathe more easily and to be able to speak. It would be morning soon.

At Indigo Cottage, everyone slept late on Tuesday morning. It had been a rough Monday, and they were exhausted. Vivian had breakfast ready when, one by one, they began to drag themselves into the kitchen.

Richard went to check on Matthew who was now delirious. Richard helped Matthew into a warm shower and then helped him back to bed. Richard was terribly concerned about his friend and fellow physician. Everyone had praised Matthew and Cameron when they'd saved the life of one of the rotten teenage kayakers. But after the incident, Richard had seen what nobody else had bothered to notice. He could see how badly Matthew was shaking from the cold when he'd arrive back at the dock in the rescue boat. Doctors are notoriously neglectful of their own health, and Richard could see that Matthew wasn't acknowledging the toll that the water rescue and saving a life had taken on himself. Then Matthew had spent hours, in the cold and damp, looking desperately for his wife. Who could blame him for that? But he'd been searching outside in cold weather without a coat. He had refused to eat or drink anything, and he'd become dehydrated. He had refused to rest. The sprinklers had come on and drenched him. It would be no surprise to anybody if he contracted pneumonia. Richard did not want to admit it, but he was almost certain Matthew had succumbed to the dreaded illness that could prove fatal to older people.

It was obvious that Matthew was quite ill, and Richard knew he had to call an internist to come to the house and examine Matthew. If he did have pneumonia, he needed to start on a course of antibiotics. The internist could prescribe those antibiotics. Vivian would know what doctor to call, and she would be able to find a home health-care company to come to the house to take care of Matthew, if he needed that.

Richard had decided he wasn't going to enable Matthew's irrational searching any more. Matthew was now too sick to do anything except lie in bed. Richard would try to organize a search party later today. He would look into engaging a PI, but the weather forecast didn't look good for any kind of outside activities.

Vivian had another feast laid out on the island, and stone ground oatmeal was ready on the stove. She was taking orders for sunny side up, over easy, and the omelet of your choice. Elizabeth was still in pain from her fall and worn out from the day before. She was taking her time getting dressed, and Richard brought her breakfast in bed, a bowl of the wonderful oatmeal with brown sugar, cinnamon, and heavy cream.

The temperature had dropped precipitously during the night, and the wind was churning and swirling dead leaves into the air. The sun was trying to peek out from behind black clouds that were rushing across the sky as if they were being chased. The crashing surf on the rocks below the porch let the residents of Indigo Cottage know that the remnants of Hurricane Gabriel were imminently upon them. It was going to be a bad storm, and Vivian, who had been through these storms on the Bar Harbor coast many times before, told them to hurry up and do what they had to do early in the day. If they had errands or shopping or anything to do that required driving anywhere, they had to do it and be back at the house before the rain got bad. No one in their right mind would go out in a car and be on the road once the storm hit. The wind would push the rain sideways, and there would be zero visibility. All roads would be flooded, and most roads would be closed.

Vivian warned her guests that at some point she would be putting down the storm shutters. These sturdy window coverings were designed specifically to protect the windows of the house during a storm. They worked, and kept the windows from being broken. The downside to the shutters was that, once they were lowered, all sunlight was cut off. There wouldn't be much light anyway, once the rain began to come down in torrents. They would have to hunker down. Search parties and visits from private investigators would all be on hold.

The news about the bad weather was the last thing Olivia wanted to hear. She was expecting another visit from her PI. He was at the Inastou now, checking out the people who worked at the lodge, recent guests, and the grounds. He had a team doing background checks on all the Inastou employees and would have a preliminary report for her this afternoon. Olivia was convinced it was someone connected with the Inastou who was behind the things that had been done to the others in the group, as well as behind J.D.'s and Isabelle's disappearance. That was what her gut instinct told her, and she was going with that when she gave instructions to her PI. She began pacing the floor and looking out the windows. She was feeling anything but cozy.

Gretchen was supposed to be at work today in Texas. She'd been scheduled to fly back to Dallas yesterday and go into her office this morning. Fortunately, she was pretty much her own boss. She could do some of her work from home, or from wherever she happened to be. She had scheduled an important meeting for today, and she intended to hold her meeting, in spite of being more than two thousand miles away. She would conduct the meeting via Facetime. She set up her computer in the bedroom and turned it into an office. She was not going to allow Bailey's involvement in some crazy international something-or-other mess or a storm or a murder or the disappearance of two close friends, keep her from doing her job. She was just as concerned as anybody. But she had work to do, and she was going to do it. She had told the others she would be incommunicado in her bedroom office for several hours.

Elizabeth finally rallied and went to the kitchen to confer with Vivian. Yesterday evening, they had planned the menus and gone online to order the groceries for the next several days. The groceries had been delivered, including the difficult-to-find Locatelli Romano cheese, the absolutely essential ingredient for the meatballs. The order from the butcher shop had also arrived. Vivian and Elizabeth were going to make Elizabeth's famous marinara sauce and meatballs for dinner tonight. The meatball recipe had been Elizabeth's mother's recipe. Elizabeth's parents had moved to New Haven, Connecticut as newlyweds. They didn't have much money, but once in a while they splurged and had dinner at Vito's, their favorite Italian restaurant. They loved the food, and Vito developed a small crush on Elizabeth's mother. He had shared his meatball recipe with her, and now the recipe belonged to Elizabeth. She was making an Italian feast for her friends tonight. It would be the perfect meal to enjoy during a storm.

Elizabeth's arthritis hampered her ability to chop and cook, but she was still very good at giving directions. Elizabeth had seen basil plants and flat leaf Italian parsley growing in the small kitchen garden behind the house. This morning, Vivian had picked the herbs they needed for the sauce and the meatballs. Vivian was the perfect sous chef, and before noon the meatballs were ready to be sautéed and the sauce was simmering on the stove. The cooks had also managed to produce two excellent salads for lunch. Many hands make light work.

Putting the food out on the kitchen island worked for everyone. There had been much coming and going that morning, and there were extra people at the house. Olivia's PI had arrived, and she'd invited him to eat with them. Elizabeth and Vivian had made orzo shrimp salad and curried Moroccan chicken salad. Vivian had ordered several quarts of lobster salad from her favorite lobster pound, and she was busy taking pans and pans of popovers out of the oven. In spite of the dire straits in which everyone found themselves, at least they would not go hungry. There was leftover tomato soup, and Vivian had also put together a pot of homemade chicken noodle soup. Even the hard-working Gretchen smelled the delicious sauce simmering and came out for a plate of salads and some warm popovers. The doctor had arrived to examine Matthew, and Richard invited him to stay for a meal.

And then the best surprise of all materialized, just as they were sitting down to the wonderful lunch. There was a knock at the front door, and Tyler hobbled to open it. There was Teddy Sullivan, standing in the doorway wearing a soaking wet raincoat. Another man in a soaking wet raincoat was standing next to him. Tyler pulled Teddy and the other man inside, out of the rain, and there were hugs and tears all over the place.

"This is my lawyer, Conrad Watson. He's the man who flew me down from Nova Scotia in his private plane this morning. He's also my guitar teacher." Teddy introduced the man who'd arrived with him.

"He looks like he might also be your bodyguard, Teddy." Nothing much got by Elizabeth. The very good looking, tall man was obviously strong and fit.

"He might also be my bodyguard, Elizabeth. He just might be." Teddy had a way of never telling you exactly what you wanted to hear. "I have heard via the Camp Shoemaker rumor mill that 'Ya Got Trouble, right here in River City.'" Teddy loved music and singing. He loved opera and Broadway shows and often made references to these when he spoke.

"I don't know what's happening in River City, but right here in Bar Harbor, we have been having a heck of a lot of trouble." Tyler raised his crutch as evidence of his share of that trouble.

Teddy and Conrad filled their plates with food and sat down at the table. Vivian was delighted to have so many people to feed. She hovered and refilled glasses of iced tea and cups of coffee. She brought second helpings of hot soup and passed around more popovers. Then she served plates of homemade cookies.

"Tell me all about it. Start at the beginning. Assume I know nothing. Teddy Sullivan, your own resident Sherlock, has arrived. I must have all the facts, so everything is important. No detail is too small to mention. We will find our missing friends. The weather be damned! The game's afoot, Watson!"

"Is your name really Watson? I'm Lilleth by the way."

"Yes, Lilleth, my name really is Watson. I'm not a real doctor, but I play one on TV."

"That's where I've seen you. I knew you looked familiar." Gretchen recognized Teddy's pilot/lawyer/bodyguard/guitar teacher from the hit television show, *How to Live Forever.* "I love the show, and I love your character. I wish you were on it more."

"Do you really play a doctor on TV?" Richard, who was a real doctor, didn't watch doctor shows on TV. Back in the 1970s and 1980s, he'd had too many people ask him if he were like Quincy.

"Yes, I play the neurosurgeon, Dr. Grey Matter."

"How do you ever have time to film a TV show and do all of this other stuff that Teddy says you do for him?" Lilleth sounded skeptical and wanted some lessons from Watson on time management.

Gretchen interrupted. "I have to know how you happened to get the part in *How to Live Forever*? If you're a lawyer, how did you become an actor? And how do you know Teddy?"

Watson laughed. "I was the legal consultant on the show. I used to be a prosecutor in L.A., and over the years I made the transition into entertainment law. Teddy is also a consultant on the show. He's the architectural historian, a very important person. That's how we know each other. The guy who played Dr. Grey Matter in the pilot episode of the program came down with some rare tropical disease when he was on safari in Africa. I was about the same size as the sick guy and could fit into his costumes. The director asked me to stand in for him and say his lines. When the actor who'd been hired to play the part recovered from dengue fever, or whatever it was he had, and came back to the show, they were going to shoot his scenes and use Photoshop, or the video version of it, to insert him into the episodes. I thought it would be fun to pretend to be an actor, so I gave it my all. The director and the producer loved my delivery and asked me if I'd like to have the part on a permanent basis. I said I would, and the rest is history."

"He knocked their socks off. They tore up the contract they'd made with the poor guy who was sick in Africa. They made Watson an offer he couldn't refuse. He's become the favorite character on the show now." Teddy was giving the details Watson was too modest to tell.

"And you are Teddy's guitar teacher, too?" Lilleth was still incredulous that this man could do all the things he said he could do.

"Okay," Teddy interrupted, "back to the business at hand. We can talk all about Watson's fabulous career after we've found Isabelle and J.D."

"Just one more question … how did you get here, really?" Elizabeth had to know.

"I received your email while we were filming in Nova Scotia. You were right next door in Bar Harbor. Watson has a plane, so we got on it this morning and flew down here. It was just a hop, a skip, and a jump. What does that mean, anyway? But I digress. I want you to start with when you made your reservations. Who made the first call to the Inastou? Who'd you talk to? Were all the reservations made in the men's names, or did some of the wives or girlfriends make the reservations in their own names? When did you all arrive, on what day and in what order? What was the first thing that happened? I agree that somebody who is connected with the Inastou is behind this. He or she knew you were coming and plotted their mischief ahead of time. This hurtful tomfoolery required at least some advance planning. So tell me everything."

They sat around the table and talked and recounted their stories. No detail was left untold. Both Teddy and Watson occasionally interrupted and asked questions. Teddy was intrigued when they talked about bringing out the old photographs from Camp Shoemaker. He wanted to see the photos, too. Nobody was exactly sure where they were right now, but they were guessing the photos were in Matthew and Isabelle's rental car that was still parked at the Inastou. Teddy asked for the keys to the car and said he would drive it back from the lodge, if road conditions permitted. "What was Isabelle doing the last time anybody saw her?"

"Isabelle was looking at the photographs on the wall in the dining room of the Inastou. I saw her there after breakfast yesterday." Richard had been the last person in the group to see her.

"And J.D. was last seen talking to the general manager of the Inastou? In other words, they were both inside the lodge. Am I right? Watson and I want to go there and take a look at the photographs Isabelle was looking at, and I want to talk to the GM about what J.D. said to him and what he said to J.D. That's where we have to start."

"You can't leave now. Look outside at the rain and the wind. It's coming down like crazy, and it's only going to get worse. Vivian is about to put the storm shutters down, and it will be dark in a few hours. And Matthew said he looked everywhere yesterday. He questioned the general manager and the chef and the desk clerk and everybody in sight." Richard was urging caution. He didn't want anybody else in the group to get lost or hurt or sick.

"Well, Matthew must have missed something. And the weather doesn't concern me. We must find our friends, and we must do it in spite of the storm. We have a Range Rover designed to go off-road and through floods. It's part SUV and part boat." Teddy was always making a joke.

Olivia's PI had been sitting in on the session. He listened to all the details and heard parts of the story he'd not heard before. He told Olivia that this complete account, told in person by those who'd actually experienced the events, had given him some fresh ideas. He was waiting for an email to come through, and he planned to return to the Inastou, if Teddy and Watson would give him a ride.

Vivian told the PI where he could find the printer. She assured him the WiFi was still working. Gretchen had been using it all morning. The PI wanted to print a copy of the incoming email for Olivia. It was the report on the background checks the PI's staff had done on all the employees at the Inastou. Teddy thought the background checks would be useful, and he decided to delay his departure for the Inastou long enough to read them. He asked the PI to print a copy for him.

Most of the group was still sitting around the table. As always happens before a bad storm, the barometer drops precipitously. Falling barometric pressure saps the energy from most people, and few had the initiative to get up from the table to do anything. The storm was ramping up outside. Vivian lowered the storm shutters and added wood to both fireplaces. Those who were inside were safe and warm, but all any of them could think about was where Isabelle and J.D. were during this cold deluge.

The doctor who had examined Matthew said he was seriously dehydrated. Matthew was running a fever and had to drink more liquids.

Matthew was not compliant, and didn't want to drink as much as he needed to drink. The doctor told Richard that after pushing fluids, if Matt's temperature began to rise, or, if it didn't begin to come down within two hours, Richard was to start an IV. The doctor had brought everything Richard would need to start the IV, but it had been years since Richard had actually done it. The doctor also left a stethoscope and some samples of antibiotics. With the storm coming, he'd said he didn't know when he would be able to get back to see Matthew again. Richard was to listen to Matthew's chest, and if it sounded like he had fluid in his lungs, Richard was to start him on the antibiotics.

The email came in and Gretchen printed it. Olivia, Teddy, and the PI all began to read. Olivia and Teddy saw it at the same time.

Chef Eugene Bonier was born Eugene Spencer Boone in 1946. He grew up in a small town in the Ozark Mountains and graduated from Pineville High School in Missouri in 1964. Bonier/Boone is a creative chef, and his culinary skills are exemplary. However, he has a great deal of difficulty working with other people and has moved from one restaurant to another over the years. He has never been able to hold a job for more than six months. He has worked at the Inastou for four months. There have been a number of complaints about his inability to get along with the rest of the staff, but everyone who works in the Inastou kitchen agrees that his food preparation and service are outstanding.

"That's it!" Olivia shouted. She knew it was the chef because of the reference to the town in the Ozarks.

"That's it!" Teddy shouted at the exact same moment. He knew it was the chef because of the mention of the town in the Ozarks and because of the chef's real name.

"His mother was Mrs. Boone. I remember it now." Teddy was absolutely certain. "She worked in food services at Camp Shoemaker. Eugene was little 'Genie.' That's what we used to call him. It made him furious. That little pest. Did you know that he tortured and cut up small animals? He trapped squirrels and chipmunks and liked to burn them alive. He was a terrible kid."

Several people at the table gasped. Lilleth spoke up. "Why didn't anybody mention that when we were looking at the pictures the other day? Why didn't somebody mention that this little boy used to torture and kill animals? That behavior is a tremendous harbinger of what a person might do later on in life. It can be an early indicator of serious mental illness. If someone had mentioned that on Sunday, we might have put the spotlight on this Boone guy."

"Nobody had put it together on Sunday. Nobody realized that the pesky, rotten little brat who bedeviled us at Camp Shoemaker had anything to do with the chef at the Inastou." J.D. wanted to set the record straight.

"But the chef was watching us and listening to what we were saying, you know. Isabelle and I both noticed his eavesdropping on our powwow in the dining room. We thought it was very odd that he got so angry all of a sudden and kicked us out. His behavior was inappropriate, bizarre really, and we should have asked ourselves why."

Olivia was energized. "He's got them. I'll bet you anything. We have to get over there as fast as we can. You have to try to get some kind of law enforcement to come out of their warm, dry donut shops and meet us there. It's hard to imagine what he might have done with them. If they are outside in this driving sideways rain that's only going to get worse, they could die." Olivia wanted immediate action, now that they knew where to look. "I didn't know anything about the animals." When she mentioned the animals, she broke down and ran out of the room.

"Watson, can you bring in our suitcases? You need to get something out of yours." Nobody asked what it was he needed to get out of his suitcase.

Vivian could see things were serious, and she spoke up and offered the two newcomers a place to stay. "There's a second, smaller, guest house attached to the other side of the garage. It's not fancy, but it's clean. It has two bedrooms and an old-fashioned bathroom. The place is pretty small and very rustic, but you won't have to walk out in the rain to get to the main house. You just have to go through the garage and the breezeway. Teddy, you and Watson can stay there, if you want to."

"We'd been planning to get reservations at the Bar Harbor Inn, but when we called, they said they didn't have a free room and wouldn't for ten days. We thought they might have had some cancellations, with the storm coming and all. They said leaf-peepers had cancelled, but the boat people are coming into the harbor in droves and have taken all the leaf-peepers' cancelled rooms. We were going to sleep in the truck. An antiquated bathroom is so much better than no bathroom at all. So a guest house on the other side of the garage sounds like home and heaven all at the same time. And if Vivian is cooking, we are definitely staying." Teddy was thankful he didn't have to sleep in the Range Rover.

"Actually, Elizabeth is cooking tonight. She's already done it. It's her spaghetti sauce you smell. And her meatball recipe. It's garlic in everything with Elizabeth." Vivian wanted to give credit where it was due.

"We're leaving now. Richard, call whoever you can get hold of on the local police force and at the local sheriff's office. It isn't going to be easy to drag somebody out in this weather, especially if they think it's a wild goose chase. But we might need ambulances, and we will definitely need handcuffs. We will get this pervert, and we will bring our loved ones home. Olivia thinks she wants to go with us to look for J.D., but that's not going to happen. She doesn't have any business being out in this storm. We don't have any business being out in it either. Nobody does. She'll be angry that we left without her, but she's not coming." The men secured their layers of raingear and left through the front door. Olivia's PI went with them. They put their heads down and fought their way against the driving wind. Because of the ferocity of the downpour, it was impossible to see their vehicle from the house. How would they ever be able to find their way anywhere on the road in this rain? Nobody could see them as they drove away, but the three were being sent on their misadventure with lots of prayers and lots of hope.

Chapter 28

TEDDY, WATSON, AND THE PI DROVE THROUGH howling wind, sideways rain, and flooded roads to reach the Inastou. Darkness arrived earlier than usual because of the storm, and Teddy was desperate to begin grilling Eugene Boone about J.D. and Isabelle. He had a sense that time was running out for his friends, and if they were anywhere outside in this rain and cold, they would die of exposure. He didn't know what it was going to take for Eugene to give up the information about what he'd done with his hostages. Teddy almost wished he'd brought Lilleth along. He wasn't a psychologist, and neither was Watson. They could have used Lilleth's expertise when they leaned on Eugene.

On the way to the Inastou, they agreed that the PI was going to interview the other employees at the lodge, and Teddy and Watson would take on the kitchen staff. The chef was, after all, the life-long nemesis of the Camp Shoemaker boys he'd stalked. They hadn't realized he had harbored hatred in his heart all these years, and they probably never would have known it, if they hadn't turned up at the Inastou for this year's reunion.

Their rain gear dripped onto the expensive rug when they entered the lobby of the lodge, and their boots tracked mud all over the shiny enoteca bar floor. Housekeeping problems at the Inastou were the least of their worries. Not a single guest was in the lobby or the bar, and it was close to dinnertime. Teddy and Watson immediately went to the GM's office and gave him a quick rundown about what Chef Bonier/Eugene Boone had done and about what was going to happen. Watson had been a criminal lawyer, and he let the general manager know the charges against the chef were more than credible. He also implied that the complicity of the Inastou in the various assaults on its guests was still to be determined. He'd hoped to scare the stuffing out of the GM, and he succeeded.

Supposedly, the sheriff and two deputies were trying to get to the Inastou. Although the sheriff's vehicle was a sturdy SUV, it was not as safe to drive on flooded roads as the Range Rover. Even relatively wealthy Hancock County was not able to afford to buy Range Rovers for their law enforcement officers.

Teddy had hoped the sheriff would be at the Inastou by the time he and Watson arrived, but he didn't intend to wait for anybody or anything. They went to the kitchen assuming Eugene would be there. They were more than disappointed to find out that it was his day off. Because weekends are so important in the restaurant business, a chef can never take off on a Friday, a Saturday, or a Sunday. Chef Bonier's day off was Tuesday. Teddy called the kitchen staff and all the waiters and waitresses together in the dining room. He told them their chef was suspected of criminal activities and was being sought by law enforcement. One of the busboys, who was fourteen or fifteen, was obviously frightened by this news. His face turned as white as a ghost's. He got up from his chair and bolted toward the back door of the kitchen. Watson went after him and tackled him on the slippery utility porch. He dragged the boy back into the main part of the kitchen and pushed him into a chair.

"Okay, spill it. Tell me what you know, and you might not have to go to jail. We know you were conspiring with Bonier to cause trouble for some of the guests. Speak to me."

The boy was terrified of the large and threatening attorney. He lost control of his bladder, and as a puddle formed underneath the chair, he began to cry. "Chef Bonier paid me to fix the bikes. He paid me a hundred bucks. I damaged the brakes and cut the steering cables on one of the fancy bikes at the bike shop. He told me exactly what to do and how to do it. He told me to be sure I got the right bikes. I only had time to bust up one of the bikes, and he wasn't happy about that. He wanted me to do four bikes, but I only had time to do one. That's all I did, I swear."

"Did you know that a man fell down the mountain and broke his ankle because of what you did to his bike? He could have been paralyzed. He could have died. He had to be flown by helicopter to the hospital in Bangor. He had to have surgery. He's on crutches and will be for a while. His ankle will probably never be completely right. The man you hurt is a ski instructor, and you may be responsible for his never being able to ski again. How does that make you feel? If that doesn't make you feel bad enough, I wonder how the multi-million dollar lawsuit he's going to file against you will make you feel?" Watson was relentless.

The boy began to cry again. "I didn't know anybody was going to get hurt. The chef said it was just a practical joke he wanted to play on some friends of his. I didn't think about it. He gave me a hundred dollar bill."

"It's going to cost you a hell of a lot more than that in legal bills, to keep yourself out of very, very big trouble. Now, where are the hostages he took? If you don't tell me, I have ways of making you talk. And you won't like my ways, trust me."

The kid looked blank. "I don't know anything about any hostages, I promise I don't. I only helped him wreck the bike. I didn't sign on for taking hostages."

Watson believed him. "Well, for your information, Bonier did take hostages, and he's hidden them somewhere. Do you have any ideas about where he might have taken them?"

The kid shook his head. Watson asked, "Where were you on Monday morning, around ten o'clock?"

"I don't come in on Mondays. I wasn't here. Chef Bonier likes to come in on Monday morning and get things ready for the week. He doesn't want most of the rest of us underfoot until it's time to prep for lunch."

"What kind of car does he drive? Do you know where he lives?"

"He drives an old green beater to work, a Honda hatchback, I think, very old, and I don't know where he lives. He carries around a lot of stuff in the back seat, and it's a tiny car. We've all wondered how in the world he gets his huge self into it. We've made jokes behind his back about how he does it, like with a crowbar or a giant shoehorn. When he's here he drives a Gator that belongs to the Inastou. They don't like for him to drive it, but he does anyway."

"Where's that Gator kept?" The GM had already told them there weren't any security cameras in the kitchen, except for right outside the walk-in freezer and the walk-in refrigerator. The cameras had been put there to prevent theft.

"It's probably in the shed with all the other Gators. The handyman has one. Housekeeping has three. Groundskeepers have five. There are others in the shed." Watson thought the Inastou Lodge was definitely oversupplied in the Gator department.

Watson took hold of the busboy by the neck of his shirt, lifted him out of the kitchen chair, and pushed him back into the dining room where Teddy was talking to the other food service workers. The boy's pants were wet, and he looked like he was about to be sick. "Junior here has peed his pants, but he's confessed to sabotaging Tyler's bike. Bonier paid him to do it. I'll tell you all about it. He says Eugene drives a Gator around the Inastou grounds, and it's parked in the shed with about a dozen other Gators." The boy hung his head and couldn't look any of the other employees in the eye.

Teddy stared at the whimpering youth who was looking at the floor. "Take him out to where the Gators are parked and make him show you the one Eugene drives. Go over it with a microscope. If he took them someplace in the Gator, maybe one of them left something behind that will prove they were in it. I haven't quite finished talking to the rest of the staff."

Watson and the busboy left Teddy to finish questioning the others.

"So, if any of you have an idea about where he could have taken my two friends, speak up now. There will be a reward in it for you. Also, anything else you can tell me about Eugene will be appreciated. I can't believe not one of you knows where he lives." Teddy looked in the eyes of each of the people who were gathered around him. He wanted them to know how serious he was.

"He's not an easy person to get along with or to get to know. He's not friends with any of us. He keeps himself to himself." One of the young waitresses who had been afraid to speak up before, volunteered this bit of information. Teddy wondered if seeing the busboy's wet pants had motivated her to speak.

"I get that. Is there any place on the grounds of the Inastou where he might have hidden two people? Think hard. This is very important. Even someplace outside, someplace where he could keep them secured and nobody would ever happen to stumble on them by accident?"

One of the older waitresses reluctantly spoke up. "There's a shed in the woods that's falling down. It was supposed to be demolished years ago, but nobody got around to doing anything about that. I don't think Chef even knows it's there, though. I only know about it because sometimes I bring my dogs over here and walk them in the back. Nobody ever goes over there, not in that part of the woods. It's really in a marsh. If anybody was inside it, they would be lying in the water by now. With all this rain, those low spots fill right up, like a lake. It used to be a shed for garden equipment, but the Inastou built a fancy new building for the yard equipment, mowers, and such. That old shed was falling apart, anyway. It used to be at the edge of the woods. But the vegetation has grown up around it so now it's completely in the woods. It's overgrown with bushes and vines. I don't think the Gator could get back there, so that's probably not a possibility."

"Why do you think a Gator couldn't get back there? A Gator can go almost anywhere it wants to go." Teddy knew about Gators.

"There are dead limbs and tons of brush, and like I said, it's in a marsh. The Gator would sink. Chef would have had to walk through some swampy water to get there. I don't think he would do that. He's too picky about his shoes. He wears covers over his shoes in the kitchen so nothing will spill on them. He would never get his feet wet."

"We will check it out. Thank you. I know you all need to get back to fixing dinner, but if you think of something, even the smallest thing, please call me immediately. My friends will die from exposure if they are out in this weather." The collapsing shed in the middle of a marsh didn't sound like a great lead, but they would have to find it, just to cover all the bases. If Eugene had hidden his hostages away in a place like the shed the waitress had described, it meant he was abandoning them. It meant he had no intentions of checking on them to see if they were all right. It meant he wasn't bringing them food or water. It meant they would die.

Chapter 29

ISABELLE WAS AWAKENED BY THE COLD RAIN pouring in on her through the holes in the roof of the dilapidated shed. The ground under her was getting wet, so wet, she realized she was lying in a puddle. Soon she would be lying in a puddle of mud. She was so thirsty, all she could think about was how to get her mouth in position to drink some of the rainwater that was coming in through the roof. She had worked some of the duct tape away from her mouth, but she was unable to maneuver her body around to get any water.

It was her thirst, her longing for a taste of rainwater that motivated her to get creative. She was lying next to an old riding lawn mower. She was being held captive by that mower, pressed up against the wall of the shed and unable to move. A mower had blades. Even an old mower had blades. The blades might be dull, but Isabelle was going to give it her best shot. The water was rising in the shed. She was out of options. She was no longer counting on being rescued. Eugene had left her and J.D. someplace that no one knew anything about, a place where no one was ever going to find them. She refused to lie down and die in the mud.

She twisted and turned and was able to get her arms, which were tied together behind her with very strong rope, under the riding mower. She moved her arms around as much as she could until she felt a sharp piece of metal. She'd found the blade. She was in an extremely awkward position, and the way she had to twist her body to reach the mower blades was painful. Her shoulder was pushed up against the mower, and every time she moved even an inch, metal parts gouged into her back. But she persisted. It seemed like she worked on cutting her bonds for hours and hours. She couldn't see anything inside the shed, and she couldn't see her arms or hands that were behind her back and now were underneath the mower. She didn't know if she was making any progress at all toward freeing herself. Every time she moved her arms back and forth, to use the mower blade as a saw, she nicked her wrist. She could smell her own blood, but she kept on. No matter how much it hurt, she had to keep on. She had no choice if she was going to free herself.

J.D. was either asleep or passed out. Isabelle was worried about him. He'd been so strong and energetic and had guided her through the tedious process of loosening the duct tape around her mouth. As a result, she was able to get more air, and she could talk. Then J.D. had gone back to sleep and hadn't wakened again. She knew he was dehydrated; they both were. She knew he was in excellent physical condition, but he was seventy-five years old. He didn't have a riding mower with a blade next to him. It was up to her.

She rested and worked, rested and worked. She drifted off to sleep, but the rising water kept waking her up. She was lying in a sea of mud. The water covered half of her prone body. She had to work faster.

Finally, she felt something slacken. She hoped it was a part of the rope that had given way. She thought her restraints had loosened by some miniscule degree. It wasn't much, but it was enough to motivate her to continue. She worked and worked harder.

After what seemed like days of effort, the blade began to cut through one of the ropes that bound her. After a few more minutes of struggling, the last of the ropes fell away, and her arms were free. She pulled them from under the riding mower. Blood from where the blade had nicked her wrists was all over her, but she didn't give a hoot about that. The next thing was to free her legs, but her hands were numb with cold and numb from having her circulation cut off by her restraints. Eugene had used a heavy hemp rope, and he'd tied her up with yards and yards of it. She rubbed her hands together and tried to wipe the blood away. She started working on the knots that bound her legs. It took her a long time to get free, but just when she thought she couldn't stand the cold another minute, she found she was able to move her legs.

She was still wedged behind the riding mower, but she was determined and found the strength to climb out over it. Her legs were weak and stiff, and she wasn't able to stand. So she crawled through the rising water. She wondered if they were in a tidal cove or somewhere near the ocean. Would they drown before they could get out of their watery grave?

She was able to reach J.D., but when she shook him, he didn't wake up and didn't move. Isabelle couldn't figure out why he wasn't responding. She wasn't a medical person, but she was able to find J.D.'s pulse. He was still alive, but he was unconscious. His pulse was thready. She shook him harder. It was dark in the shed, and she couldn't see his face. The shed had no windows, but there were plenty of holes in the roof. It was dark outside. The wind was ferocious, and the rain was definitely coming down harder and faster. She carefully removed the remains of the duct tape from J.D.'s face. Then she began to work on the ropes that bound his arms and legs. When she had him free, she shook him and yelled at him to wake up.

"I can't carry you out of here, and I'm not going to leave you here. So wake up. Your arms are free, and your legs are free. We can get out of here now, but I need your help." Isabelle was afraid that dehydration had caused J.D. to lose consciousness. She knew she was desperately thirsty. She looked around for something to catch the water that was gushing through the roof. She found a can that smelled as if it had once held gasoline or motor oil. She rinsed it out as best she could and filled it with rainwater. She drank from the can and then filled it again. She held it up to J.D.'s mouth and poured it down his throat. He began to choke on the water, and then he opened his eyes.

Isabelle was thrilled to see him look at her, but he was confused.

When he finally spoke, he wasn't making sense. He didn't seem to know what was happening or where he was. "What's going on? What are you doing here?" Isabelle reassured him and explained to him what had happened and where she thought they were. She told him they were now free to leave the shed and try to find their way back to civilization.

Isabelle was on her last legs, but she knew she had to pull J.D. into the present. She needed his help, and she was not going to leave him behind. She briefly considered leaving and bringing back help to get J.D., but she had no idea where they were. She didn't know what would face her when she walked outside the shed. They might be on a cliff on the side of a mountain. They might be in the middle of a swamp or in the middle of one of the ocean's tidal flats. The tide could be coming in as she was sitting there, trying to talk to J.D. She kept urging him to drink water, and finally he did. He lay back down.

"We have to get out of here. I think we might be in the tidal flats of the Atlantic Ocean. The water is coming up on us rapidly. You have to get yourself together. You have to help me save your life." She didn't really know where they were, but she thought the threat of the tidal flats might get his attention. In exasperation, she shook J.D. again. Maybe it was the water she'd made him drink. Maybe it was the shaking. Maybe it was the talking to she'd given him. Or, maybe his adrenalin was finally kicking in. He began to come around. They were both exhausted and dehydrated, and all of their energy reserves had been used up long ago. Isabelle was several years younger than J.D., but neither one of them was young. They would be lucky to get out of this alive.

He pushed his body into a standing position and was finally able to stand on his own. His resilience was driven by pure will, and he seemed to be almost himself again. They made their way to the door of the shed, but nothing about their situation was going to be easy. There was a padlock on the outside of the door. They could see it through the holes in the door. Eugene had done everything he could to keep them from escaping.

"I'm going to knock out one of the panels of the door. This place is about to come apart at the seams anyway. Let's look for a hammer or an axe or some kind of a tool that we can use to knock this door down." J.D. had his wits about him again. They searched, and all they could find was a shovel. It wasn't ideal, and neither one of them had the strength left to use it effectively. They took turns battering the door with the shovel. Finally, they got one board of the door down, and then they pulled a second board loose. It was then they ran into their worst nightmare.

Eugene had rigged explosives, some kind of a bomb, to go off, if anyone crossed the threshold of the shed's doorway. Isabelle knew nothing about bombs, but J.D. did, from his military training. After looking at what Eugene had assembled at the door to the shed, J.D. said he didn't think they were going to be able to get out of the shed by exiting through the door. The bomb was made from plastique explosives, and it looked surprisingly sophisticated. J.D. shook his head. "I had no idea the guy had the expertise to build something like this. I know he used to tie bunches of cherry bombs around the necks of baby bunny rabbits and light them on fire, but this is way, way more sophisticated than that. We are in a whole different ball game here. Now I'm glad nobody came to rescue us. He's hidden these explosives in such a way that nobody would have noticed them as they approached the door. As soon as anybody stepped across the entrance to the shed, they would have been blown to kingdom come — before they knew what hit them. We're darned lucky we didn't blow ourselves up, trying to take the door apart."

"The man's evil knows no bounds, does it? So how do we get out of here? The water is rising very fast. I can tell my body's core temperature is going down, and I will soon be suffering from hypothermia. It happened to me once on the ski slopes, so I know the symptoms and what it feels like. When that happens, I won't be any help to anybody. If it gets bad enough, I won't be able to walk anymore. We have to do something, and we have to do it quickly." Isabelle was insistent.

"We're going to take this shed apart. We are going to exit this miserable place through a hole in the wall, a hole we're going to make. Eugene won't have put explosives all around this worthless building. I think if we work on another side of it, we'll be okay. Those explosives are there to keep somebody on the outside from getting into the shed through the front door. The bomb is meant for our rescuers."

They found a second shovel, and both of them worked hard to try to save themselves. They banged the shovels against the wall for a while. Then they had to rest. They pushed themselves to continue working with their shovels. The temperature outside was going down, and Isabelle was fading. She knew she was getting much too cold and had to stop pounding on the wall. J.D. worked faster. He finally pulled one board away from the wall. Then he pulled away another board. They were almost free.

Chapter 30

"I FOUND A FEW BLONDE HAIRS IN THE GATOR, BUT it looks like he cleaned it out pretty well. She's a blonde, right? Isabelle? But the blonde hairs could be from anybody. I put them in a sandwich bag. If the worst happens, maybe those few hairs will hang the bastard." Watson was disappointed that his meticulous search of the Gator hadn't yielded any real evidence that J.D. and Isabelle had ever been in it.

"What did you do with the busboy? I'm determined that little bugger is going to juvie. He's got to be held accountable for his actions. If they let him get off when he's young, I'm afraid he will end up where Eugene has ended up." Teddy was not going to shrug off the bad things the busboy had done to his friends.

"Eugene sounds like he was pretty sick as a kid. We know he messed with animals, but as far as we know, he didn't hurt people when he was little. He was mostly a brat and a pest when it came to humans. Animals were another story. Of course, nobody knows what Eugene was up to when he was a teenager. Who knows what kinds of mischief he'd gotten into by then? The busboy has already assaulted someone and caused bodily harm. Tyler may not be able to ski again, and that's his life. This is serious business, even if Tyler wasn't a skier. The kid has to be punished. He may not learn anything if he's prosecuted, but we have to make sure he pays in some way for what he did. He has to pay in a way that gets his attention. A slap on the wrist won't do it. Right now, he's handcuffed to one of the Gators in the garage. He's not going anywhere any time soon, but I wish the sheriff would hurry up and get here." Watson had been both a prosecutor and a defense attorney. He was adamant about this young criminal. This was personal.

"I don't want to wait any longer to go out looking for J.D. and Isabelle. I think he's got them somewhere on the Inastou grounds. From the description of his car, I don't think he could have transported both of them, or even one of them, anywhere in that hatchback. He's huge, and his car is tiny. And he's got it full of junk, according to the kitchen staff. You heard them say they didn't know how he gets himself into and out of it. Maybe he lives in his car. Maybe that's why nobody knows where he lives. That sounds about right for somebody like Eugene — to be living in his car. The trouble with my theory, that he's got Isabelle and J.D. someplace on the Inastou grounds, is that supposedly Matthew searched every possible place on the grounds yesterday and came up with nothing." Teddy didn't want to sound like a downer, but he wanted to be realistic.

"I don't know Matthew, so I don't know how thoroughly he would have searched. I know he was frantic to find his wife. Carpenter said he was wandering around in circles. Maybe he was too emotionally distraught to do a methodical and systematic search. Of course, he had much better weather than we've got."

"I want to try and find that shed in the swamp or in the woods, or wherever it is. Matthew would not have known about that shed, so he wouldn't have looked there. I'm going to get the waitress and ask her to come with us. She knows where it is because she's walked her dogs out there. We'll take one of the Inastou's Gators. Bring the biggest, heaviest one in the garage. Can you get the keys from the GM? I'll talk to the waitress." Teddy was not giving up the hunt without pursuing every possible lead, no matter how unlikely.

When Teddy found her, the waitress had on a raincoat, but it wouldn't stand up to this storm. Teddy questioned the waitress. "I'm surprised you came in to work tonight. Will you be able to get home?

This seems like the kind of night when the dining room would have closed down or a skeleton staff would have put out soup and crackers."

"My name is Rita, by the way. My last name is about to change, so it's not important. Chef runs a tight ship. He's very difficult about time off, and if you are sick for more than one day, he's always threatening to let you go. He's not an easy man to work for, even if he is great with food. He's terrible with people."

Teddy handed her a waterproof poncho with a hood that would do a better job of keeping her dry than her thin raincoat would. The Gator that Watson brought didn't have a top, so they were all going to be at the mercy of the storm. "I'm Teddy Sullivan. Put the poncho on over your raincoat. You'll need them both. We'll bring you back to your car when we've had a look at the old shed. That's all we really need you for, to show us where it is."

"You can bring me back here to the lodge. Even if there aren't any customers eating here, I can't leave until eleven." Just then, the young waitress who'd spoken up in the dining room meeting came running after them carrying two large catering thermos jugs and a plastic bag.

"Here's the hot chocolate and the chicken broth. The Styrofoam cups are in the bag. I hope you find your friends." She handed the thermoses to Rita.

"Was this your idea, Rita? What a great thought, and how nice of you to get it together."

"I feel bad that Chef did this to your friends. I thought they could use something warm and nourishing, if they've been out in this weather since yesterday morning."

"You're a good person, Rita. I hope that next last name will be good to you."

"Oh, it will be. I'm taking back my maiden name. No more husbands for me. I've exhausted my options in that department, and I'm not trying again." Rita shrugged and smiled a sad little smile.

"Hop on the Gator. Watson, this is Rita. Let's get going."

The rain hadn't let up at all, and the wind was howling. They all had to lean into the wind to make any progress walking forward. Teddy tried to call the sheriff again before they left, but he still wasn't able to get through. Cell service was spotty on Mount Desert Island under the best of circumstances, and with the storm, it wasn't surprising that there wasn't any. Teddy realized they were on their own. It was a small town, a quiet town, and missing persons and potential murderers were not part of this community's agenda or the agenda of their law enforcement officials. Rita climbed into the Gator's passenger seat, and Watson climbed in the second seat. Teddy was driving. They'd taken a big Gator, hoping against hope they would have two passengers to bring back with them on their return trip.

The going was extremely rough. Before they reached the edge of the woods, the water was already halfway up the wheels of the Gator. There was thick brush and dead wood all over the ground, and the woods were almost impassable. Rita was sure she knew where the old shed was, but she'd said it wouldn't be easy for the Gator to get there. Rita was always on foot when she had her dogs, and she could go around or climb over whatever blocked her path. The search party had to take several detours to dodge fallen limbs and avoid the water they knew was too deep for them to drive through. At one point, they were literally driving through a swamp, just like Rita had said they would be. It was hazardous, and the Gator finally got stuck in the mud and came to a stop.

They climbed out and began walking. Because they didn't really expect to find anything in the shed, Watson stayed with the Gator to try to get it out of the mud. If he could move it, he would follow later.

"How much farther do we have to go?" It seemed impossible to Teddy that anyone could have brought two hostages out to this Godforsaken place, even with a vehicle.

"Not much farther now ... just a few more yards. Chef might have been able to drive the Gator up to the shed in good weather. It looks to me like somebody has been back here. I come here pretty often with my dogs, and I think somebody has driven back here in an ATV or a Gator. Let's hope."

They saw the shed up ahead. Teddy started running. If his friends were inside the ramshackle building, he wanted to get to them as soon as possible. He shouted over his shoulder. "Rita, go back to the Gator. Tell Watson I've found the shed. He needs to get up here." Rita turned around and started back. Then she heard more shouting.

"I think we are just about out of here. Are you okay?" J.D.'s voice was hopeful and excited.

"No, I am not really okay at all, but I can climb out of this shed. I'm right behind you." Isabelle was completely exhausted, but she was not about to give up now.

"I hear something. It sounds like a golf cart or an ATV. Do you hear it?"

"Yes, I can hear it, and it's getting louder. It's coming in this direction. Do you think it's somebody on their way to find us?" Isabelle had not lost hope.

"It probably isn't, but if it is, we have to stop them before they reach the front door of the shed."

"Oh, my God. I was so excited about getting free, I'd almost forgotten. We have to get out of here and go around to the front." Isabelle listened again. "Now the sound has stopped. I don't hear it any more, do you?"

"No, I don't hear it now. But we still need to get out there, to keep anyone from trying to go in through the door." J.D. pushed the third board away, and stepped through the opening in the wall. He grabbed Isabelle's hand and pulled her outside after him. The rain was coming down so hard, they couldn't see anything at all. They grabbed hold of the walls and made their way around toward the front of the shed. They saw two people a short distance away. One of them was running toward the door of the shed.

J.D. screamed at the running form, "Stop! Stop! Don't touch the door. There's a bomb! The door is booby-trapped. It's going to blow up." He didn't think the person had heard him over the roaring wind, and he ran to try to intercept whoever was running before he reached the doorway. The man did make it to the door, and J.D. flew at him from the side. The second figure had been headed away from the shed, but when J.D. started to shout, it turned around. Now the smaller figure in a poncho was also rushing toward the door of the shed. Isabelle gathered her last bit of strength, digging deep for the umpteenth time of digging deep. She ran to intercept the second figure, to try to keep that person from reaching the door.

J.D. was too late to keep the bomb from going off, but the tiny delay in the ignition mechanism of the explosive device saved his life and the life of the person who had pushed against the door. J.D.'s flying leap carried the two of them far enough from the explosion that they were both only singed by the heat and covered up with debris from the exploding shed. Shards of metal and wood and balls of fire cascaded down on top of them. Isabelle had tackled Rita in time and kept her from dying in the explosion. The two women were not badly hurt. Watson came running.

"What the hell was that? Teddy, Teddy, are you all right?" Watson was sprinting toward the pile of rubble.

Isabelle helped Rita get up off the ground. She looked at Rita and then at Watson. "Who are you?" Isabelle asked. She'd expected to see Matthew or at least somebody she recognized.

Watson ignored her. He rushed toward the two men who were underneath the burning debris. Thankfully, he was wearing gloves as he dug through the wreckage and pulled away the fiery pieces of junk to get to them.

J.D. had thrown Teddy to the ground under him and had taken the brunt of the explosion. Teddy hadn't been badly hurt by the pieces of the shed and garden equipment that had come flying through the air. J.D.'s clothes were burned, and his head was bleeding. He looked down at the man whose life he had just saved and recognized his old friend Theodore Sullivan. "What the hell are you doing here, Teddy? I thought you were in Timbuktu or someplace like that."

"I was in Timbuktu, J.D., but I heard you were in trouble. So I flew down here to rescue you and give you a chance to be a hero. And now you are." Even in the worst of circumstances, Teddy always kept his sense of humor.

They were all alive.

Isabelle was shivering dangerously. Watson wrapped her in blankets and a waterproof tarp. He lifted her into the Gator. Rita had twisted her ankle, but she limped to the back of the Gator and retrieved the thermos jugs of hot liquids.

"Chicken broth or hot chocolate?" Rita asked Isabelle.

"Both!" Isabelle was lying down in the rear of the Gator where Watson had put her, but when she was offered something hot to drink, she sat up.

Watson had been able to dig the Gator out of the mud, and he loaded Teddy and J.D. into it. With difficulty, Rita climbed into the cargo area with Isabelle. Watson drove like a bat out of Hades as he headed for the Inastou. The ground was soaked, and it was impossible to see where he was going. But he kept his foot to the floor.

"I heard the shed was scheduled for demolition anyway." Teddy tried to make a joke, but no one was laughing at this one.

When they got to the Inastou, there was still no sign of the sheriff or anybody else. At this moment, Watson was in the best shape of any of the people in the group, so he started issuing orders. "We're going to the local hospital in Bar Harbor right now. Of course my phone is down, so I can't use Google maps. I do know how to get to town, and Bar Harbor is not that big. Somebody will be around who can tell us how to find the hospital. How hard can it be? Rita, get in the far back of the Range Rover, if you can make it with that ankle. You need to come with us and have yourself checked out."

"I don't think I really need to go to the hospital. I don't want to ride with you because I don't want to be somewhere without my car. I would drive myself and meet you there, but I don't think my Neon can get through in this rain." Watson was impatient and wanted to get on the road. He was thinking about a lot of things at the same time. He wondered when anybody would find the busboy who was handcuffed to a Gator in the garage. Watson was determined that the little punk was not going to get away with his crimes. He knew he shouldn't leave Rita behind, but she refused to get in the Range Rover.

Watson loaded everybody else into the SUV and turned up the heat full blast. He was driving, and Teddy was trying once again to use his cell phone. He wanted to let his friends at Indigo Cottage know that J.D. and Isabelle had been rescued. He couldn't get through.

The roads were flooded and visibility was zero, but they were on their way to the ER. With all the difficulties they encountered on the road, Teddy worried about Rita in her little Neon. She wouldn't be able to drive home from the Inastou. They owed her, and he wished they'd brought her with them. A sprained ankle was not a minor injury for a waitress. Many roads were completely closed, and they had to try three different detour routes before they were finally able to get to the hospital. Most people had heeded the warnings and stayed off the roads.

There was no one else waiting at the ER, but there was only one doctor to take care of the three victims. They triaged themselves and decided that J.D. needed to be seen first. He was bleeding. He wanted to defer to Isabelle, but she was feeling a little better after the chicken broth and the hot chocolate. An ER nurse started an IV, covered her with warm blankets, and had her lie down. She was sound asleep on the gurney in a treatment room before the doctor got to her.

In addition to the big gash in his head, J.D. had minor burns and lots of cuts and contusions. The IV in his arm had rehydrated him, and he was doing better. He needed quite a few stitches. Teddy also needed stitches in his hand, and he was already lamenting what would happen to his guitar career as a result of his injuries. His guitar teacher and lawyer told him to button his lip and be thankful it wasn't worse.

The ER doctor listened to the whole story about Isabelle's and J.D.'s abduction. When he learned they'd been drugged, tied up and held hostage in the swamp for two days, almost died in an explosion, and all the rest of it, he insisted they spend the night in the hospital. They protested, but were both too weak to argue. Teddy had tried to call the landline at the cottage from the land line in the hospital, but of course all land lines were down. Isabelle and J.D. were in good hands. There were hugs all around, and Teddy and Watson left for Indigo Cottage. The only way to let everyone know that the lost had been found was to give them the news in person.

Chapter 31

They'd had a big antipasto with their spaghetti dinner. They had offered a toast to Elizabeth's sauce and meatballs, her secret recipe salad dressing, and her garlic butter that had been slathered on the Italian bread. They had heaped lavish praise on Vivian's antipasto and the luscious Italian cream cake she'd made for dessert. The electricity had gone off, but within a minute or two, the whole-house generator had kicked in and turned the lights back on. In spite of all the lovely food, somebody asked every three minutes why Teddy hadn't called. Then they would remember how bad the cell phone service was in the area. Didn't Teddy have a satellite phone? Somebody thought he did. Discussions ensued. Because of the wind velocity, Sidney and Cameron's plane had been forced to land in Boston. They would arrive in Bar Harbor when the weather permitted.

This time, Teddy and Watson came in through the back door. Vivian was in the kitchen doing dishes and putting food away in the refrigerator. Watson picked her up and whirled her around in the air. She giggled.

Teddy was gleeful. "We found them, and they are fine. They are staying overnight at the hospital in Bar Harbor. It's a joyous day ... a joyous night! Halleluiah! Where is everyone? Where is Olivia? Where is Matthew?"

"They're sitting in front of the fire in there, except for Matthew.

Matthew has never come out of his room. He's quite ill. They're all pretty down. We had a really nice dinner, and everything was going well. Then somebody turned on the short wave radio. The reports of the storm were so dire, it made everybody depressed. They will be overjoyed to hear the news."

Teddy walked into the great room and stood in front of the fireplace. Always dramatic, he raised his arms in praise. "They are safe and almost completely sound! Isabelle and J.D. are at the hospital in Bar Harbor. The doctor wanted to keep them overnight, for observation. They are fine. Dehydration is their worst problem, and both have IVs. J.D. managed to save my life and get a big gash in his head doing it. So, he's got a bunch of stitches to show off as proof of his heroism. I will never live it down. They have been through a terrible trauma, but they're both champs. I will tell you all about it."

Tears of relief and gratitude were shed, and not all of those were shed by the women. Olivia couldn't stop laughing and crying at the same time. She wanted to go to the hospital immediately, but she knew that wasn't possible. Teddy pulled up a chair, and, being the excellent raconteur that he was, he told the story of the rescue in all of its terrible and wonderful detail. He spared nothing because they wanted to know everything. He told them about the busboy peeing his pants, the waitress Rita who had alerted them to the presence of the shed in the woods and had so kindly provided thermoses of hot chocolate and chicken broth, the Gator's journey through the swamp, the doorway full of explosives, Isabelle saving Rita, J.D. saving Teddy, and the wild ride through the storm to reach the hospital.

Vivian brought champagne flutes and several bottles of chilled champagne she'd found somewhere. Somebody set up folding trays for Teddy and Watson in front of the fire, and Lilleth brought each of them a large bowl of spaghetti and meatballs and several pieces of warm garlic bread. It was a night for rejoicing. Teddy kept asking where Matthew was, and Richard told him that Matthew had pneumonia. Richard assured Teddy that he'd gone to Matthew's bedroom and, even though his friend was asleep, Richard had told him several times that

Isabelle had been found and was fine. Richard didn't know if his words had penetrated through to Matthew's consciousness.

Nobody had yet brought up the big loose end that was on everyone's mind ... Eugene Boone. Where was he and when would he be brought to justice? They were disappointed that the sheriff had not been at the Inastou to help Teddy and Watson. But they realized the storm, with its downed trees, flooded roads, roads blocked by fallen limbs, and people who needed rescuing from their homes, all took precedence over hunting for two missing persons. Everyone at Indigo Cottage was determined, however, that Chef Bonnier/Bad Boy Boone had to be found and punished.

No one was even thinking about the one important reason why they were all still here in Bar Harbor. The state police had told the group they were not allowed to leave until they had all given witness statements about Elena Petrovich's death. Captain Trimper had insisted that Cameron and Sidney fly all the way back to the East Coast to give their statements. For now, the storm raged outside, and they were completely incommunicado with the rest of the world. Teddy had fallen asleep and was snoring in his chair beside the fireplace. Somebody had tucked a blanket around him. Everyone else went off to bed. Tomorrow was only a day away, and tomorrow was another day.

It would in fact be two days before anybody from law enforcement showed up to talk about Elena or about Eugene Boone. Even though the storm still raged outside on Wednesday, Teddy drove Olivia in the Range Rover to the hospital in Bar Harbor to pick up Isabelle and J.D. When she saw her husband, Olivia threw her arms around J.D. and clung to him and wept. She tried to speak, but the words wouldn't come to her. She had been so afraid she would never see J.D. again, and to have him safely in her arms was a miracle beyond belief.

Olivia had brought clean clothes for both Isabelle and J.D., and they looked remarkably normal when they climbed into the Range Rover to drive back to Indigo Cottage. Isabelle didn't understand at first why Mathew hadn't come to the hospital with Olivia and Teddy. She'd expected her husband to be there to welcome her, and he would have been, if he hadn't been sick in bed. Olivia could see that Isabelle was very worried when she heard the news about the pneumonia.

"Pneumonia? How in the world did he get pneumonia?"

"Looking for you, like the crazy person that he is." Teddy didn't mince words. "He completely lost it when you disappeared. Everyone tried to get him to rest, to drink some water, to eat something to keep up his strength, but he was a man obsessed. He searched for you late into the night until he collapsed on the grounds behind the Inastou. Richard found him, passed out, and brought him back to Indigo Cottage. Richard called a doctor from town to come and examine him. Matt was running a fever, and the doc left antibiotics and everything Richard would need to start Matthew on an IV. Richard had to start the IV because Matthew's temperature kept rising. He was delirious for a while, but he's going to be fine. He'll be elated that you've been found, but he will be furious that somebody else actually found you. I think he was so panicked that you were missing, he wasn't thinking clearly at all. His hunting skills, at least when he was searching for you, left a great deal to be desired. But it's the thought that counts, right?" Teddy was trying to lighten the mood.

Isabelle didn't think his remark was funny. She was both touched and annoyed by her husband's frantic search for her. "He's a hunter. If the quail aren't where he is that day, he stays in the field and keeps on looking until he finds them. He's been known to keep on, even when the sun is going down." Isabelle understood better than anybody else why Matthew had searched for her until he had driven himself to the point of becoming ill. His friends might tease him for his obsession with Isabelle and his inability, a compulsion really, to give up looking for her. Isabelle understood that this was part of Matthew's personality. He was like this with everything he really cared about. His fixation on finding her was also an expression of his deep devotion to his wife. He was terrified of losing her, and he would not rest until he found her. Isabelle knew her husband well. She understood his extreme determination and his inability to give up the hunt, whether it was for the wife he adored or for the quail that he also adored.

Teddy was worried about Rita. He was ashamed that he didn't know her last name. He was concerned about whether or not she had made it home in the storm. He felt guilty that they'd not insisted she go to the hospital with them in the Range Rover, but she'd wanted to have her own car. He wondered if the busboy was still handcuffed to the Gator in the Inastou garage and if his pants had ever dried out.

Teddy had sent a text message to the sheriff about what Chef Eugene Bonier had been up to. He'd followed up his text with a long and detailed email about how they had figured out that Eugene was behind the troubles at the Inastou. Teddy explained the hostage-taking to the sheriff and told him how the hostages had been found and rescued. He gave the sheriff all the information he would need to prosecute the man. Teddy urged the sheriff to pick up and arrest Eugene Boone, and the sooner the better. He let the sheriff know about the busboy who was tethered to the Gator at the Inastou. Teddy emphasized that the busboy was complicit in an assault that could have been deadly and that charges should be filed, either in juvenile court or in adult court. That little twerp was not going to get off scot-free, if Teddy had anything to do with it.

As far as anyone knew, Chef Bonier wasn't aware he'd been exposed as the kidnapper and hostage-taker that he was. He didn't know his hostages had freed themselves and were already on their way to be reunited with their spouses and friends. Or, maybe he did know what had happened, had piled his belongings and his enormous self into his fifteen-year-old green Honda hatchback, and left town. Teddy had been emphatic with the kitchen staff at the Inastou that they must not try to contact Chef Bonier. He thought they were sufficiently frightened by what the chef had done that Teddy was pretty sure none of them would get in touch with Bonier/Boone. Teddy had sensed that they were already afraid of the chef at some level, even before they heard about the hostages he'd taken.

The Range Rover arrived back at Indigo Cottage in the middle of the afternoon. There was more champagne, and even though the former hostages might have wanted to climb into their beds and sleep for a week, they knew the others needed to see that they were all right, physically and mentally. They gathered around the fire and told their friends the story. They gave a detailed account of how they had managed to free themselves from the duct tape and the miles of rope that Eugene Boone had used to immobilize them.

Isabelle went to Matthew's room and hugged him. She told him she was fine and was there by his side. He briefly opened his eyes and smiled when he saw her standing there. Isabelle felt better and was reassured by the smile. She was certain her husband was going to recover from his illness.

Vivian and Elizabeth were in the kitchen making a special welcome-home dinner to celebrate the homecoming of the hostages. It was to be a Thanksgiving feast, complete with turkey and two kinds of stuffing, mashed potatoes, gravy, three green vegetables, three yellow vegetables, and Elizabeth's grandmother's cranberry relish. Vivian was making pies. It would be another glorious feast, served up with terrific food and with lots and lots of love and gratitude.

The others were napping or reading when there was a loud knock at the front door. It was still raining and the storm shutters were down. So who in the world was coming to the front door? It must be officials or law enforcement of some kind. Everybody else came in through the kitchen door. Tyler was sitting in his usual spot in front of the fire with his leg on a footstool, and he was closest to the door. He grabbed his crutches, and when he opened the door, he was shocked to see Bailey standing there. Bailey had been MIA for days, and although the group knew he was all right and purposely hiding out, they were relieved and delighted that his ordeal, whatever the heck it had been, was apparently over. He was back. Bailey had brought two men with him. They looked like government types to Tyler. Sure enough, the government-issue sedan was parked outside in the driveway.

Gretchen appeared in the great room and ran to embrace Bailey. She was so glad to see him, but she was also furious with him. "Bailey MacDermott, you are going to tell me, right now, exactly where you have been and what you have been doing. I've been worried sick. Why do you do this to me?" She ignored the two men who had come into the house with Bailey. "Start talking!"

Bailey introduced the two men he'd brought with him. They were from the U.S. Department of the Treasury. They'd brought Bailey to Indigo Cottage and were there to help him explain to his wife why he'd disappeared for a few days. Bailey knew that Gretchen was upset and wouldn't forgive him until he'd told her everything.

Chapter 32

"It's a long and involved story. I don't know how much you all know about money laundering." Bailey looked around and saw that every face was eager to hear what he had to say, so he continued. "I know more than I'd really like to know about money laundering, because I deal in commercial real estate." Tyler nodded his head. Pretty much retired now from the buying and selling aspects of the commercial real estate business, Tyler, too, had run up against plenty of money laundering schemes in his day.

"These gentlemen from the Treasury Department have given me the okay to share my latest adventure with you. It will all eventually come out in federal court proceedings, so it's not like I'm telling you anything that's top secret. In other words, I'm not going to say anything that will get any of us in trouble." The attentive faces wanted him to get on with it.

"As some of you may know, years ago, before I ever met Gretchen, I was involved in a money laundering court case. I put the finger on a guy who was trying to use me and a real estate deal I was setting up for him, to launder millions of dollars. I reported him to law enforcement and ended up testifying against Sato Nakamura. Partly as a result of my testimony, he was sentenced to twenty years in prison for his attempts to defraud. The charges against him included the transaction that I reported and testified about, as well as other activities the feds uncovered when they investigated him. I hadn't thought about Nakamura in years, and if I had, I would have assumed he was still serving his prison sentence."

Baily's audience was hanging on every word, and he continued. "When I walked through the lobby at the Bar Harbor Inn on Saturday afternoon, I saw a man I thought I recognized. I was almost sure it was Nakamura but didn't think it could be because he was supposed to be in jail. But it was the crook from Indonesia. With prison overcrowding and the fact that his was a white collar crime, some judge had decided he was not a threat to the public and released him early. After I testified against him in court, Nakamura threatened to track me down and kill me. So when I first saw him, I thought he'd come after me. I overheard him talking to the desk clerk at the Bar Harbor Inn. He was getting directions to the Inastou Lodge. When I heard that, I was convinced he'd followed me to Maine and intended to kill me because of my testimony years ago. I was frightened and didn't want him to see me. I hid in the cloak room for a while, and then I decided to get a room at the Bar Harbor Inn. If Nakamura was headed for the Inastou, I knew I couldn't go back there. I left a note for Gretchen on our rental car. I didn't want to go into details, but I told her I was hiding out. I didn't want her to worry about me. I know she, and probably the rest of you, thought I'd gone completely nuts. And I almost thought so myself at first. I hated to miss the fun you all were having, and I wanted more than anything to go to the Down East Café. It's my favorite restaurant in the area. That's why I showed up at the restaurant in a disguise, and I admit that was pretty stupid. I'm not sorry I did it because I really craved their Lobster Newberg. I know I didn't win any points with my wife for my appearance that night." Bailey glanced at Gretchen and winced. "So, moving on …."

Bailey continued his explanation about money laundering. "There are as many schemes for money laundering as there are money launderers. The basic goal is to exchange 'dirty money' for 'clean money.' Dirty money comes from some kind of illegal activity, usually drugs, but it can also come from prostitution, gambling, human trafficking, or some other nefarious endeavor. And it's cash. If someone has buckets of cash and tries to deposit it in a regular bank account, alarms will sound all over the place. The feds will be on the bank's doorstep in seconds.

"The person with all the illicit cash has to find a way to 'clean' their ill-gotten gains. There are countless schemes for exchanging dirty money for clean money. Many with ill-gotten cash choose to do this through real estate deals. If we are talking millions of dollars, expensive real estate is a great way to launder money — if the person with the cash can find a co-conspirator who will make a deal with them."

Bailey looked around and saw that his friends were still interested in his story. "I'm going to tell you what Sato Nakamura's scheme was for laundering money here in Bar Harbor. A real world example is much easier to follow. Nakamura is not a drug dealer. He's a middle man. He works for the drug dealer or the person who runs the prostitution ring, to clean their money. He finds a client with clean money or real estate who is willing to do a deal.

"Nakamura found someone in Bar Harbor who had a bunch of older condominiums for sale. The condos are not in great shape and need work. They've been on the market for almost two years, and the seller hasn't had many potential buyers show an interest. The asking price for the condos was too high. The seller needed to get his money out of the property, so when he was approached by Nakamura, he was willing to do business. Nakamura offered to pay the owner of the condos two million dollars more than the condos were actually worth. It was a great deal for the guy who was selling the condos, and it was a great deal for Nakamura's client. The seller of the condos will be paid an inflated price, way too much money really, for his property. Here's the tricky part of the deal. How does he accept the cash from the buyer at the closing? The payment for the real estate could be in the form of actual cash, maybe in hundred dollar bills in a suitcase. The seller could, theoretically, accept this large suitcase full of cash at the settlement table. He could drive directly to the airport and fly to the Cayman Islands or to Switzerland to deposit the money in a numbered bank account. That is a very risky way to transact business, and whoever chooses this method might very well be arrested before he gets out the door of the real estate agent's office.

"Or, the cash could be converted into several cashier's checks. Once again though, it is very difficult to take a duffle bag of cash into a bank and convert it into cashier's checks. The critical step and the most difficult part to accomplish in the money-laundering process is to somehow manage to deposit the dirty cash into a bank account where it can be turned into cashier's checks or transferred electronically.

"As you can imagine, the help of an unscrupulous banker would be of inestimable value in getting the questionable cash into a bank account. The cash would be deposited into his bank, and it would never be reported as cash. It would just be reported as a regular deposit, and it would never be reported in any official accounting the bank does to governmental agencies. The crooked banker sets up the bank account for his crooked clients and issues electronic funds transfers, EFTs from the account.

"Another useful ruse in the money-laundering world, for the person who needs to clean up their money, is to buy or use a legitimate business that routinely deals in cash. This might be a laundromat, ha ha, that requires quarters and other cash to use its machines. Another example of a cash business would be a casino. Owners of laundromats and casinos are expected to deposit large amounts of cash into their bank accounts. A gas station and convenience store, a company that owns and services vending machines, or a car wash would be examples of other businesses that deal in lots of cash.

"A professional money launderer like Nakamura has probably set up a number of dummy corporations, inside the United States and in other countries around the world. These are companies that don't do anything or make anything. They are incorporated for the sole purpose of laundering money. They are vehicles for turning dirty money into clean money. They take in the cash, deposit it into their bank accounts, and report the deposits as income from their non-existent business. In some countries, there is no oversight about where the money comes from that flows into these dummy companies' bank accounts. Cash from dealing drugs or prostitution can be deposited into the bank account of a bogus LLC in a number of foreign countries. These pretend companies transfer funds electronically from their bank accounts all around the world as needed.

"When the real estate settlement takes place, electronic transfers are used to pay for the multi-million dollar property and might come in from a bank account in Tokyo that is owned by one of these dummy corporations, an investment account in Singapore that is also owned by a dummy corporation, and so on. You get the picture. There are many layers in the transactions, and the electronic transfers might have been combined and split up and combined again many times before the final transfer of funds arrives at the settlement table. The point is to clean the money and make it untraceable.

"The most likely scenario is that the money at the settlement table would be in the form of one or more electronic funds transfers, EFTs. With today's global economy and the digital age, business deals and large transfers of funds across international borders are not unusual. The goal is to get the money into the seller's account. When this has been accomplished, the deal is done, and the seller has just made a bundle on his crappy condos.

"The client, who has purchased the property at an inflated price through Nakamura, now owns a building of old condominiums. They aren't worth what he paid for them, but the buyer doesn't care. He cares that they are clean. They are a real commodity, not cash. Nakamura has traded seven million dollars in dirty money for five million dollars' worth of clean real estate. The client who has purchased the condos turns around and puts them on the market for a realistic price. He or she sells the condos and gets five million dollars in clean money. He has traded seven million in drug money for five million that he can now legitimately claim as proceeds from selling the condos.

"It can get complicated and happens in an infinite number of convoluted ways. In this case, Nakamura had his daughter acting as his front man — in this case, his front woman. She has a different last name from Nakamura, and no doubt she has multiple false identities.

"Nakamura's daughter buys the condos from the man who was originally selling them. Then the daughter resells them at a lower price, and the proceeds from the second sale go to the drug dealer who wanted to get rid of his seven million dollars in dirty cash. The clean money proceeds go to the drug dealer, the client. The final payment would probably amount to about four million dollars, after Nakamura deducts his fee for laundering the money. Some drug dealers launder their own money. Some hire middle men like Nakamura to do it for them. Nakamura used his daughter in this transaction because he has a prison record. The real estate/money laundering arrangement is a family affair for the Nakamuras."

"What does this have to do with you, Bailey? I don't see how you got involved with all of this." Elizabeth asked the question that everyone wanted answered.

"That's the fascinating part, and that's how I got involved with my Treasury buddies here. I had to know what Nakamura was doing here in Bar Harbor. I followed him, and he never mentioned my name or asked anybody about me. Since he didn't seem to be interested in me, I came to the conclusion that he wasn't here to kill me. But, as I was following him, I figured out that he was in Bar Harbor to do a deal, to buy real estate for a client. The leopard doesn't change its spots. I saw him meeting with a local real estate broker, and then I saw him talking to a person I found out was interested in selling a property. That property was the older condos that had been on the market for ages. I made some discreet inquiries. The guy trying to sell the condos was in financial trouble. He'd mortgaged and remortgaged the condos several times. The property was so heavily leveraged, it wasn't possible to reduce the price too much. The owner was getting desperate. He was the perfect co-conspirator for the money laundering scheme.

"I contacted somebody I knew who used to be connected with law enforcement in Texas. He's now retired, but he'd been involved in Nakamura's case from years ago and helped to put him in jail. My guy in Texas contacted the Treasury Department, and the Treasury Department contacted me at the Bar Harbor Inn. I explained what I thought was going on, and Treasury talked to the real estate broker who was putting together the deal between Nakamura's daughter and the guy who was selling his condos. It all happened very quickly. Because the settlement was scheduled for today, my friends from Treasury had to move fast.

"Texas has a lot of money laundering going on, so honest real estate people are more likely to spot it there. Bar Harbor is a sleepy, resort town. Real estate people here are used to the very rich buying properties at outrageous prices. Rich people are willing to buy places above market value because they fall in love with a place, want to invest their money in something, or have more money than they know what to do with. It really is an untapped market, partly because the real estate people up here in Maine are not looking out for money laundering schemes. They're used to buyers being willing to overpay for a piece of real estate. And, of course, the higher the sales price, the bigger commission the real estate agent gets.

"The real estate agent in Bar Harbor was not in cahoots with the Nakamuras. The agent was new in real estate and just starting her business. She was young and naïve, an unwitting and innocent party in the transaction. I'm sure the Nakamuras chose her to handle the deal because of her youth and inexperience. They figured she wasn't savvy about money laundering. Once Treasury approached her and told her what they suspected was going on, she was very cooperative and did everything she could to help reel in Nakamura and his daughter. When everybody showed up at the settlement today, and the transaction to buy the condos for seven million dollars was completed, the buyer and the seller were both arrested. Nakamura wasn't present at the settlement, but the Treasury guys knew he was staying at the Inastou and had been keeping tabs on him. I am delighted to tell you that Sato Nakamura, or whatever name he is going by this week, and his daughter are both in federal custody. The money was confiscated, and all the guilty parties have been charged with conspiring to launder money. So now you know." Bailey was tremendously relieved that the whole thing was finally over.

"I was trying to lay low and stay out of sight until the transaction was completed and the principals were arrested. I couldn't take a chance that Nakamura would see me in the area. My advisors from the federal government were afraid Nakamura would freak out if he happened to see me hanging out up here in Bar Harbor. They were worried he would go to ground or cancel the deal if he caught sight of me. He's operating in a new geographic area, because he's known in Texas. He's using his daughter to buy the properties, because he has a prison record."

The two Treasury officials had been silent and allowed Bailey to tell his story his own way. One of them now spoke up. "Mrs. MacDermott, we know you were very worried about Bailey, and we know you are angry with him for disappearing and going into hiding. We know you're angry because he didn't let you know what was going on. He was very concerned about that, but we were the ones who insisted that he communicate with you only occasionally and always very cryptically. He was acting on our instructions. Bailey helped us put a very corrupt bunch of people out of business, and we are grateful that he contacted us and assisted us in our sting. I know this was hard on you, but Bailey was just doing what we told him to do. Please forgive him."

The expression on Gretchen's face softened a little bit. She looked at her husband with fondness, shook her head, and said, "I forgive you, Bailey. But don't you ever do anything like this again, ever! You have to promise me." Bailey smiled and promised her. But he knew, if given the chance, he would do it all over again in a microsecond.

The two Treasury officials were invited to stay for dinner, but they graciously declined. They shook hands with Bailey and left the group to their gathering of thanks. It was time for cocktails, and dinner would be ready shortly. It was Thanksgiving in September. They had much to be thankful for, and everybody knew it. Even Matthew, as weak as he still was, had dressed and made his way to the dining table to sit next to Isabelle. Richard Carpenter gave a heartfelt blessing of gratitude, for the safe return of the hostages, for Matthew's improved health, for Bailey's return, for the help of all who had contributed to finding their missing friends, and for the absent Rita. Richard said a special prayer for Darryl's recovery. The men cared about their friend who had been involved in a dangerous and risky relationship. Everyone said "amen" when Richard prayed that he would recover from his shock and grief and from the effects of the stroke.

They ate their wonderful turkey dinner with two kinds of stuffing — Yankee stuffing made from regular bread and Southern stuffing made from cornbread. They drank wine and told their stories. Matthew hadn't heard the details about how his wife and J.D. had been rescued. The group insisted on a retelling of Isabelle's and J.D.'s escape. Their friends were once again captivated by the descriptions they gave of how they'd freed themselves from captivity. As Vivian began to bring out the desserts, there was a knock at the door. It was Cameron and Sidney. A cheer went up all around the table as they walked into the great room. Their plane had been able to land in Bangor, and they had driven the rest of the way. Vivian had been expecting three people, but the pilot had decided to stay in Bangor with the plane. Two more places were laid, plates and glasses were filled and refilled, and the guest list at Indigo Cottage was complete.

Chapter 33

WATSON HAD TOLD EVERYONE GOODBYE THE night before, and Teddy drove him to the airport in the morning. Watson had to fly back to Nova Scotia to resume filming on his hit TV show. Shooting on the Showtime series had been interrupted because of the storm, but now that the sun had reappeared, Watson had to go back to work. The lawyer turned actor knew he would probably have to return to Bar Harbor to make a statement to the authorities. Because he was an attorney, he thought maybe a long-distance deposition would satisfy the sheriff and the courts. If he did come back to Bar Harbor, he hoped the sheriff had captured and charged Eugene Boone by then.

Teddy had decided to stay in Bar Harbor with his old friends for another day or two. Teddy was advising the production company in Nova Scotia about the historic buildings in Shelburne County, the site where the current episode of *How to Live Forever* was being filmed. The series involved time-travel, both backward into the past and forward into the future. Teddy knew everything there was to know about historic buildings. He was the architectural historian who made sure the buildings the production company used in their exterior shots were from the correct time periods. Teddy would have to return to the set in a couple of days.

The rain had finally stopped, and the sun was out. Most roads were still covered with water, and the air was cold and uncomfortably damp.

But the storm was over, and law enforcement was beating a path to the door of Indigo Cottage in droves. First to arrive was Sheriff Carney Dodd with two deputies in tow. Dodd wanted to interview everyone who'd ever known Eugene Boone, even those who'd only known him when he was a kid. The sheriff also wanted to take detailed statements from those who had participated in the search for and rescue of the hostages. Most of all, he wanted to interview Isabelle and J.D.

His deputies would hold their interviews in the Indigo Cottage library. To insure some privacy, he insisted that the heavy wooden folding doors between the library and the great room be closed. With the recent wet weather and given that the doors had probably not been closed in many years, the doors protested mightily. They creaked and groaned and refused to budge. With some WD-40 on the hinges and a little elbow grease, the doors finally yielded to the sheriff's wishes. Elizabeth wondered what all the secrecy was about since they'd shared everything with each other and talked over every detail multiple times during the past several days. The sheriff had arrived very late to the party, but the group members were respectful of the law. Carney Dodd would call his witnesses one at a time.

But Teddy had questions for the sheriff and insisted on speaking to the man before the interviews began. "Please tell me you have Eugene Boone in custody."

The sheriff had the grace to look chagrined. "No, we haven't been able to locate Chef Bonier. We've had an APB out for him and his Honda hatchback since I received your email late Tuesday night, but so far we've had no sightings."

Teddy gave the sheriff a hard look. "Tell me you have arrested and charged the busboy from the Inastou."

"We have charged him, and he's out on bond. He's a good kid, and his parents have promised to keep an eye on him." It was a small town, and Sheriff Carney Dodd knew the busboy's family.

Teddy was incensed. "He's not a 'good kid,' Sheriff. Just because you know and like his parents doesn't diminish the seriousness of the crimes he's committed. I will not tolerate your failure to prosecute him. I am already in the process of having my lawyer prepare a civil suit against the boy. He needs to be taught a lesson. He did a very, very bad thing."

The sheriff was clearly on the side of "boys will be boys," but he could see that he was not going to be able to convince this crowd to go for any degree of leniency. Teddy knew that J.D. would hold the sheriff's feet to the fire when they had the chance to bring a multi-million dollar lawsuit against the boy.

"You have to find Boone as soon as possible. I think everyone here is at risk for their lives until you have him locked up. Have you even been to his house?" Teddy was not going to let the sheriff off the hook.

"Somebody is going over there today. We didn't know where Boone lived, and then we couldn't get there because of the storm."

"You didn't help us out much when it came to rescuing our friends. Have you seen the explosives Boone prepared for whoever tried to enter that shed where he was holding them hostage?"

"I personally haven't been to the scene, but we have a forensics team from Bangor there this morning, collecting evidence." The sheriff had not, in fact, done anything at all so far. He was blaming his lack of progress on the storm.

Teddy snorted, gave the sheriff a disgusted look, and left the library. He was angry that Boone wasn't in custody and angry that Carney Dodd wasn't taking the busboy's part in the crimes more seriously. Because Teddy was going to have to leave to return to Nova Scotia, he wanted to be the first person the sheriff interviewed. He walked back into the library, presented himself to the sheriff again, and insisted that the sheriff talk to him. If he were the first witness, Teddy knew he would be able to help Dodd and help the inquiry. He swallowed his anger and made the decision to do everything he possibly could to help Sheriff Carney Dodd catch Eugene Boone.

The next knock on the front door came from the FBI. When Teddy answered the door, he didn't know why they'd come at all. He had missed the murder of the Russian in the Inastou parking lot, and that's what the FBI was there to talk about. Somebody official had discovered what everybody else already knew, that the mystery man, who had died from three gunshot wounds, was a Russian national. The FBI had taken over jurisdiction of the case. Sheriff Dodd had told the FBI where to find Elena's friends. The feds set up for their interviews in one corner of the great room. They wanted to interview everyone who had been on the back porch of the Inastou the night of the argument between Elena Petrovich and the now-dead Russian man. Interviewing Elena, the person they would most like to have been able to question, was now impossible.

The FBI took statements from everyone who had witnessed the argument between the two Russians. They questioned Tyler for almost an hour and spent an even longer time talking to Gretchen. Both Tyler and Gretchen had confidential information they would share only with the FBI. The special agents took a long time with Richard Carpenter, who in turn had questions for them. The FBI also wanted information from him about Elena Petrovich's death at the Cuban restaurant, and because he was a physician and had spent time working in the Philadelphia Medical Examiner's Office, they knew his testimony would be dependable. Because both people who had argued in the parking lot on Saturday night were now deceased, the Bar Harbor piece of the investigation did not have any place to go. The FBI, of course, knew much more about the dead Russian man, and probably much more about Elena Petrovich, than they were willing to share with anybody.

Richard knew his friends would want to know as much as he was able to find out, and he turned on all of his considerable charm with the investigators. He asked as many questions as he thought he could get away with. The FBI, as they always do, was holding everything very close to the vest. Richard concluded that, because they seemed to know so little about the Russian and why he was in the United States, the final result of the investigation into his murder would undoubtedly be "death by person or persons unknown."

If Elena hadn't killed the Russian, Richard was sorry, for his friend Darryl's sake, that the real killer might never be found. Failure to solve the case would forever leave some question about whether or not Elena had done it. The possibility that she was the murderer would, by default, hang over her head and impugn her reputation. Richard knew that Elena had never liked him, but he didn't want her to be blamed for something she didn't do. She wasn't alive to defend herself. Richard didn't want to believe Elena had shot the Russian, but it was always a possibility.

The two FBI agents finished their interviews, and Vivian invited them to stay for lunch. She had a pot of vegetable beef soup and a pot of turkey soup with wild rice on the stove. She'd made an enormous plate of sandwiches — turkey, ham and cheese, and tuna fish. Everyone had been smelling the soup all morning, and the FBI agents were not able to resist accepting her invitation. Even federal investigators have to eat. Sheriff Dodd and his two deputies also joined the group for lunch. Vivian was the consummate diplomat, and her delicious food worked better to smooth ruffled feathers than all the conciliatory words in the world. Any hostile feelings the law enforcement people might have had toward the group at Indigo Cottage were mostly put to rest after one of Vivian's lunches.

The FBI agents were gracious, and without revealing anything they considered to be classified, they particularly praised Tyler and Gretchen. The federal agents said they'd been waiting to hear from FBI headquarters in order to positively identify the man who'd been killed at the Inastou. The verification from Washington had been slow to arrive and was still uncertain. But because Tyler and Gretchen had both been able to independently give the man an identity and a nationality, the investigation was on much more solid ground than it otherwise would have been. Their information had moved things forward more quickly because the agents had not been required to wait to make an identification or depend on information being processed at their bureaucratic headquarters.

Gretchen took the praise in stride. It was just another part of the day's work for her. Tyler was especially gratified that he'd been able to make a contribution. He was used to being constantly active, on the go, and the first one to rise to any occasion. He was used to taking the lead and leading the charge. Because of his ankle and the crutches, he was having a difficult time sitting on the sidelines. He was delighted that his memory and his brain had been able to help, while his physical self was temporarily out of commission.

The third group of law enforcement officials arrived in the early afternoon. This pair, Captain Dryden Trimper and Detective Creighton Laurence of the Maine State Police, were already known to some of those staying at Indigo Cottage. The state policemen had come to ask questions about the night of Elena Petrovich's death at Cuba LIbre. They had already conducted a few interviews at the Inastou Lodge on Monday. They were delighted to hear, they said, that the two missing friends had been found. Vivian had finished cleaning up the kitchen from lunch, so Trimper decided to conduct his interviews there.

Even Bailey was not exempt from Captain Trimper's scrutiny. Trimper wanted to know why Bailey had not been with the rest of the group at dinner Sunday night. Where had he been and what had he been doing? After interviewing everyone about that night, Trimper announced that the next afternoon, there was going to be a reenactment of sorts. They all groaned. Cameron and Sidney were ready to leave town. Gretchen needed to get back to her office.

But the Captain was adamant. He said that for him to get an accurate idea about what had happened that night, they had to actually show him. He wanted to see where each person was sitting at the table. He wanted to know what each person had ordered for all courses of the dinner, as well as what they had ordered to drink. He had arranged with the restaurant's manager for everyone to be at Cuba Libre the next afternoon at 2:00. They had to be finished and out of the restaurant before 5:00. Tomorrow night was Friday night, the biggest night in the restaurant business everywhere, including at Cuba Libre.

Teddy had never met Elena, and he was finally able to convince Captain Trimper that he wasn't needed for the Cuba Libre demonstration. Teddy had hoped to stay in Bar Harbor until Eugene Boone was securely in jail, and he was disappointed the chef hadn't been apprehended. It didn't look like that was going to happen in the next day or two. Teddy would call Watson to pick him up the next morning.

Sheriff Dodd's crew was the last to leave. Just as they were about to go out the door, Dodd's phone rang. Teddy was walking them out, and the conversation the sheriff was having caught his attention.

"You've found his car parked at his house, right?" Teddy asked the sheriff.

The sheriff had been going to say he wasn't able to comment about an ongoing investigation, but when he saw the expression on Teddy's face, the sheriff decided not to say that. "Yes, they've been to Eugene Boone's cabin, and his Honda hatchback is parked there. Boone, however, is nowhere to be found."

"That means he's got another car and probably left town a long time ago. When was the last time anybody saw him? Have you talked to the people at the Inastou?" Teddy wanted answers.

"The dining room was closed all day Wednesday. The storm was just too severe, and none of the employees could make it in to work. Boone was off on Tuesday, as you know, so nobody has seen him since Monday. The dining room reopened today, but Boone never showed up this morning. A waitress, a Rita somebody, who was supposed to work today hasn't shown up either. According to the general manager, Rita has been working at the Inastou for a long time, and she's the most dependable of all the waitresses."

"Wait, you're saying that Rita's missing, and she didn't report for work today?"

"That's what the GM was telling me. He's concerned. She's never late and never misses a day."

"I'm concerned, too. We sent Rita off in her Neon Tuesday night when we shouldn't have. We should have driven her to the hospital to have her sprained ankle looked at in the ER. She wouldn't go with us in the Range Rover because she didn't want to be without her car. I'm worried that she might have driven off the road in the storm and is stranded somewhere. Can you give me her address? I hate it that I don't know her last name."

The sheriff got Rita's home address from the Inastou and gave it to Teddy. Teddy was out the door before the sheriff could put his cell phone back into his pocket.

Chapter 34

Rita's neon wasn't parked outside her house. There was a dog pen at the side of the small bungalow, but the pen was empty. Teddy had a bad feeling. He knocked on the front door, but there wasn't any answer. No dogs barked. He went around to the back door and looked through the glass panes into the kitchen. What he saw there brought him close to panic. The kitchen chairs were turned over. Cups and plates were broken, and other kitchen utensils were lying helter skelter all over the floor and kitchen counters. Pots and pans of food were overturned. The place was a mess. There had clearly been an altercation in the room. The back door was unlocked, and Teddy let himself into Rita's house.

He yelled for Rita. "Rita, are you here? It's Teddy Sullivan, from the other night. You helped us find our friends in the shed on the Inastou grounds. I'm coming into the house to look for you." There wasn't any response to his shouting, and he dreaded what he would find. She was lying on the floor in one of the bedrooms. She'd been tied up and gagged. The duct tape wrapped around her head looked like what had been used on Isabelle and J.D. Teddy knelt beside her and felt for a pulse. She had one. He called 911 and told them where to send the ambulance. He sat down next to Rita, intending to remain there until the ambulance arrived. He loosened her bonds and held her hand. Her eyes opened, and she looked up at him.

"My dogs. He drugged them, tied them up, and threw them down the basement stairs. They're down there now. Please, go see if they're still alive. He may have killed them. I love my dogs. They are everything to me. I'm okay. He just wanted my car. He threatened to kill my dogs if I didn't give him the keys. Please, go and see about the dogs."

"What are their names, Rita? I will go right now to the basement and see about them."

"They are 'Teddy' and 'Bea.'" Rita gave Teddy Sullivan a small, sheepish smile, but Teddy just chuckled.

"I'll bet that Teddy is a real cutie."

"He is for sure. Check on them, please. Chef drugged them both and tied them up. My dogs are my family, you know." Teddy Sullivan could tell Rita's concern for her dogs was deeply felt. He was suffering some guilt because he realized his pursuit of Boone was responsible for Rita's being hurt and her dogs being threatened. He'd involved her in this predicament. If it hadn't been for her, they might not have found Isabelle and J.D. in time. Teddy felt as if he'd inadvertently dragged her into the search, and he knew he owed her. He also felt guilty because he wished he'd been more insistent that she go with them to the hospital on Tuesday night. Teddy wondered how Eugene Boone had become aware that he was in trouble and that the sheriff was after him. He'd somehow learned the authorities were looking for his car and realized he needed a different one. Figuring out who'd tipped him off would have to wait.

Teddy hated to leave Rita's side, but he knew she wanted to know about her dogs. He unlocked the front door for the emergency responders and hurried down the basement steps. He found an enormous Bernese Mountain dog and a tiny Pomeranian lying on the floor. They were both tied up like Rita had been tied up, with lots of rope and miles of duct tape. The Bernese was clearly very angry and struggling to get out of her bonds. The Pomeranian wasn't moving. Teddy cut the rope and duct tape away from both dogs with his pocket knife. He tried not to pull out too much of their hair when he ripped off the tape.

The Bernese was fine, but the Pomeranian was limp. Teddy didn't know how to find a pulse on a dog, and he was afraid the little dog was dead. The Bernese began to nudge the smaller dog with her nose. She licked and nudged and whined, and after a few seconds, the little dog moved. But it wasn't good. Teddy picked up the little one and carried it up the basement steps. The big dog followed right behind him.

The EMTs were coming through the front door. Teddy told them where to go, and they rushed to Rita's aid. He followed them, holding the little Pomeranian named Teddy in his arms. Rita was being hooked up to an IV, and the EMTs said she was going to be all right. All she wanted to know about was her dogs. The huge Bernese, Bea, was obviously okay, but she told Teddy to rush the Pom to the vet. Rita knew the vet's address by heart, and the office was only two blocks down the road. In less than a minute, they were on their way. Teddy shouted over his shoulder that he would meet Rita at the hospital ER.

Bea wasn't about to allow the human Teddy or the canine Teddy to get away without her, and she jumped into the Range Rover's passenger seat with the unconscious Pom. The vet attended to the little dog immediately. She obviously knew the canine Teddy well and called an assistant to help her. After several minutes of working with the little dog, the vet told Teddy Sullivan that Rita's Teddy was going to make it. The vet wanted to keep the Pomeranian overnight to be sure he was okay.

Bea and Teddy Sullivan left the vet's office and were on their way to Mount Desert Island Hospital. Teddy was eager to see and talk to Rita. He wanted to assure her that her little Pomeranian was going to be all right, and he wanted to ask her about her interactions with Eugene Boone. If Boone had taken her car, no wonder the green hatchback had been left behind at Boone's cabin. Law enforcement's APB/BOLO had described the wrong car and given out the wrong license plate number. Teddy realized he didn't even know what color Rita's Neon was. How far away would Eugene be by now?

Rita had been admitted to the hospital, and Teddy Sullivan went to see her in her room. She was hooked up to an IV and all kinds of monitors. Teddy told her about the dogs, and he could see she was already better after hearing the good news. Then a shadow crossed her face. "Can you take Bea to a kennel overnight? I will be out of here by tomorrow, and the vet will keep Teddy until I can pick him up."

"Don't worry about Bea. I have the perfect place for her. It's the least I can do. I'll be sure Bea is well taken care of until you are out of the hospital." Rita's shoulders relaxed.

"You want to know about Chef and why he came after me, but I don't really know why he did. My best guess is that Chef has a police radio. Maybe somebody on the kitchen staff disobeyed your orders and told him what was going on. Or maybe the busboy that helped him with his crimes sent him a text. I made it home all right on Tuesday night, after we rescued your friends. The roads were flooded, and I couldn't see anything with the rain pouring down. Driving was almost impossible, but I don't live that far from the Inastou. Even so, it was very scary. I didn't try to go in to work on Wednesday. It was too treacherous to be out on the roads, even for the little ways I had to drive. Then Wednesday night, Chef comes pounding on my door. I didn't know who it could possibly be, outside my house in the driving rain and wind. When I opened the door to see who was there, Chef pushed his way inside. I'd have kept him out if I could have. I'd seen the evil he could do, and I was frightened to find him at my door."

"Why did he come to your house? How did he find out the authorities were looking for him? Did he know his hostages had been rescued?"

"I think he came to my house because I live close to the Inastou. I don't know where he lives. He had to have walked to my house so he must live close to me. He's very overweight, and I can't imagine he walked very far, especially in the storm. I don't know if he'd found out the hostages had been rescued, and I don't think he knew I was the one who told you about the shed in the woods. He never mentioned any of that. But he knew there was an ABP out for him and his green hatchback. That's what makes me think he has a police radio at his house. That must be how he knew the sheriff was looking for his Honda."

"I hadn't thought of a police radio, but that makes sense. He must know the hostages have been found, if he knows the sheriff is after him. But he might not know they were found alive. He might think he succeeded in letting them die there in that Godforsaken shed."

"Like I said, he never mentioned the hostages to me, and I certainly didn't bring it up. He wanted my car. He threatened me. I didn't want to give him the keys, but he said he would kill my dogs. He knew they were important to me because I was always talking about them at work. He had a hypodermic needle and said he was going to kill them with drugs. I begged him, and I finally had to give him the keys to my car. He tied me up and then he tied up the dogs. Then he threw them down the basement steps. I didn't think Teddy could survive that. I was sure he was dead. I thought Bea would make it, if anyone came in time to feed her and give her water."

"Both dogs are going to be fine. When I took Teddy in, the vet gave Bea water and food and checked her over, too. Now, you only have to worry about you."

"I'm sorry I gave the keys to Chef, but I didn't have a choice. He took my cell phone, too. I was tied up and couldn't call anybody, anyway."

"Give me a description of your car and the license plate number. I'm going to call the sheriff while I'm here with you in case he has any questions. He needs to know to look for your car and to put out a new APB." Teddy called the sheriff and gave him the details about what had happened to Rita. He gave Dodd the details about Rita's white Neon. Rita had drifted off to sleep while he'd been on his cell phone with the sheriff. Teddy Sullivan slipped quietly out of her hospital room.

He had to leave the next morning to go back to Nova Scotia. He'd wanted Eugene Boone in custody and on his way to a long prison term before he left Maine. That wasn't going to happen. Teddy felt like he'd done all he could do to motivate the sheriff to try to capture Eugene. Since Boone had now attacked, not just a couple of tourists, but Rita, who was a local person, Teddy was hoping the sheriff might try harder to bring Boone to justice.

The sheriff had assured him that Rita's house and the Boone/Bonier house were both being investigated as crime scenes, whatever that meant in this town where apparently no crimes were ever committed. Rita would not be able to go back to her house for a couple of days, so Teddy would have to talk to Vivian about that. He knew his friends were grateful to Rita and would be happy to host her and her dogs at Indigo Cottage.

Teddy hadn't had a lobster yet, and he'd been in Maine for three days. On his way home from the hospital, he stopped off at a favorite lobster pound for a solitary dinner and joined his friends back at Indigo Cottage for dessert. He told them all about Rita and the dogs, everything he knew about the hunt for Eugene Boone, and everything he'd said to the sheriff. He was sorry he couldn't stay, but he had a job he had to get back to. Everyone was sorry to see him leave, and they would be forever grateful that he'd helped to find Isabelle and J.D.

Bea was welcomed with great enthusiasm. Vivian loved dogs and was already spoiling the Bernese. The group would take good care of Bea until Rita was back on her feet. The next morning, Vivian would get the guest quarters that were attached to the garage, the rooms where Teddy and Watson had been staying, ready for Rita and her dogs. Richard and J.D. would pick up Rita at the hospital when she was discharged. J.D. had really never had the chance to thank Rita for her role in saving his life.

The group of friends at Indigo Cottage were not looking forward to the next day. They were going to have to meet Captain Trimper at Cuba Libre and relive what had happened the night of Elena's death. Nobody wanted to do that. They'd all hoped they would never again have to enter the restaurant as long as they lived. Matthew was stronger, but he wasn't completely back to his usual energetic self. He'd tried to beg off participating in the Cuba Libre drama, but Captain Trimper was having none of it. Everyone had to be there. No exceptions.

Teddy Sullivan drove to the airport early the next morning. Watson was flying in to take him back to Nova Scotia. The mood around Indigo Cottage was gloomy. Richard and J.D. collected Rita and brought her back before lunch to meet everybody. Rita's ankle was taped, and she was limping and using a cane. The encounter with Eugene Boone had not been a positive thing for her already-injured ankle. Bea was overcome with joy to welcome her mistress. Rita's arrival was the bright spot in the day, and everyone expressed their gratitude for her part in the hostage recovery. Vivian produced another wonderful lunch, to give them strength, she said, for their afternoon ordeal. Rita told the group about the attack by Chef Bonier, but meeting all the new people and recounting her story exhausted her. She needed to rest, and Vivian took her and Bea to the guest house to settle in. Vivian knew Rita's vet and volunteered to pick up the Pomeranian later that afternoon.

The weather had grown colder. None of them had brought the heavy coats, scarves, and gloves these unexpectedly chilly early October temperatures required. Everyone was cranky and angry that the sheriff was putting them through what they all considered to be a charade. They wondered if his motive really was, as he'd said, to gain a better understanding of what had happened that night. Some wondered if he was hoping to spook or scare somebody into a confession with his theatrics. Could he possibly believe that one of them had murdered Elena?

It wasn't a surprise to anybody that Elena had been poisoned. Richard had spoken with the medical examiner and confirmed it, but anybody who'd been in the restaurant that night and watched Elena die, had to know she'd died from poison. The ME wouldn't reveal exactly what poison had killed her, and Richard hadn't been able to find out that information. The general consensus of opinion was that Elena's death was connected to the death of the Russian mystery man who'd been shot at the Inastou. That murder had happened just the night before Elena died, and the two had been arguing publicly and loudly. Elena was Russian, and everyone who knew her suspected that she had something secret in her past that she didn't want to talk about. Two people had died in almost the same location in two days. They were both Russians. Why wouldn't these deaths be related? Why was there any need to bring the rest of the Camp Shoemaker friends and their wives and girlfriends into the whole thing? The opinion of those who didn't want to go back to Cuba Libre, which was everybody, was that Elena's death didn't have anything to do with the rest of them, and the sheriff needed to turn the case over to the FBI.

Darryl wouldn't be at Cuba Libre that afternoon. He'd been transferred to a long-term care and rehabilitation facility where he was receiving treatment and therapy for the effects of his stroke. Nobody knew exactly how bad the stroke had been or what his current medical condition was. Because of HIPAA, it wasn't possible to find out that kind of medical information about anyone, unless you were next of kin or on a list of those who were privy to such information. Darryl didn't have a list, or if he did, none of the reunion group was on it. Richard was going to try to pull some strings to find out something, but so far, he'd not been able to learn much of anything.

In cases of murder, the amateur sleuths in the group speculated, the first person the police usually suspect is the spouse or partner. Elena's spouse would not be at the meeting this afternoon. His devastation at her death had been obvious, but perhaps he had been giving a superb performance. Maybe his extreme grief response was something other than shock and surprise? Could anybody feign a stroke? Or maybe he hadn't really had a stroke? Maybe he'd really had some kind of a nervous breakdown. Maybe he knew more about the death of the Russian man in the Inastou parking lot than he'd let on. In the absence of real information, speculation ran wild.

Chapter 35

They trailed into Cuba Libre, dragging their feet all the way. No one said anything, but every one of the group looked like he or she wished they were anyplace except where they were that afternoon. The person who had called 911 was there, and the two people who had given CPR to Elena were there. None of the participants were happy. Captain Trimper had everyone sit in exactly the same places they'd been sitting on Sunday night, the night of the murder. He asked each person what they'd ordered to eat. Had the food they'd ordered been the food that was served to them? Had any mistakes been made in serving the food or the drinks? Captain Trimper walked them through the timeline of the night's events — the time they'd all arrived, the time each course had been served, the time when Elena had stood up on her chair and sung *The Internationale*, and the time she had fallen into the beautiful blueberry and strawberry Cuban flag cake.

"Did anyone see Elena's cake being put on the table in front of her?" Captain Trimper asked. No one had, or at least no one could remember it. "Did anyone notice the waiter or waitress who put her serving of cake on the table?" No one remembered that either. "Did you see anyone put anything into or onto Elena's cake?" Again, no one had noticed anything. Elena had made such a spectacle of herself and had embarrassed the group in a public place to the extent that no one had wanted to look at her or even turn a head in her direction for the rest of the evening. They'd wanted to pretend they didn't know her. The Captain established that no one had seen anyone tamper with or add anything to Elena's dessert after it had been put on the table in front of her.

Trimper moved on to what had happened after Elena collapsed. Richard and Matthew had rushed to see if they could save her. A person at another table had called 911, and the good Samaritan couple had lowered Elena from her chair to the floor and begun CPR. They'd been through all of this before. This time was for Trimper, and he finally seemed to understand what had happened.

"I spent all morning interviewing the waiters and waitresses here at Cuba Libre, as well as the entire kitchen staff who worked on Sunday night, including the woman who assembles the Cuban flag cakes on the plates. None of them saw anything suspicious. None of them knew Elena or had any reason to want to kill her. We are back to where we started. We have no motive, and we have no suspects.

"Why don't you look in the obvious places, Captain." Cameron was exasperated. He was a busy man and didn't have time for any of this. "She was a Russian national and had a murky past. Everybody knew this about her. A Russian man was shot in the parking lot of the Inastou the night before Elena was killed. The dead man and Elena argued … in front of all of us. Don't you think these things have to be related? Why aren't you talking to the FBI about their investigation? We don't know anything about Elena's death. We didn't poison her cake."

Sidney was out of sorts. She was missing her grandson's birthday party, and she was not at all happy about that. She was also not happy to be back at Cuba Libre. She'd never liked Cuban food and didn't think the food at this Cuban restaurant was very good. Even before Elena had embarrassed all of them with her singing and even before Elena had fallen dead into her plate, Sidney had decided she was never coming back here again. But here she was, back again.

She blocked out whatever the sheriff was droning on and on about. Her mind was someplace else. Sidney had been sitting directly across from Elena the night she'd died. Because of where Sidney was at the table, she'd had a front row seat to every second of the horror. It had not been possible to look away. Sidney felt sick to her stomach as it all came back to her.

She looked again at the antique mirror she'd gazed into Sunday night. She thought of the large woman, dressed in the black silk caftan and wearing heavy gold jewelry, the woman she'd seen staring back at her through the mirror. Sidney knew the woman had not been looking at her, but at Elena. Because of Elena's bad behavior, Sidney had been afraid the woman was going to come to their table and kick them all out of the restaurant. But the woman hadn't done that.

Sidney didn't think the woman who'd been standing at the back of the restaurant had known she was being watched. She didn't know Sidney could see her through the cloudy mirror. Sidney remembered the expression on the woman's face. It was pure hatred. Sidney had thought at the time, no matter how badly Elena was behaving and no matter how much the woman in black might have wished their group of older folks had never crossed the doorstep of her restaurant, the look on her face was extreme and not appropriate to the situation. As Sidney looked back on Sunday night's events, she realized there had to be something more going on than was apparent at the time. There was more to the woman in black than anyone knew, and there was more to her murderous expression. And that is exactly what it had been, Sidney now realized, a murderous expression.

Sidney could read people. She knew what was appropriate, and she knew when something was off, when something wasn't right. She knew without a doubt that there was more to the story of Elena's performance in Cuba Libre than Sidney was able to understand. There was a backstory to this, and Sidney wanted to find out what that backstory was. The woman must have recognized Elena from somewhere. But how was that possible? Elena had never been to Maine before, and she had mentioned that fact several times during the weekend as she sang its praises and devoured its lobster.

Captain Trimper was still talking and talking, and Sidney was lost in her own thoughts. She tried to half-listen to the questions.

She wasn't sure, but she thought several other people at their table had ordered the cake. Somebody had ordered flan, she thought. Not everybody had ordered dessert. Trimper seemed to be trying to figure out if the poisoned cake had been intended for somebody else. If somebody else at the table had ordered the cake, maybe the plates had been mixed up, and the cake with the poison had been put in front of the wrong person.

Cameron was still not able to understand why Trimper wasn't looking into Elena's past for the person or persons who might have wanted to kill her. He didn't feel like he could stress this again with the Captain. He'd already voiced his opinion about where he thought the investigation should be heading. Cameron had connections with people in high places, and he'd decided if Trimper kept them in Bar Harbor for another day, he was going to make a few phone calls to try to get this wrapped up. He couldn't figure out why Trimper hadn't called in the FBI. It was Russians! Maybe it was some old KGB rivalry that had outlasted Glasnost and the dissolution of the USSR and Boris Yeltsin. Or, maybe it was something to do with the Russian mob. Cameron knew the Russian mafia played the hardest of hardball and had few scruples about killing off their rivals, their friends, and their own. Elena's death definitely didn't have anything to do with the Camp Shoemaker reunion group. It was time for all of this to come to an end. It was time to go home. They couldn't get out of Cuba Libre fast enough.

Isabelle was worried about Matthew and knew he needed to get back to bed and rest. Trimper had put him and Richard Carpenter through an especially grueling session of questioning, both yesterday at the house and today at the restaurant. The two were physicians and were in the business of saving lives. Neither one of them was a murderer. Isabelle knew that none of the people at the table had murdered Elena, and she was so tired of answering questions. She wondered why nobody in law enforcement was willing to spend their time looking for Eugene Bonne. She was sorry Elena was dead, but she didn't think anybody would ever find out who had killed her. Just like nobody would ever find out who had killed the Russian in the parking lot of the Inastou. This group didn't have anything at all to do with Russians ... except for poor Darryl.

Bailey hadn't attended the Sunday night dinner, but he'd come along for the reenactment and sat on the sidelines, giving some support to Gretchen who was chomping at the bit to get back to Texas. She was openly furious with Trimper for keeping them one more day. It was clear to her and to everybody that they were never going to catch Elena's killer. All of this was a waste of time. Gretchen figured whoever had poisoned Elena and shot the other Russian was back in Moldova or Kiev or Timbuktu by now.

Everyone in the group had a theory. Everyone knew none of them had done it. But Trimper had yet to be convinced. They were tired and wanted to get out of Cuba Libre. Finally, the Captain told them they were free to leave. He said they did not have to stay in Maine any longer. A cheer went up, and the group got in their cars and trucks to return to Indigo Cottage. Vivian was making Lobster Fra Diavolo for dinner tonight. It was her own special recipe, and she was baking blueberry pies for dessert. They were all going to miss Vivian and her wonderful food.

Elizabeth had recovered from her fall, but she, along with everybody else, was worn out — physically, mentally, and emotionally, from the ordeals of the past few days. She was looking forward to the pasta dish and was eager to get back to Indigo Cottage to rest before dinner. Sidney and Cameron had ridden to the restaurant with Elizabeth and Richard.

They were pulling out of the parking lot next to Cuba Libre when Sidney said, "She did it. I know she did it! I don't know why, but I do know who."

"Who did what?" Richard was driving and was anxious to get back to the lobster dinner. Vivian was making her Fra Diavolo recipe with his favorite pasta, bucatini.

Cameron knew by Sidney's tone of voice, that she had figured it out. He inwardly groaned because he knew what was coming. Sidney wouldn't give up until she had righted a wrong. She was a bulldog. If she knew something was rotten, she kept on until she'd done everything humanly possible to remedy whatever it was. Cameron was certain Sidney had figured out who had killed Elena. He had no idea how she'd figured it out or if she could prove it. And he didn't want her trying to prove it. He wanted the FBI to prove it. The last thing in the world he wanted right now was to get involved in this murder mess. But he knew his wife, and he knew she wasn't wrong. He also knew he wasn't going to be able to leave Bar Harbor the next morning.

"Richard, turn the car around. You have to take me back to the restaurant. I know who murdered Elena." Sidney was adamant. Richard turned the car around, but he gave Cameron a pleading look that begged him to try to talk some sense into his wife.

Cameron knew he was going to lose this one, but he gave it a shot. "I think we should call Captain Trimper and meet with him first. You can tell him your theory, and then leave it up to him to pursue it and arrest somebody. It isn't smart for us to go charging back into the restaurant and begin questioning people. Or, heaven forbid, start accusing people of murder. Come on, Sidney, be sensible. I support whatever you want to do, but we can't do this on our own."

"I have to know why, Cameron. She's an old woman, even older than you." Sidney smiled at her handsome husband who was almost fifteen years older than she was. "She had to have had a good reason for doing it. I don't know how I know that, but I know it. I'm not sure I want to see her punished."

"What do you mean, you don't know if you want to see her punished? If she murdered somebody, she has to be punished." Cameron was a law and order kind of guy, but likewise, Sidney was a law and order kind of woman. It was very out of character for her to say something like that.

"I think she had a good reason for killing Elena. I think she was avenging a terrible crime, or something that had damaged her soul."

"Come on Sidney, cut it out. You can't possibly know that."

"Yes I can, and you know I can."

Richard and Elizabeth had kept their mouths shut until now.

Elizabeth spoke up. "Sidney, you can't go in alone. You need someone to go in there with you, and I don't think it ought to be Cameron. I can't do it because it's too much walking, and I'm no help in a fist fight. Richard will have to go with you." Elizabeth knew Sidney was serious, and she was concerned for her friend's safety.

"Cameron is going in with me. Richard has to stay out of the fray and treat the casualties after it's all over. You two wait here. Don't call Trimper until I tell you to call him. Will you agree to that?"

Richard was going to say something, but Elizabeth intended to respect Sidney's wishes. "We won't call him until you say so, but if we hear gunfire, we reserve the right to call him without your okay. Is it a deal?"

They pulled up to the rear of Cuba Libre, and Sidney and Cameron got out of the Expedition and walked into the kitchen without knocking on the back door.

Chapter 36

THE KITCHEN SMELLED WONDERFUL … OF GARLIC and cumin and fresh herbs and roasting meat. It briefly occurred to Sidney that maybe the restaurant food wasn't so bad after all and maybe they'd just ordered the wrong things. Sidney knew the woman in black was somewhere in the kitchen. She found her looking down into an enormous pot. Sidney tapped her on the shoulder, and the woman turned around. She was wearing a huge white coverall over her clothes tonight.

She turned around to face Sidney. "I thought it would be you who found me out. I could tell that first night when you came to the restaurant with your friends that you have second sight." The woman had no accent. She spoke perfect American English. Sidney had expected something different, a Spanish flavor of some kind to the woman's speech. This woman who looked so exotic was all American. "And you want to know why, don't you?"

"Yes, I want to know why. I believe you had a good reason for killing Elena, and I want you to tell me what that reason is."

"It's almost time for dinner. This is my special version of seafood gumbo, with a Cuban twist on the dish. Don't worry, it isn't poisoned." The large woman pointed to Cameron and pointed to the chair. He sat as directed. Sidney pulled out a chair at the table. The woman served three bowls of the delicious-smelling concoction and put them on the table. She put a soup spoon and a cloth napkin beside each bowl and sat down with Cameron and Sidney.

"You want to hear my story? First, let me tell you that I am not sorry at all for what I did. I have no guilt and no regrets. I know who this Elena was, and she deserved to die a hundred times over for what her family did to mine."

"How could you possibly know who she was? She's never been to Maine before? Where have you met her?" Sidney wanted to hear every detail.

"I am Daniela Garcia. I'm from Cuba, as I am sure you know. I came to the United States in 1960, when I was twenty-two years old. Fidel Castro had briefly pretended he was a revolutionary who was fighting for a more democratic Cuba. He overthrew a self-aggrandizing, totalitarian dictator named Batista and replaced him with another self-aggrandizing, totalitarian dictator — himself. One reason Castro was worse than Batista was because of the economic ideas he espoused. There was income inequality under Batista. There were upper classes, it is true. But Castro's socialist and communist ideologies forced on Cuba the outcome these corrupt economic systems always produce — poverty for all. Socialism always makes everybody poor. And Castro was more brutal than Batista ever was. He imprisoned or murdered anyone who opposed him. He was Stalin's clone. Cuba used to be a prosperous and exciting place. Now Cuba has been left behind in the dustbin of history, thanks to the Communist brothers who have spent the last sixty years raping and pillaging my country. I won't bore you with more politics, but you must know that since Fidel seized power in 1959, I have despised the Castros to the depths of my being. And I know whereof I speak."

Daniela continued. "My father was not particularly a supporter of Batista's, but he saw Fidel for the wolf in sheep's clothing that he was. My father always knew he was a pawn of the Soviet Union, a collaborator with the despicable Che Guevara. My father was a doctor and an intellectual. He spoke out, and he paid the ultimate price for that. Fidel Castro's sycophants came to our house in the middle of the night and murdered my father and my mother, in front of me and my grandmother. I was twenty-two. They would have murdered me, but I was young and pretty. So instead of killing me, the stinking, wretched, vile Communist bullies, Fidel's minions, raped me and made my grandmother watch. There were five of them, and they raped me over and over again. When they left the house, I was bleeding to death. I was almost dead. My grandmother called a colleague of my father's to come and save my life. I wish she had let me die. I did not speak a word out loud for almost six months."

Cameron and Sidney were completely shocked and horrified by Daniela's story. They said nothing because there was nothing to say.

The Cuban woman resumed her monologue. "My grandmother did not know if I would ever speak again, or if I would ever be able to function again. She made arrangements and transferred our wealth. To the extent that she could, she moved our assets out of Cuba. Many middle-class and upper middle-class people were leaving and making plans to leave. They knew their property, their savings, and everything they had worked so hard for would be confiscated by the monster who now ruled the country. I finally recovered to the extent that my grandmother decided I was well enough to travel. She and some others who felt compelled to leave their beloved country behind chartered a boat to make the journey from Havana to Key West. From Key West, we drove to Miami. Many Cuban expats, all of whom had left their homes and fortunes and families behind, were making new lives in Miami. We settled there and tried to find some contentment in the United States. I continued to recover, and I grew stronger. But I would never be the same. How could I be?"

Sidney started to interrupt, then stopped.

"I will skip over the transformation that took place within me. I will just say that the only way I was able to function again with any normalcy was to direct my rage against the fiends who were in power in Havana. I embraced revenge and put that energy into fighting those who had destroyed the Daniela I once had been. I knew that I would find no peace of mind until I had done everything in my power to fight these beasts. I joined a resistance group in Miami, a group that was passionately committed to destroying Castro and everything he stood for. Then the Bay of Pigs happened, and I was angry — not only with Castro but also with the President of the United States. The country we thought would save us, had run away when the chips were down. So I volunteered to leave the United States and return to Cuba to fight against the Castro regime. We lived in huts in the jungle. I learned to be an excellent marksman. I learned to make bombs, and I learned about poisons. I knew how to kill a man who weighed twice as much as I did by slicing his throat with a paring knife. I knew where to cut so that he would die within ten seconds.

"I spied on Russian military installations and the Russian troops that were pouring into Cuba daily and in huge numbers. I saw the Russian advisors who filled the streets of Havana. There was no more pretense. It was clear that Fidel and his revolution were firmly up the asshole of the Soviet Union. Then the Russian nukes began to arrive in Cuba. I watched the Soviets set up their death missiles, and I took photographs and made notes. I passed everything I observed along to my controller in the resistance who was reporting it all to the U.S. government.

Sidney interrupted. "You have endured and prevailed through unspeakable horrors, and you certainly did all you could do to fight back against Castro and his tyrants. But what does any of this have to do with Elena? She wasn't even born at the time of the Cuban Missile Crisis. What was your motivation for killing her?"

Daniela continued. "If you can spare me a few more minutes, I will make it all perfectly clear to you. Are you listening?"

Cameron answered. "Of course we're listening. Yours is an astonishing story."

"I was trained as an assassin, and I was a crack shot. I was given an assignment to assassinate a high-ranking KGB official who was coming to Havana for talks with Fidel. The talks had to do with arming the nuclear missiles the Soviet Union was bringing to Cuba. I knew I was good, and I was confident I could accomplish the mission. I was already in place to take my shot, but there had been a leak in our organization. Someone had betrayed me, and just before I was going to pull the trigger to kill my mark, a Russian woman discovered me in my assassin's nest. She was an expert in the martial arts and was much more accomplished in that kind of fighting than I was. We struggled. She broke twenty-three bones in my body, including all of my fingers, both my arms, and both my legs. I don't know why she didn't shoot me with the rifle I had planned to use. I can only conclude that she wanted me to die a painful death, rather than mercifully finish me off quickly as I begged her to do. I prayed that I would die. But my broken body would be the smallest price I paid.

"The Russian woman knew my name. She knew there were many members of my extended family who still lived in Cuba. She said she would not rest until every member of my family was dead. I lost consciousness before she could tell me everything she was going to do to punish me for my assassination attempt. And she followed through with her threats. Sixteen of my family members, including small children and two infants, were slaughtered in their beds that very night. Because I was in a coma, lying on the ground waiting to die, I did not learn of this carnage until much later.

"My compadres in the resistance rescued me and saved my life. I have wished many times that they had never found me. They somehow commandeered a boat and took me back to the United States. I don't remember any of that part of my journey. They gave me morphine to kill the tremendous pain I was in from all the broken bones. I endured three years of surgeries to repair what doctors could salvage of my body. I have countless metal rods and screws and plates, everywhere inside this wreck of myself, and I have walked with a cane since I was twenty-six years old. And, I have lived with constant pain since I was almost killed by the Russian woman. My work for the resistance was finished. I could never return to Cuba. My grandmother finally decided I was well enough that she could tell me the terrible news. Everyone related to me by blood who'd remained in Cuba, everyone that the Russians and Fidel's men could find, had been slaughtered. They were all dead because of me. I have had to live with that guilt for the last fifty-five years.

"I did not know the name of the Russian woman who had destroyed my body and ordered the destruction of my family, but I will never forget her face. I searched for a long time and spent a great deal of money until I was able to discover her name. Her name was Elena Petrovich. She was an agent of the KGB.

"I saw her face again last Sunday night, here in my restaurant. I almost fainted when I saw her walk through the door. There she was, sitting with your group. At first I thought I was hallucinating. And then I thought it had to be a fluke, a coincidence. But the resemblance was too striking. She had to be Elena's daughter; she could not possibly be anybody else. I kept telling myself that it was impossible for Elena's daughter to be here in Maine, in the United States, in Cuba Libre.

"And then she stood up on her chair and sang the Communist national anthem, and I knew it was no coincidence. I knew that God had sent to me the child of the woman who had destroyed my life. I wished I could have prolonged her death and made her suffer, like her mother has made me suffer for so many years. But I didn't want to miss my opportunity. I can no longer kill with a paring knife. The only useful weapons I had at my disposal, to use in this emergency, were my poisons — cyanide and strychnine. Strychnine to inflict suffering, and cyanide to be sure she died quickly, before anyone could save her. I had to strike and strike immediately. There was no time for elaborate planning or for any planning at all. Strychnine is bitter and sometimes takes a little while to act. So I put it in her main course and then a larger dose in her dessert. The cyanide was in her dessert. It was ad hoc and seat of the pants all the way. Elena Petrovich's daughter had to die that night. And so she did."

Sidney and Cameron were speechless. They had many questions. It took everything they could muster to absorb the amazing narrative of Daniela Garcia's life and the story of how and why she had murdered Elena.

Finally Cameron found his voice. "How did you happen to come to Maine? It's a long way from Miami."

"I came to Maine *because* it is a long way from Miami. I could not live in the Cuban expat community anymore, and with the anger and the guilt that consumed me, I really couldn't live anywhere at all. My grandmother was a fabulous cook. She taught me how to make all of her dishes, including the beautiful Cuban flag cake." Daniela smiled the smile of an angel when she mentioned the cake. "When my grandmother passed away, I moved to Maine and opened a small store. I lived here in Bar Harbor for many years under another name. I married twice and divorced twice. Trust, which is essential in any marriage, was not my strong suit. I married a third time, and my husband died. I gave up my store and decided I wanted to run a restaurant. I also decided I was tired of hiding behind a name that was not my own. I realized that anyone who had known me in Miami under the name Daniela Garcia was either dead or too old to care. So I took back my own Cuban name and opened Cuba Libre. I have loved being the owner and the chef here. But I am ill. I am eighty years old, and I am going to die."

"You don't look ill, Daniela. You are the picture of health, and you certainly don't look anywhere close to eighty years old. Why do you say you're going to die?"

"Fat people never look sick." Daniela glanced scornfully at Sidney's young and shapely figure. "I was diagnosed with pancreatic cancer three weeks ago. I have four to six months to live, at the most."

"Can't something be done? Has it metastasized?" Cameron always wanted to find a way to fix whatever it was that had gone wrong.

"It has metastasized to my liver. Nothing can be done. I will be dead before my next birthday. You can call the police. You can call the FBI. You can call whoever you want to call. I will be dead before they can convict me of Elena's murder."

"I don't know that a jury would ever convict you, Daniela, if they heard the story you've just told us." Sidney was on Daniela's side, or at least she thought she wanted to be.

"Don't be ridiculous! Of course a jury would convict me. Elena The Second had nothing to do with the sins of her mother. I knew my only chance for revenge was to kill her myself, to take her out of this world as swiftly as possible. I feel that God sent her to me, during my last days on earth. I acted as His avenging angel."

Sidney and Cameron just sat there, in the kitchen, staring at Daniela, trying to make sense of it all. Daniela finally spoke, "I am glad you came. I wanted somebody to know my story. I wanted somebody to know why I killed Elena. She is also KGB, you know. She may have pretended not to be, but I know she is. I can smell them. I can smell KGB. I have one question of you. How did you know?"

"I watched you in the mirror on Sunday night. I saw the expression on your face when Elena stood up on her chair and sang. I couldn't help but look at you. You were standing there at the back of the restaurant with a look in your eyes that, in retrospect, I now know to be the look of a woman who is going to kill."

"But you didn't know for sure until today?"

"It all came together for me when we came back this afternoon and did the reenactment. I remembered watching you through the mirror on the wall."

"That mirror was the only thing my grandmother was able to take with her on the boat that brought us to the United States. It is the only relic from my beautiful home in Havana, the place that was a happy home until Castro's men murdered my parents there before my eyes. Now that one last remnant has become both my undoing and my redemption."

"How is it a redemption?" Sidney got the undoing part.

"You coming here today has given me the courage to do what needs to be done. I can die, knowing that God is on my side and that I have done His work for Cuba." Daniela put something into her mouth and drank from a glass that sat alongside her now-empty bowl of gumbo. It was a few seconds before Sidney and Cameron realized what she had done. It was too late to stop her.

Chapter 37

DANIELA FELL FROM HER CHAIR ONTO THE kitchen floor. Someone came running to help her.

"I think she's had a heart attack." Cameron wasn't sure what to say or do about Daniela's death. It looked like a heart attack, so he said that.

"I knew she was ill, but I didn't know she had a weak heart. I thought it was something else. Is she dead? Should I call 911?" The kitchen assistant was obviously very upset and confused about what to do next.

"Go ahead and call 911. But there's nothing we can do. She's dead." Cameron had recorded the entire conversation with Daniela on his cell phone. He had the hard evidence of her confession that she had murdered Elena Petrovich. But what good did that evidence do anyone now? The only thing Cameron could imagine his recording might be used for would be to keep Captain Trimper from arresting someone else for Elena's murder.

Sidney was in shock and had tears in her eyes. The story Daniela had told them had stunned her. She walked out the back door and motioned for Richard Carpenter to come inside. "She'd dead, Richard. Someone is calling 911, but just check her pulse to be sure." Sidney climbed into the back of the Carpenter's SUV.

"Sidney, are you all right? What's happened?" Elizabeth had never before seen Sidney so shaken.

"I will tell you all about it, but not now. I don't want to talk. I can't talk. Just let me be, okay?"

"Of course. I won't ask any questions, and I won't blabber." Elizabeth knew when to stay silent.

The two women waited a long time. An ambulance arrived, and two EMTs ran into Cuba Libre. Cameron and Richard eventually came out and got into the car. No one said a word.

When they arrived back at Indigo Cottage, Sidney walked directly to the guest house in the back yard where she and Cameron were staying. Cameron followed her. Elizabeth and Richard went inside where the rest of the group was seated at the dining room table, already enjoying Vivian's lobster and pasta feast. The Carpenters had really been looking forward to this dinner, but they didn't have much appetite now.

"Where have you been?" Tyler wanted to know. "The last thing we knew, you were leaving Cuba Libre with the rest of us, and the next thing we knew, you were nowhere to be found. We started to wonder if you'd been taken hostage. Don't do that to us again."

"We've been at Cuba Libre. Actually, Elizabeth and I have been waiting in our car in the parking lot most of the time. Sidney and Cameron were inside, and they should be the ones to tell you what they've learned. I don't know all the details, but they do. It's serious and not a happy story. It does clear up the mystery of who killed Elena." Richard tried to enjoy the lobster and pasta, and he gave Vivian an apologetic look. "And I do so love bucatini," he said. His appetite did rally enough, however, to allow him to eat a large piece of blueberry pie when dessert was served.

They were drinking coffee when Cameron came through the back door. He didn't say anything, just put his cell phone on the table, put it on speaker phone, and turned up the volume so everyone could hear. The group listened to every word and sat in stunned silence after the recording ended. No one knew what to say.

Matthew was the first to speak. "What do you intend to do with your recording, Cameron? Are you going to give it to Trimper?"

"I don't know what I'm going to do about anything. You all have heard Daniela's story, but you didn't see her as she told it. I've never heard anything like what she had to say, and I have no doubts whatsoever that every word is true. It overwhelmed Sidney and me. I'm completely drained and have to get some sleep. I'll deal with this tomorrow." Cameron, who was always in control and always master of his fate, looked sad and a little lost as he left through the back door.

"He has to give the recording to Trimper." Matthew had already made up his mind where he stood. "It's only fair to Darryl and to Elena for Daniela to take responsibility for her death."

"It's not quite that simple, though, is it?" Lilleth was able to see more than one point of view in this tragedy. "Is it fair to anybody for this whole sordid and tragic story to come out? I'm just asking. Elena is dead. Who benefits from these revelations? Who gains anything from hearing the truth in all of its horror? Does Elena really benefit?"

"I thought you were a psychologist, not a philosopher." Richard was trying to lighten the mood.

"A psychologist has to be a bit of a philosopher, too, don't you think?" Lilleth looked Matthew and Richard directly in the eyes. Matthew was married to a psychologist, and he ought to know this.

Elizabeth jumped in. "I think you're right, Lilleth. A psychologist must be a philosopher, as well as many other things. And this 'truth' must be handled carefully. Cameron and Sidney are convinced that Daniela was telling her story from the heart, as she remembered it. I have no doubts that the Castro regime was as ugly and brutal as Daniela says, and there is no reason to deny that part of her story. But as we all know, with social media and all news all the time on television, there's very little that can be left undisclosed these days. More's the pity. Or, maybe it's a good thing to let it all hang out. Let everybody know how horrible life was for Daniela and what she did about it in the end." Elizabeth hadn't helped resolve anything with her remarks. If anything, she'd muddied the waters even more.

"I think we need to sleep on it. We are all tired and strung out over this, and we can't possibly make a good decision right now. And it isn't our decision to make. Daniela made her confession to Cameron and Sidney. They have the recording. They're the ones with the difficult choices. What we think really doesn't mean a thing." J.D. wanted everybody to quit talking and go to bed.

Gretchen and Bailey were leaving very early in the morning from Bangor to fly back to Texas, and they said their goodbyes. J.D. and Lilleth were leaving after lunch the next day. They would drive to Portland and fly to Colorado on Sunday. Tyler had an appointment to see a sports medicine specialist in Colorado Springs. He had to be ready to ski when the first snow fell.

The others were staying in Bar Harbor for a few more days. It didn't seem possible that almost a week had passed since Elena's death. Cameron and Sidney, who had been the most eager to get out of town, were going to have to stick around and answer more questions from Captain Trimper. Elizabeth and Richard were driving back to Maryland, and they would be leaving day after tomorrow. Elizabeth thought her bruised ribs would have healed sufficiently by then, and she would be able to endure the long car ride.

They all hated that Eugene Boone was still at large, but they felt they'd done everything they could to motivate Sheriff Carney Dodd and get him moving on the case. He was probably a pretty good sheriff, but he was a good old boy and not used to dealing with serious crimes. His loyalties were to the local people, so no one really expected anything to happen to the busboy who had sabotaged Tyler's bike. But, the busboy's family might sit up and take notice when he was served with a big fat law suit. Going to court might force the parents to admit their little darling was a juvenile delinquent and headed for trouble.

It was three o'clock in the morning when Matthew heard noises outside his bedroom window. He was almost fully recovered from his bout with pneumonia, but he found himself sleeping during the day and then not being able to sleep at night. He'd watched a late movie tonight, hoping that would tire him out and let him sleep. He tried to ignore the scratching at the side of the house, blaming it on a raccoon or a deer or some other curious critter. It was only when he heard the explosion that he realized human mischief was responsible for the noises.

The explosion brought everyone running from their bedrooms, and sure enough, the garage was engulfed in flames. The fire was shooting high into the air, and the pine trees close to the garage were in danger of burning. None of their cars were parked in the garage. Only an old lawn mower and an even older pickup truck to take brush to the dump were inside the burning building. Rita and her dogs were staying in the guest house that was attached to the garage, but they'd escaped before the garage had become consumed. Rita and her dogs were huddled together, outside in the cold, watching Indigo Cottage burn. Everyone was shivering as they gathered in the early morning air, but no one was about to go back inside to get a coat.

"I've already called 911. It's a volunteer fire company, but they're very good about responding quickly." Rita, who knew quite a few of the firefighters in town, had left everything but her purse, her phone, and her dogs inside the burning guest house. The Ryan's garage was attached to the main part of Indigo Cottage by a breezeway. The garage was going to be a total loss, as was the attached guest house, but if the fire department got there in time, the main house might be saved.

They stood and watched the flames shoot higher and higher. The fire was moving very fast, and a few trees had already caught fire. It could be very bad, but nobody wanted to run back into the house to try to save anything. "He's close by someplace. I know he is." J.D. was sure it was Eugene Boone who had started the fire. "It had to be him. I'll bet anything he's not too far away, watching to see what happens. He intended to murder us all and watch us burn to death in our beds."

There was a strong smell of gasoline everywhere, and the fire was obviously the result of arson. Vivian came running from her house next door and was visibly shaken to see the garage destroyed and the house threatened. She was the caretaker for the house and had been its steward for decades. How could this be happening to her beloved Indigo Cottage?

The volunteer firemen arrived and made quick work of putting out the fire. There was no wind that night, or it might have been a different story. The detached guest house where Cameron and Sidney were staying was untouched, and the main part of Indigo Cottage was fine. The garage and the attached guest quarters were a total loss. Rita had come to Indigo Cottage directly from the hospital, and the few clothes that had burned belonged to Vivian. Vivian didn't care about the clothes she'd lent to Rita. She was enormously relieved that the main house had been spared.

Once the fire was out and the firefighters had left, the Ryan's houseguests began to think about the consequences of the fire. They were certain Eugene Boone had been responsible. Because of his hatred for the Camp Shoemaker boys he'd felt had shunned him, he had tried to kill them. He had attempted to destroy the house where they were staying. How had he found them? Why had he stayed around and not taken off for parts unknown when he'd had the chance? Would the Ryan's homeowners' insurance cover the cost of rebuilding the garage and the guest house? Would homeowner's insurance cover the damage from a fire that had been deliberately set? They were devastated, and they were frightened. Where would Eugene strike next?

Vivian offered them one piece of good news about the fire. The garage and its attached guest house were old and had been infested with dry rot for years. The Ryans had put off updating this antiquated part of Indigo Cottage. The garage and guest house were scheduled for demolition later in the fall. A new and larger garage and a larger, nicer guest house were to be built in the spring. The breezeway that joined the garage to the house was to be enclosed, protected from the weather. A fire was never a good thing, but at least this fire had destroyed only parts of the house that were going to be torn down and rebuilt anyway. Vivian said she would be the one to tell the Ryans what had happened to their garage. She would schedule workmen to immediately begin the clean-up from the fire.

The members of the Camp Shoemaker reunion group wondered to what extent Eugene would keep up his attacks on them, even after they'd left the area. He somehow had tracked them to the Ryans' house. Would he bother to track them even further and follow them to their own homes, in other cities and other states? Would he pursue them, one at a time, and find them … in California? in Texas? in Colorado? They decided he had to be stopped. He had to be found. If they didn't stop him now, would they ever feel really safe?

Cameron and Sidney were staying in Bar Harbor anyway, because of their part in the investigation into Elena's murder. Richard and J.D. decided they would stay, to put more pressure on the sheriff and to hunt for Eugene. Matthew said he would stay, too, but he wasn't sure how much help he would be in his weakened condition. Elizabeth was happy to stay and give her ribs a few more days to heal. Isabelle was eager to get back to her store in Palm Springs, but she felt Matthew needed more time to rest and recuperate. She did not want him hunting anything right now, least of all Eugene Boone, but she knew her husband was stubborn and would do whatever he wanted to do.

Bailey wanted to stay behind and help search for their nemesis, but Gretchen was determined to leave that morning so she could return to work. Tyler was sick with worry that he wouldn't be able to ski this year because of his ankle. Held captive by his crutches, he wouldn't be any help at all hunting for Eugene. He and Lilleth still intended to leave for Portland after lunch.

Cameron called the sheriff and told him what had happened. He told Carney Dodd they were all convinced the fire had been started by Eugene Boone, and they wondered why nobody had been able to apprehend him. Cameron told the sheriff they were going after Eugene themselves, since nobody in any official capacity had been able to do anything. Dodd protested and cautioned Cameron about interfering in an ongoing investigation. Dodd warned Cameron against doing anything best left to law enforcement.

"I don't think there's anything whatsoever that's best left to law enforcement. You aren't doing squat." Cameron was tired of tiptoeing around the sheriff's feelings.

Rita told Cameron that she had LoJack on her car, the Neon. She'd not wanted it because of the extra cost, but it had come with the car. She hadn't paid extra for it and had forgotten all about the fact that she had it until her car was stolen.

"Could we find my car and find Chef, if we can track the LoJack?"

"You're darn right we can." Cameron was instantly on his phone. He was calling in a few favors to find the location of the Neon. Enough was enough. He was going after Boone, no matter what the sheriff threatened.

It wasn't long before Cameron had a call back about the LoJack, and they had a location on Rita's car. Sure enough, it was parked less than mile from Indigo Cottage, on a long-forgotten dirt road in the woods. Vivian knew about the old logging road that had been abandoned before Indigo Cottage was built. It approached the Ryan's property from the opposite direction and came to a dead end by a pond in the woods. The only way for the men to get close to the pond where the Neon was parked, was to make their way through dense forest. There was no path. Heading out from Indigo Cottage, they would have to cut their own track through the woods to reach the car.

No one knew if Eugene Boone was anywhere near where the car was parked, but they were betting he was. The men were all seventy-five years old, but Eugene was not much younger. They had no weapons with which to defend themselves, but they were all determined to put an end to their nightmare.

What if Eugene had a gun? Richard Carpenter and Matthew Ritter were hunters, and they were both skilled in the use of shotguns, and to a lesser extent, rifles. But they didn't have either. Both J.D. and Olivia were expert markspersons with handguns. They never went after people, just paper targets at the shooting range. But no one had a gun here in Bar Harbor. Almost everyone in the group had flown to Maine, and no one would have had a reason to travel with a firearm. Cameron didn't hunt, and he'd never been interested in guns of any kind. They were a motley crew when it came to tracking down a criminal on their own. They knew they probably shouldn't do it, that it was worse than foolhardy. But they were all, including the women in the group, fed up with Eugene Boone and his trouble-making. The ragtag irregulars were going after the elusive criminal that no one could seem to find. The guy was huge. How could he have managed to hide himself for this long?

Vivian was making an early breakfast as they discussed their options. She had pancakes and waffles, sausage and bacon, scrambled eggs and hash browns. But she had something else, and she was debating with herself about whether or not to tell anybody about the secret cache in the house. She was furious about the arson and the fire that had nearly destroyed Indigo Cottage. As she listened to them talk about going after Boone, she decided to show them Cabbott Ryan's gun collection that was locked in a closet on a lower level of the house. When everyone was on their second cup of coffee, she said she wanted to take them to a hidden room in the basement.

"This might be a mistake on my part, but it also might be the answer to your problem. Mr. Ryan had an extensive gun collection. He was a hunter, and he loved antique guns. I never actually saw him fire any of them, but they are all down there, locked up in a fire resistant, temperature and moisture-controlled room. Once a year, two men come to clean and oil the guns. I just let the men in the house, and somebody else pays their bill. I'm telling you this because you need to know, if you decide to use any of them, that all the guns have been well-maintained and are in good condition. The annual gun cleaning has been going on since before I started working here. I don't like guns and don't know anything about them, but I'm going to give you the keys to the gun closet."

Vivian showed them where the guns were kept and returned to her comfort zone — the kitchen. She was making beef barley soup and ham salad sandwiches for lunch. She had a butterflied whole leg of lamb that she intended to stuff with spinach, fresh mint leaves, and feta cheese to roast for dinner. She knew what she was doing when it came to food. She was at a loss around guns. These old guys were on their own with the weapons, but she had grown fond of every one of them and didn't want them hurt. She didn't want them to be hurt by Eugene Boone, and she didn't want them to hurt themselves. She hoped she hadn't made a big mistake.

Chapter 38

"Do you think you could shoot him, if it came to that?" Cameron asked J.D. who was armed with a loaded handgun.

"He tried to kill me. He drugged me with a hypodermic full of tranquilizers, tied me up, and left me for dead. Of course I could shoot him, if it came to that. I'd prefer to take him alive, though. At least, I think I would. But considering the sheriff who pretends to be in charge around here, I'm not entirely sure I want to turn him over to Carney Dodd. If we get Eugene, maybe you can find somebody else we can turn him over to. We could call Captain Trimper, but in the end, I'm afraid he'll just hand him over to Dodd. Nobody wants to step on anybody else's toes, but I think this guy needs to be investigated by the feds. Maybe you could trade your recording of Daniela's confession to the FBI in exchange for arresting Boone and taking him into federal custody … once we've caught him that is."

The four men had found warm coats, boots, and gloves to wear, clothes that belonged to the Ryan family. Matthew carried a shotgun, and Richard had a deer rifle. J.D. had the handgun, and Cameron was carrying rope and duct tape and an axe to use to cut their way through the woods. They'd even found a box of handcuffs in the gun closet. They loaded their weapons and took off through the woods in search of the white Neon and, hopefully, Eugene Boone. The woods were swampy, still flooded with water from the recent storm. It would have been rough going for anybody, but it was especially difficult for a bunch of men who were in their mid-seventies.

"How did Boone ever make his way through this marsh? He's in terrible shape and must weigh more than three hundred pounds. He's not an outdoorsy type." Cameron was in good shape, and he was finding it almost impossible to cut his way through the thick vegetation and dead trees. "I guess he was coming from the other direction and drove the Neon to the pond on the old logging road, but I'm surprised he could even fit into the Neon."

"I know I've had pneumonia, so I'm not keeping up with you guys like I wish I could. Boone must be going on pure adrenalin to be able to make his way through this kind of terrain. Even driving on the logging road wouldn't be easy. Nobody has driven on that road for dozens of years, according to Vivian." Isabelle had not wanted Matthew to go out into the cold and damp, but he was determined to participate in the capture of Eugene Boone. They were fighting for every inch of progress as they approached the dirt road where Rita's car was parked.

Matthew was the most experienced outdoorsman and best tracker of the group, an expert at finding birds in the southern Arizona desert. Now he was committed to finding his prey in the woods and swamp of northern Maine. "We have to be quiet when we get near the pond. I'll do some reconnaissance and get as close as I can to the car, to see what's going on. We need to get the lay of the land before we go stumbling into the unknown. The rest of you stay back and don't move around or make any noise. I'll see if he's anywhere near the car. I'm worried that he's strapped dynamite onto his body or something stupid like that. He's crazy enough that he might have made a bomb out of himself. I really do think he's that far gone. If I see him in the car or anywhere around the car, I'll come back to you, and we can make a plan. We need to decide ahead of time exactly what we're going to do. I probably won't be able to see if he has a handgun or a long gun, but if all he's armed with are a couple of hypodermic needles full of tranquilizers, we should be able to take him. He's a big guy, but there are four of us."

All agreed to allow Matthew to check out the car to determine if Boone was anywhere nearby. They kept quiet as directed, and Matthew went on ahead to try to find out what he could. He saw the Neon sitting on the dirt road, the road that was completely overgrown. Boone somehow had been able to drive Rita's car down the logging trail, but just as Vivian had said, it didn't look as if anyone else had been on the road for years. Once again, Eugene Boone was MIA. How could the guy just disappear into the mist at will?

Matthew was careful to watch for trip wires and other booby traps. He was concerned that the car itself might be a booby trap. The Neon was in a small clearing, and Matthew didn't want to get too close for fear Eugene was in the woods, watching to see if anyone approached the car. Boone might have a gun and shoot at anyone who came to check it out. They knew Boone had some expertise with bomb-making. Matthew was worried that Eugene had filled the Neon with explosives and would use a remote control device to trigger an explosion. There were a number of possible scenarios, and none of them were good ones.

Matthew crawled slowly through the underbrush toward the car. He wished he had a ghillie suit, but a very old camo hunting jacket and a camo hunting cap were the best he'd been able to come up with. He was used to sneaking up on birds, not cars or crazy people. He got close enough to see that no one was inside the car, but Matthew was cautious. He found a piece of wood on the ground and threw it at the door of the Neon. Nothing happened. Then he found a long stick, and with a piece of duct tape, he attached his hat to the end of it. It wasn't really going to fool anybody, but Matthew thought it was worth a try. He crawled forward, a little closer to the car. He raised the stick in the air and moved it around as if it were a puppet or a moving scarecrow.

He inched closer to the Neon, still crawling forward on the ground. He crept to where he had a good view of the car's undercarriage and was horrified to see it was packed with what looked like plastique explosives. This was big trouble, much bigger trouble than they'd been expecting. If Eugene was anywhere around and intended to blow up the car, the resulting explosion would leave a huge crater in the ground. How far the force of the blast would reach was anyone's guess. Matthew had to get his friends out of the area before the car blew up. The heck with capturing Boone; they needed to save their own lives. Matthew briefly wondered where Eugene had learned to make bombs with plastique.

Before he'd seen the bomb underneath the car, Matthew had wondered if his hat on a stick would attract Boone's attention, and it had. Just as he dropped the stick, he heard a clicking sound, the sound one might hear at the moment a detonating signal was sent to set off a bomb. Matthew instinctively knew he wouldn't be able to crawl fast enough to get away from the car before it blew, so he stood up to try to run away. He shouted, "Bomb!" and screamed at his friends to take cover. As he stood up and began to run from the exploding Neon, out of nowhere came an enormous body that took him to the ground. Eugene, all three hundred plus pounds of him, tackled Matthew and held him down. Debris from the explosion rained down on them. Matthew was being crushed under Eugene's tremendous body.

The three who had taken cover watched with increasing alarm as their friend was attacked by the enemy. Richard Carpenter was finally able to see through the falling dust and rubble, and he aimed his rifle at Matthew and Eugene as they rolled around and struggled in the dirt. Richard was a very good shot, but he was not confident enough that he could hit Boone without hurting Matthew. He held his fire. J.D. was an excellent marksman, but he was also reluctant to fire a shot that might hit the wrong moving target.

The three decided to try to overwhelm Boone and advanced as a gang to attempt to save their friend. They pounced on the blob that was Eugene Boone and wrestled him away from Matthew. But Boone was moving with the energy and momentum of the crazed and insane. His adrenaline was pounding. The three did everything they could to subdue him. They would have him under control for a few seconds, and then he would break free. He seemed to have superhuman strength. Cameron and J.D. finally thought they had him pinned to the ground, and Richard went back for his rifle. He was going to hold the gun on Eugene while the others tied him up. But Eugene was not going to be taken or tied up. Just as Richard returned with the rifle, Boone broke free again and headed for the trees. He wasn't able to run very fast, and Richard aimed the rifle and fired at the escaping form. He thought his shot hit Boone in the leg. Boone fell to the ground. No one could see him very well as he made his way on his hands and knees, crawling back into the cover of the woods, but Cameron was certain Eugene was bleeding from his leg or foot.

Being shot had not stopped the madman. He continued to limp through the brush. Cameron was enraged that they'd not been able to subdue Eugene, and he took off after him, armed only with his axe. Cameron caught up with Eugene just as he reached another clearing farther down the road. Eugene had hidden an old ATV there, and with blood gushing from the wound in his thigh, he jumped onto the vehicle and turned on the ignition. He was going to get away. Cameron made one last lunge and threw the axe at Eugene's head. Cameron had never thrown an axe before in his life, but he miraculously scored a hit. The blade of the axe hit Eugene Boone's head and bounced off onto the ground. Eugene, now bleeding from his head and from his leg, drove away from his pursuers. He was badly injured, but he had managed to escape again.

The evening fog was closing in, and the four deeply disappointed men were forced to give up their quest to capture Boone. They'd done their best, and he had eluded them. They would be licking their psychological wounds for some time, as they chastised themselves for losing him. They had walked almost a mile through the woods to the pond beside the old logging road, and now they were going to have to find their way back to Indigo Cottage in the "pea soup" fog at dusk. Feeling down and completely exhausted, they gathered their weapons and the ropes they'd hoped by now would be holding Eugene Boone, securely bound for some kind of law enforcement officials to take away to jail. The ropes were now only useless artifacts, empty and without a function.

Vivian heard a noise outside the kitchen door. She knew the four men had gone on foot to the logging road, and she thought the women were in the great room in front of the fire. Rita, who'd been helping her prepare dinner, had left the house to walk her dogs. Vivian thought the noise she'd heard was some kind of vehicle. It sounded a little bit like a Gator, but not exactly. The sound was not from a vehicle she recognized. She was not expecting anybody, and Vivian was concerned. She opened the back door. Standing before her was an enormous man with blood streaming down over his head and face and body. She knew exactly who he was. She screamed and tried to run. He caught her apron and pulled her outside onto the back porch. He put a knife to her throat and then pushed her ahead of him into the kitchen.

He dripped blood along his path across the kitchen floor. The women in the great room had come running when they'd heard Vivian scream. The behemoth who was covered with blood was shouting something, but no one was able to understand what he was saying. They did understand that he was threatening to cut Vivian's throat if any of them approached him. Eugene was not thinking rationally, and he wasn't counting accurately. He thought he was keeping the wives of his victims at bay by threatening to cut Vivian's throat. But he had forgotten about Elizabeth. The other three women had run to the kitchen when they'd heard the screaming, but it had taken Elizabeth longer to get there. She was slower because she had to use her cane. Elizabeth didn't run anywhere anymore. Eugene was completely focused on the three women and on Vivian. A slip of his hand could mean the end for Vivian. The man was completely deranged. It was a very dangerous situation.

Eugene didn't see Elizabeth slip into the pantry. She came at him from behind. She used her cane and hooked it around his ankle. Gathering all of her upper body strength, she gave the cane a mighty tug, and pulled Eugene Boone down. The floor was slippery with his blood, and he tripped as he stumbled backwards and fell to the floor. Vivian was free, and she grabbed the closest weapon she could reach, a large cast iron skillet that was sitting on the stove ready to be used to saute the asparagus for dinner. Vivian had turned on the gas burner to warm the olive oil in the skillet when she'd gone to the back door to investigate what the noisy vehicle was all about. The skillet was fiery hot, and the olive oil was ablaze. Vivian grabbed a dishtowel that lay on the counter, took the burning skillet by the handle, and began to beat Eugene Boone over the head with her weapon. The burning olive oil spilled on Boone's face, and he started screaming. Elizabeth freed her cane from Boone's ankle and began to hit him with it. Isabelle and Sidney grabbed pots and pans. Olivia lifted the toaster oven from the counter and brought it down on Eugene's head.

The man was raging, and at some level he realized he was finally beaten. He covered his face with his hands and scrambled away from his attackers. They kept after him, and he slithered on his fat stomach, through the olive oil and the blood on the floor toward the back door. The women never relented and followed him outside, across the back porch, and down the ramp. They kept going after him with their kitchen implements. Eugene was in the final stages of his adrenalin surge. He would soon be spent. To the extent that he realized what was happening or where he was, he knew he would soon be unable to fight back. He scrambled once again onto the ATV and turned toward the front of the house. He was heading for the water, heading for the Atlantic Ocean.

The tidal flats are some of the most beautiful sights on the coast of Maine. They leave the sand and dirt teeming with sea life as the tide recedes. Tourists are warned to walk on the flats at their own risk. Every season, more than one person is caught by the incoming tide that can swiftly overcome an unsuspecting explorer. Eugene drove his ATV through the thick dune grass that grew between the house and the water's edge and continued out onto the swampy muck. He was out of his mind. Anyone who knew anything about the tidal flats knew it was like driving into quicksand to take a heavy vehicle out there. But he kept driving until the AVT had sunk into the wet mud up over its wheels. Sidney and Isabelle were ready to go after the man as he abandoned the ATV and took off across the flats. Olivia, who was a sailor and knew about tides, shouted at them to stop. Vivian, who had kept up with the daily tides on the coast of Maine ever since she'd been a little girl, yelled that the tide was coming in.

They all stopped and stood on the shore. They watched as Eugene Boone left the ATV behind and scuttled, like the crazed madman he was, back and forth across the tidal flats. Blood was pouring from his head and from his leg. He resembled the monster that he had probably always been inside. Hate had consumed him, and finally it had destroyed him. He was shouting and waving his arms and cursing as the tide rushed in to take him down one final time. He had been able to escape his human opponents, but the rage of the ocean overpowered him at last.

Just as Eugene was struggling in the swiftly moving water which had now reached his waist, the four hunters dragged themselves in the direction of the house and joined the women who were watching the former nuisance from Camp Shoemaker being carried away in the surf. He was finished. There would be no arrest, no formal vindication or conventional punishment. Eugene Boone would never have to face the kind of justice meted out by society for his crimes. But he would never again threaten the boys from Cabin #1 or anyone else. He was gone.

Epilogue

How could anyone possibly think of eating, after everything they'd been through? But they found they were famished. How could Vivian possibly finish cooking dinner after everything she'd been through? But she'd always found her solace in cooking. Rita had returned from walking her dogs and taken up the reins in the kitchen. She scrubbed the mess from the floor and made the kitchen shipshape again. She'd put the potatoes in the oven to roast, set the table, and made the gravy. Several bottles of wine were opened, and the spectacular leg of lamb was carved. Rita and Vivian ate with the others. Everyone loved Rita's crispy potatoes that had been roasted with just a touch of rosemary and just a hint of thyme.

Vivian was pleased to announce that she'd persuaded Rita to work for the Ryan family. The family had grown so much, with the addition of spouses and now grandchildren and great grandchildren, Vivian wasn't able to do the cooking by herself any more. She needed a full-time assistant and hadn't found anyone she wanted to hire until she'd met Rita. Rita was great with food and with set up and serving. She would be a Godsend during the holidays, when the Ryan family gathered to spend Christmas at Indigo Cottage, and she would be Vivian's savior when the family arrived en masse for the summer. Rita's salary would be twice what she'd been making at the Inastou, and she didn't want to go back there anyway. It was a great solution all around.

Everyone proposed a number of toasts to both Rita and the much-loved and much-appreciated Vivian.

At the end of the meal, there was not a drop of wine left nor a scrap of food to be found on any of the platters. The chocolate almond mousse likewise had been completely devoured. They'd decided to heal themselves tonight and call the sheriff in the morning.

Trimper came the next day to talk to Sidney and Cameron, and Sheriff Carney Dodd arrived to talk to everybody. The FBI didn't show up today. Even after sleeping late that morning, everyone was worn out. The men were seventy-five years old, after all. It had been a marathon of trouble.

Cameron played the recording for Captain Trimper. Trimper had known Daniela Garcia for many years and had tears in his eyes when he heard the story she'd never told anyone until just before she died. He shook his head in horror and dismay. He didn't know what he was going to do about the recording or about Daniela.

Sheriff Carney Dodd was incredulous when he heard the details of what had happened to Eugene Boone. Those who gave him their statements knew he was overwhelmed by their story, and they didn't really care what Sheriff Dodd decided to do about any of it. Boone was no longer a threat to them or to anybody. They realized he'd been suffering from mental illness since he was a child. His obsession with the boys from Cabin #1, as well as his abuse of small animals, had all been part of that mental illness. He was a man destined for destruction. They could wish they'd never known Eugene. As much as they might have preferred their paths hadn't crossed, either when they were young or when they were old, Eugene was a part of their shared experience. Eugene Boone's body was never recovered from the sea.

They said goodbye to each other and went home to their regular lives. It had been an unforgettable trip to Maine. They wondered if they would all be around to see seventy-six. Where would they decide to go for their reunion the following September? Every one of them was determined that there would be a trip next year. Their friendship was unassailable. They'd vowed to continue their reunions until there was no longer anyone left to attend. They accepted their approaching mortality, but they wanted to make the most of this last chapter, this last hurrah. No matter how old and decrepit they might become, they would never stop believing that they were still #1. Attitude is everything.

WHEN DID I GROW OLD?

When did I grow old?
    It is now so still around me.
    When did all the noise turn to quiet?
    The cacophony of busyness that engulfed me
        for so many years, has subsided.

When did I grow old?
    Did it happen slowly as the years passed by?
    Did it happen as I filled my time with immediacy …
        moving from one crisis to the next?
    Did it happen all of a sudden when I found I had to use
        a cane to get up and down the steps?

When did I grow old?
    Did I fill those years that passed with goodness and giving
        and love?
    Did I spend too many days in anger and hoping for retaliation
        for things in life that didn't go my way?
    Did I spend too many hours organizing and cleaning and
        worrying about my material possessions?
    How much time did I spend shopping? Sorting out my closet?

When did I grow old?
    Was it when I learned that I was deaf in one ear
        and there was no help for that?
    Was it when I realized there were so few days ahead
        and so many already gone?
    Was it when I accepted that I would die?

When did I grow old?
> Was it a gradual process as the hairs on my head
>> one by one turned white?
> Or did it happen overnight? And what night was that?
> Was it when I became a grandmother?

When did I grow old?
> Did I spend this precious time I have been given
> To make a difference?
> To make the world a better place?

When did I grow old?
> Is it today when I know that however this life was spent,
>> it cannot be respent?
> It was what it was ...
> Full of imperfections and mistakes and trying hard
>> and often struggling and falling short
> And full of joy and good luck.

When did I grow old?
I just don't know.
Or, maybe I'm not old yet.

MTT 5-7-2014

Acknowledgments

Heartfelt thanks to my readers and editors. I couldn't have done this without you. Thank you to my talented cover artist, the photographer who always makes me look good, and Open Heart Designs. Thank you to my fans who have encouraged me to continue writing.

CPSIA information can be obtained
at www.ICGtesting.com
Printed in the USA
LVHW080526190819
627955LV00002B/5/P